PLAY WITH FIRE

Into The Fire Series

J.H. CROIX

*This one goes out to MG, my dear friend. You are one of the strongest women I know, and I'm so blessed to have you as a friend. Keep kicking a**.*

Sign up for my newsletter for information on new releases & get a FREE copy of one of my books!

http://jhcroixauthor.com/subscribe/

Follow me!
jhcroix@jhcroix.com
https://amazon.com/author/jhcroix
https://www.bookbub.com/authors/j-h-croix
https://www.facebook.com/jhcroix

PLAY WITH FIRE

Jasmine

I lost my job, lost my fiancé, and started a bar fight. That's how I met Donovan Ryan. Don't worry. I gave another guy a bloody nose, not Donovan.

Donovan is way too handsome for my own good, certainly for my peace of mind. He's also one of those save-the-day hotshot firefighters. You know the type. Strong, protective, dangerously hot.

Now isn't the time for me to fall for anyone. I won't. I definitely won't.

Donovan

Jasmine Phillips has a solid right hook. She's also crazy beautiful with a fiery temper. I can think of quite a few things I might enjoy about *fiery*.

But Jasmine's off limits, and I don't do love. Then, she kisses me and sets me on fire. There's lust, there's love, and then there's *this*.

Jasmine makes me question everything. She makes me want to move mountains. I would—for her. Only her.

Maybe it's crazy. Or maybe it's the only thing that makes sense.

*This is a full-length, standalone romance with a guaranteed HEA.

Chapter One

DONOVAN

Leaning against the bar at Wildlands Lodge, I took a long pull from my beer and scanned the bar and restaurant. It was a busy night here, but then, even a slow night was crowded. I was tucked into a corner with a good view of the room. As I glanced around, my gaze landed on a woman playing pool in the corner nearby.

I idly wondered if she was a tourist. Willow Brook, Alaska was a small town, but it was smack dab in the middle of summer, which meant the town was teeming with tourists. Pushing off the bar, as if drawn by an actual force, I found myself walking in her direction.

Her dark amber hair glinted under the dim lighting in the bar, and fell down her back in a cascade, almost reaching her waist. With a flick of her hand, she brushed it over her shoulder as I approached. She wore jeans and cowboy boots paired with a loose red blouse. Somehow, I just *knew* there were curves to die for hidden beneath that silk.

She was in the midst of a game with several men and looked well on her way to being tipsy. While I'd initially walked over here without thinking much about it, as I got closer, I noticed the hum of tension in the air. Two of the men near the table were leering at her.

There were different kinds of men. It was one thing to appreciate a woman—hell, that was what I'd been doing—and it was another thing to look at them as if you could do whatever the hell you wanted. I felt as if I'd walked into a pack of dogs jockeying for position. To make matters worse, this woman wasn't paying the least bit of attention to it. She was focused on the game. My hackles rose.

As she leaned over to take a shot, one of the men slid his hand over her ass. In a flash, she spun around, pulled her fist back, and clocked him right in the nose.

"Get your hands off of me!" she declared, swinging her pool stick in his direction.

She clearly didn't need help.

"What the fuck?!" The guy who'd been the recipient of her fist wiped blood off his nose.

"Don't grab my fucking ass."

One of the other guys snickered. "Well, sweets, you can't just waltz in here and show off your ass like that."

"Oh, *hell* fucking no," the woman said.

I threaded through the cluster around her. I didn't even know who she was, but I needed to get her out of the middle of this mess.

"I'm playing pool. That doesn't give any of you idiots the right to touch me," the woman stated, swinging her pool stick around again.

I caught the end of it and tugged it out of her hands. While I'd be happy to watch her whack a few of these assholes, it might not work out in her favor. Glancing around at the guys, I said, "Okay boys, break it up."

"Hey, she fucking hit me," the man with the bloody nose retorted.

"Yeah, well, you grabbed her ass, and she didn't appreciate it. So, like I said, back the fuck off."

The bartender, Mike, stepped to my side and leaned over.

"Heads up, that's Jasmine Phillips, Levi's sister. She drove here, so I'm about to take her keys. Mind giving her a ride home?"

Ahh fuck. Levi was a friend of mine. We were both firefighters at Willow Brook Fire & Rescue. I wasn't so sure I wanted to be the one giving his sister a ride home, but more than that, I didn't want to see her caught in the middle of this.

"Not a problem," I replied, glancing at Mike. "I'll call Levi once we get her out of here."

Wading into the cluster, Mike dealt with the guys, while I stepped to Jasmine's side. Just as I was about to open my mouth, she spun to look at the guy who'd copped a feel. "And don't grab my ass again."

With a huff, she turned back to face me. Sweet hell. She was fucking beautiful. Her cheeks were flushed, and her eyes snapping fire. My body had all kinds of thoughts about her. She was flat-out gorgeous, with that fall of dark amber hair and those deep sapphire eyes.

Before I had a chance to speak, Mike stopped in front of Jasmine. "Hand 'em over," he said, holding his palm out.

"Hand what over?" Jasmine asked, narrowing her eyes at Mike.

"Your keys. This is Donovan Ryan, if you haven't met him before. He works with Levi, and he's giving you a ride home," Mike explained matter-of-factly.

"What the hell?" Jasmine asked, her gaze bouncing between us.

"Look, you've already hit one guy. You're drunk, and you're not driving anywhere," Mike said flatly.

Jasmine glanced between Mike and me, clearly not pleased with this turn of events. After a taut moment, she shook her head. "No, I don't need a ride."

"You climb behind the wheel of your car, and I won't hesitate to call the police. They can probably walk here faster than you can back out of a parking spot," Mike said, not even the least bit ruffled by how pissed off she seemed. "Way I see it; you've got three choices. One—ride home with Donovan. Two—I call Levi and he'll come get you. Three—the guy you hit might actually decide to call the police because you hit him. Take your pick."

Jasmine rolled her eyes and sighed. "Fine. Do I have to give you my keys if he gives me a ride?" she countered, thumbing in my direction.

When Mike shook his head, she turned her attention to me. "Nice to meet you, Donovan."

I simply nodded, too busy trying to tell my body not to notice she was sexy as sin.

Mike cocked his head to the side. "So you're riding with Donovan?"

Jasmine nodded and then spun around, stalking across the floor ahead of me.

"Looks like I'm outta here," I said with a chuckle.

"Levi will appreciate it," Mike murmured as I walked past him.

Jasmine's hair swung just above her hips as she threaded her way through the tables before disappearing down a hallway in the back. I caught up to her quickly, reaching her just as she stumbled slightly in the hallway when she tried to dodge a group of people walking in from the parking lot.

"Dammit," she muttered under her breath.

I caught her elbow to steady her but the moment she shook me loose, she promptly stumbled again, bouncing into the wall. Leaning against it, she rolled both shoulders against the wall, eyeing me. Her dark blue gaze swept up and down my body.

"Damn, you're handsome," she said, her mouth lifting at the corner in a slow grin.

I took a breath and kept my eyes focused on her face. "You like to swear when you're drunk," I countered.

I was acutely aware of the shadowed valley between her

breasts with her red silk blouse slipping and sliding when she lifted a hand to brush a loose lock of hair out of her eyes.

"What the hell is wrong with swearing?" she asked.

"Nothing at all."

Jasmine stared at me, her rich blue gaze assessing. "You must be new to Willow Brook. I don't think I know you."

"Depends on what you mean by new. I moved here about two years ago when I joined a hotshot crew. That's how I know Levi. How about we get going?"

Jasmine eyed me for another few beats and then pushed away from the wall. When I lightly gripped her elbow this time, she didn't shrug me off. We stepped out into the cool summer air. It was going on nine p.m., the sun only now making its final bow for the night, leaving a crescent of orange just above the mountains in the distance. The sky was streaked with orange, red, and gold.

Jasmine came to a quick stop when we were about halfway through the parking lot. She lifted her head and took a deep breath, letting it out with a gusty sigh. "I love the air here. It's the best air," she murmured softly.

The summer air in Alaska was earthy, scented with spruce and the crispness of the mountains surrounding us. Swan Lake stretched out in front of us just beyond the parking lot behind the lodge.

Jasmine looked toward me, her gaze considering. "I bet you're not an asshole," she said flatly.

"I'd like to think not," I offered, uncertain where this topic was headed.

The anger, bravado, and recklessness with which she'd carried herself up to this point disappeared in a flash. It was as if she was deflated by nothing more than a thought.

After her announcement, she stepped closer. Before I even realized what the hell she was doing, she leaned up, slipped her hand around my nape, and kissed me. For a flash, I was so startled I didn't even move, and then her mouth was moving over mine, and I reacted.

Threading a hand into her glorious hair, I tugged her to me and swiped my tongue across the seam of her lips. She moaned into my mouth, the sound nudging me back to sanity. I tore my lips free and gave my head a shake.

"What the hell was that?"

She smiled, her eyes glittering. "I couldn't help it. Your mouth is too damn sexy."

At that, she traced my lips with her fingertip, the feel of her touch like fire.

"You're gonna have to take me to Levi's," she announced next as her hand fell away.

"I'll drive you wherever you need to go. Come on," I said, turning away because I couldn't keep looking at her and not want to kiss her again.

She walked along with me, her stride slower now. She gave off a sense of weariness and sadness. Once we were situated in my truck, she let out a deep sigh and leaned her head back against the seat.

"Levi doesn't know I'm here, by the way," she murmured.

Great, just great. I was going to take her to Levi's, but I had a feeling that there was some kind a story behind why she was in town without her older brother knowing, and I had no idea what it was.

All I knew was Jasmine was beautiful, she drew me to her like a fucking magnet, and the second her vulnerability flashed in her eyes, I wanted to take care of her. That was a dangerous feeling.

I knew where Levi lived, so I simply started driving in that direction. Jasmine was sound asleep by the time I arrived at Levi's place. I climbed quietly out of the truck, considering whether I should go knock first, or carry her in.

Glancing to the darkened windows of Levi's home, I realized I'd likely be waking him and Lucy up as it was. Rounding to the passenger side, I opened the door. Carrying the delectable Jasmine Phillips was not something I wanted to do, or rather it was something I *definitely* wanted, so that wasn't smart. Steeling myself, I reached around her to unbuckle her seatbelt, gritting my teeth when she sighed softly in her sleep.

Her body was warm and lush. I could feel her lithe build and the soft curve of one of her breasts against my chest. Fuck me. I ordered my cock down and walked swiftly to the door. After a quick knock, I waited. Several moments passed before Levi answered, a look of confusion on his face.

"What are you doing here? And what the hell is Jasmine doing with you?"

"Short version—she was at Wildlands, the bartender took her keys and asked me to take her home."

All in all, that summed it up nicely, minus the messy details.

Levi's eyes widened as he ran a hand through his rumpled hair. He and Jasmine shared the same blue eyes. It was obvious I'd woken him up. "What the hell?" he finally muttered.

"Yeah, she mentioned you didn't know she was here."

Levi looked completely flummoxed, but he nodded and opened the door, gesturing me through. With Levi pointing the way, I carried Jasmine to the couch and set her down. Between her unexpected kiss and the way it felt to hold her in my arms, I was doing battle with the state of my body.

I followed Levi into the kitchen. "Thanks, man. Anything I should know about?" he asked.

Standing there, I contemplated whether it would be better if he heard from me that Jasmine hauled off and punched a guy who grabbed her ass, or through the grapevine.

I decided hearing it from me was better. "Well, the bartender asked me to take her home after some guy grabbed her ass, and she hauled off and punched him."

Levi's eyes widened, and then he shook his head slowly back and forth. "Do you happen to know who the asshole was?"

"Nope. She can hold her own though."

"Oh, she can," he said with a wry chuckle. "Thanks for bringing her home."

"Not a problem. See you at the station."

Driving home through the falling darkness, the only thing my mind tripped over was the feel of Jasmine's lips against mine. With a hard shake, I forced my attention off of her, watching as the moon rose ahead in the sky, stars claiming the fading light.

Chapter Two

JASMINE

Bright light woke me, the sun warm on my face. Ugh. My head was pounding. It took me a moment to get my bearings. Opening my eyes slowly, first one and then the other, I glanced around, realizing that I was in Levi and Lucy's guest bedroom. I was fully dressed with my blouse twisted around my waist. I vaguely recalled waking at the sound of Levi's voice last night and shuffling up the stairs from the couch to the guest bedroom.

My mind flashed back to the evening before. A man—a classically handsome, tall, dark, and sexy-as-fucking-hell man —had driven me here last night.

For the life of me, I couldn't remember his name. But I had a crystal-clear picture of what he looked like and the way his mouth felt against mine.

I flung my arm over my face, my cheeks getting hot. Said man had almost black hair and rich hazel eyes. I remembered looking into them, the layered colors of green and gold mingled with nutmeg. His face had clean lines— sculpted cheekbones, a square jaw, a slightly crooked nose as if he'd been in a fight, and a sensual mouth with a dimple in the center of his chin.

Even though my memories were blurry, I recalled that he'd made me feel safe. As mortified as I was that I'd kissed him, I was positive I'd seen a flicker of desire in his eyes.

Who the hell was he?

I'd have to figure that out later. For now, I had to sort out who I would be facing here. I wasn't quite ready to face my brother, especially not with a hangover. I adored Levi, but he could be overprotective. I'd come home unexpectedly, without any advance warning, so I knew there would be questions. Levi thought I was too wild, too reckless, or so he'd said once upon a time. I hoped my options were no one, or my sister-in-law, Lucy. I could handle Lucy.

I slowly dragged my arm away from my face and rubbed my eyes with my fists. Moving carefully and trying not to jostle my pounding head too much, I swung my feet over the side of the bed and straightened up gingerly.

Opening the door a crack, I listened to see if I could hear any voices. Silence greeted me, so I pulled the door open and walked toward the bathroom. I paused for a moment when I rounded the edge of the balcony upstairs. I loved this house. Levi had built it himself. The upstairs had a balcony that wrapped along three sides of the house with windows extending from the lower floor to the peak in the roof upstairs in the front of the house.

Mist rose off the field outside, the sun angling across the dew-covered grasses and flowers in the field. The home offered a view of a field with a small pond to the side. Spruce and birch trees were scattered in the field and gradually thickened into forest with the mountains rising tall in the distance. My heart gave a hard thump. Alaska was home to me, and my heart knew it.

Glimpsing over the balcony railing, I scanned the living room below. As far as I could tell, it appeared no one else was here. With a sigh, I shuffled into the bathroom and paused to take a look at myself. My hair was a tousled mess, and my cheek had an imprint of the wrinkled sheets against it. My eyes were puffy and bleary.

In short, I looked like hell. I could only hope that when I'd made a pass at *tall, dark, and sexy* last night. I hadn't looked this bad. I was about to strip out of my clothes when I saw a note taped to the shelf by the shower in front of a clean stack of towels.

Morning, Jasmine. Levi's off at the station, and I'm out running a few errands. Here's a change of clothes. I'll see you when I get back. To start the coffee, just turn it on. There are bagels and cream cheese in the fridge. Glad you're home.

Lucy

PS: Levi's wondering what the hell is going on.

I started laughing. Because what else was there to do? Lucy was the best sister-in-law. She was also sarcastic and kind of quirky, which made her even better.

Peeling out of my clothes, I climbed in the shower, sighing at the feel of the hot water pouring over me. That alone eased my headache a bit.

As I showered, a few more memories filtered in from last night. Specifically, of the idiot who grabbed my ass before I punched him.

I *couldn't wait* to hear what Levi had to say about that.

After I showered, I downed two Ibuprofen I found in the medicine cabinet and made my way downstairs in the clothes Lucy had left for me. She was smaller than me, but she tended to wear loose clothes. Her comfy sweatpants and T-shirt fit just fine.

Seeing as I couldn't go anywhere, it didn't really matter how I looked. After I started the coffee, toasted a bagel, and slathered it with cream cheese, I sat down at the kitchen table to eat. I felt halfway human after some coffee and a few bites of my bagel.

The tension bundled inside of me started to ease slowly. Five days ago, I'd stopped by my apartment to pick up my lunch after I forgot to bring it to work. My life in San Francisco consisted of working my ass off at a pottery cooperative because I loved it and working at an art gallery to make ends meet. I worked insane hours and was rarely home during weekdays. My mind spun back to the memorable, ugly afternoon that set the wheels in motion for me to return to Alaska.

I arrive at the apartment I share with my fiancé to grab my lunch. Fucking starving. As soon as I unlock the door and step inside, I hear a thumping sound. Because I could be a spectacular idiot sometimes, I do exactly what they tell you not to do in horror films and follow the sound, right to our bedroom door. Unsure if I'm about to walk into the middle of a robbery, I'd grabbed a vase from the table by the front door, ready to throw it at someone if I had to. I start to open the door when a cold prickle runs up my spine and my gut clenches.

With the door swung fully open, a sick feeling overtakes me as I see Glen, my fiancé, on his back, and Lisa, the assistant manager from the gallery where I worked, straddling him, in all her naked glory. To say they were going to town might be an understatement.

That thumping sound? That's the headboard hitting the wall, over and over and over again. She's gripping it with her hands, so every time she moves, it bounces against the wall. I'm in such a state of shock, I just stand there, watching them, trying to recall the last time Glen and I'd had sex. About three weeks, maybe?

I'd chalked it up to being too busy. We both had crazy schedules and sometimes passed like ships in the night for days at a time. Obviously, that wasn't the issue.

In the throes of their rather enthusiastic fucking, it takes them a moment or two to notice my presence, and the tension I'd been feeling before I walked in quickly morphs into anger.

Lisa, my now former sort of friend, looks over her shoulder. "Oh shit!"

She starts to move, desperately looking around for something to cover up with, but I'm surprisingly calm. "Just carry on. I won't be hanging around."

I walk out of the room, calling over my shoulder, "Be out of here within the hour. I'll be back to get my stuff, and I don't want to see either one of you."

I hear someone scrambling off the bed, and then footsteps.

"Jasmine, it's not what you think!" Glen calls out.

I spin back to find him hurrying out of the bedroom, wrapping a sheet around his waist. I take a moment to stare at him. "There's not much to think about for me to interpret what I just saw. We're done."

Tears are threatening, but I'll be damned if I'm going to let them see me fall apart. I cling to my anger like a shield. Because it's all I have. "Be out of here in an hour."

He hurries after me, but I leave, slamming the door in his face.

That was five days ago. Thinking back, I couldn't quite believe I managed to think at all. At least he'd had the decency to be gone when I came back. I'd packed up all my clothes, took all my pottery and put it in my car, and left. I'd spent the night with another friend and then drove home to Willow Brook. I'd considered staying, but I managed to get myself fired on the same day.

I had a bit of a temper sometimes. That same afternoon, it wasn't a shocker that I was in a pissy mood at the gallery after my lunch break. Working in an art gallery wasn't really a great fit for my personality, to be honest, but I'd needed the money.

I preferred to have my hands dirty while throwing pottery, not dolling myself up and being polite and gracious to the rich people who spent money on art. I'd been a little emotionally overwhelmed and so out of sorts inside that I'd publicly confronted Lisa when she returned to the gallery. I couldn't believe she'd had the nerve, but then she *was* a step above me there. The manager didn't appreciate me calling her second-in-command a whore, and fired me on the spot. No job, no fiancé, and no money.

I hadn't been thinking it through, but the next morning, I pointed my car north and drove home to Alaska. It took me four days to get here.

Just now, emotion finally pushed through that shield of anger, the cracks in it spreading rapidly. Hot tears rolled down my cheeks as I cried, so hard I was hiccupping. While trying to catch my breath, I felt a tickle on my foot. Glancing down, my brother's hamster, aptly named Ham, was sniffing at my feet. Brown and white, little Ham looked up at me as if he somehow understood how upset I was. I sniffled, dragging my sleeve across my face, and managed to smile at Ham. Leaning over, I stroked my fingertips across his back. He sniffed my hand and then scurried away.

I watched as he climbed up a step stool that Levi left there for him to scurry across the windowsill and into a little pillow bed. Only my brother—my hotshot firefighter, badass brother—would have a hamster he let run loose in the house and treated like a king.

My tears subsided. I didn't like thinking about all the reasons why I was back in Willow Brook. Instead, I took a sip of my coffee and contemplated my next steps. I'd come here in a huff and had no plan. For a huff, I sure had to drive a long damn way to get here.

I'd left Willow Brook straight out of high school. Our family had moved here from Juneau, right before my freshman year. I was an Alaskan girl born and bred, and had yearned to see the bigger world beyond it. I landed in San Francisco and loved many aspects of the place I'd call home for the foreseeable future—the hum and busyness of the big city, the eclectic mix of people, the quaint buildings, and the art ... so much art. I'd finished college and started working at a studio, falling in love with making pottery. There were some things I hadn't loved so much though. For example, apparently lots of people were gluten sensitive and most of them were vegan. I loved bread and I ate meat, and I didn't intend to change that anytime soon.

I never quite felt like I fit in. I was perhaps too rough around the edges, and certainly not glamorous enough. While I wasn't a full-on tomboy, I definitely bordered on it. I preferred to wear jeans and boots and T-shirts while I worked, dressing up only when necessary. Cowboy boots were practically a uniform for me.

I'd also missed Alaska. Once the novelty of seeing the wider world had worn off, there was always a little ache in my heart—longing for the midnight sun of summer days, the crisp snowy nights, and the sense of feeling like I belonged, no matter who I was.

That was a funny quality here. Alaska was filled with so many transplants that you could find every kind of person. There were plenty of gluten-free vegans, but they rubbed shoulders with the fishermen and hunters and then some. There was a high tolerance for *to each their own* here.

And, oh my God, I'd missed the view. Just now, looking out over the field outside the kitchen window, that tight ball of tension and hurt eased. Oddly, I was more hurt by Lisa's actions than Glen's. While she'd sort of been my boss, until the other day, I'd have considered her a friend.

That was like a rule, right? You didn't fuck your friend's fiancé.

Chapter Three

JASMINE

I decided I needed another bagel because—oh my God—
they were good. They must've gotten them fresh from Firehouse Café. Janet was known to sell them occasionally when
she was in the mood to make bagels. Levi had made a batch
of fresh smoked salmon cream cheese to go with them,
which was simply divine. I knew Levi had made it because
Lucy didn't cook, hardly at all.

Most people paid a fortune for that anywhere outside of
Alaska. Yet, locally, Alaskans smoked their own salmon and
made it themselves. After toasting another bagel, I generously slathered it with the cream cheese and sat back down
just as Lucy came in the kitchen door.

She smiled the minute she saw me, pulling me into a big
hug as soon as I stood up from the table. Stepping back, she
let a grocery bag slip off her arm onto the counter. "You look
like you're doing just fine."

"Were you worried?" I asked.

"Well, according to Levi, you were, um, passed out when
you got here. He figured you'd wake up with a hangover, and
he wasn't so sure you'd remember what happened last night."

I fought my smile, but this was Lucy, so I burst out laughing. "Yeah, I might've had a little too much to drink. You don't happen to know who brought me home, by the way?"

I tried to make my question sound casual, but I was curious, really curious.

"Donovan Ryan. He's a friend of Levi's, well, of ours. He's a firefighter. I know that'll come as a shock," she said with a wry grin as she turned to put the groceries away.

As she turned, I noticed the slight curve of her belly, just now remembering she was pregnant. "Oh! You look great!" I squealed.

Lucy glanced over her shoulder, her gaze confused. "Uh, thanks?"

"You're so cute pregnant," I added.

Her cheeks went pink, and she rolled her eyes as she reached up to put some cans away in a cabinet above her head. Lucy looked a bit like a fairy, with her almost white-blonde hair, fine-boned features, and bright blue eyes. She was small and petite. With the soft curve of her belly, she looked even more feminine, which I'd bet was annoying to her. Lucy was a total tomboy—I mean, she put most men to shame—and worked in construction. In a rare moment, she wasn't actually covered in dirt.

Levi absolutely adored her, and he was beside himself about their baby. I was so happy for them.

For now, I was relieved I was dealing with Lucy first. She could ease the blow of telling Levi why I was here. I helped her finish putting away the groceries, and she made some tea before joining me at the table as I slipped back into the chair to finish my bagel.

"So, I'm guessing there's a reason you showed up and got drunk at Wildlands before letting anybody know you were home," she said with a sly smile.

"Hey, no sense in taking it slow, huh?" I countered with a grin.

Lucy shrugged and rolled her eyes. "I figure, let's get right to the point. You can tell me what the hell happened, and then we can figure out how to tell Levi. He called your parents, by the way. Your mom asked you to give her a call when you're up."

I sighed and paused to take a sip of my coffee between bites. "Okay, I'll call her in a little bit. I should've figured Levi already let them know I was here." After a fortifying gulp of coffee, I steeled myself. "Here's what happened. Five days ago, I forgot to bring my lunch to work, so I stopped by the apartment to pick it up, and I found Glen fucking Lisa from the gallery."

Lucy's eyes widened and then promptly narrowed. "That fucking asshole. And what a fucking bitch she is. I hope you hit her just like that guy last night."

I almost spit my coffee out at that. I paused and then shrugged. "Did Donovan tell Levi about that? I don't remember much," I added with a sheepish shrug.

I didn't quite remember how Donovan ended up taking me home, although I did remember hitting the guy. I vividly remembered kissing Donovan, however.

Lucy shrugged. "Yeah, he told Levi about some guy being an ass. Sounded like the guy deserved a fist to his face. Donovan's a good guy. You don't need to worry about that."

Little did Lucy know, the only thing I was thinking about was the fact I kissed him and wanted to kiss him again.

"So, back to Glen. I walked in on them and left. I don't know if you recall, but Lisa's the assistant manager at the gallery where I worked. After I went back to the gallery, I got fired because I told my boss her bitchy friend was fucking my fiancé. In front of the customers," I explained with a bitter laugh.

That was the only part about all of this that was satisfying.

Lucy burst out laughing. "Oh, that's perfect! She gets to be embarrassed." She paused to take a sip of her tea. "The last part is funny, but it sucks. It totally sucks he did that. How are you?" she asked, her gaze sobering.

I shrugged and suddenly wanted to cry again.

"You can cry. An ugly cry is probably worth it right now," she said gently.

I swiped at my tears and laughed softly. "Already took care of that this morning. I'm not really okay. I broke up with Glen, so that's done. I lost my job, so I just came home. I wasn't really thinking too far ahead. I probably look like an idiot."

Lucy shook her head. "Not at all. I think coming home was the right thing to do after all that. You can stay here as long as you need. You know we'd be thrilled if you stayed for good."

I swallowed through the knot in my throat and took a deep breath, letting it out on a sigh. "I know. Thank you for that. I'm sorry I showed up the way I did. I suppose I should track down Donovan and thank him for taking me home last night."

"You can find him at the station."

"He's not from Willow Brook, is he?"

Lucy shook her head. "Not originally. He moved here about two years ago. He started on Ward's crew and then switched over to foreman on Levi's. They're pretty good friends."

"Oh," was about all I could manage. I was all kinds of curious about Donovan. I couldn't believe he worked with my brother, although I should've known. He definitely had the whole alpha-man-rescue-vibe going on.

"So, what's your plan?" Lucy asked, as she sipped at her tea.

"I don't know. I'm here for now, and I'll figure out what's next."

Lucy was quiet as she regarded me. I felt so lucky to have her as a sister-in-law. I'd never had a sister and considered her one. While she was opinionated and wouldn't hesitate to tell me what she thought, she definitely had a "live and let live" kind of personality. Levi, on the other hand, tended to have an opinion about everything I did.

"Are you going to just hang out here today, or do you need a ride into town for your car?" she asked, immediately moving on.

"A ride to my car would be great. I'd like to stop by and see my parents. And I suppose I should go by the station to thank Donovan. I can say hi to Levi when I'm not passed out drunk," I offered with a wry laugh.

Lucy flashed a quick grin. "Well, let's go then. We'll swing by the station together and then I'll take you to your car," she said, standing from the table.

"Don't you need to work?"

Lucy shook her head. "Nope. I called Amelia and told her I wouldn't be in today. You've got me all day."

It felt good to be home, if only because I had friends like this. No matter what, I wasn't worried any friend here would end up in bed with any guy I was seeing.

DONOVAN

Later the following afternoon, I leaned against one of the trucks at the station and tossed a rag into a bucket on the floor.

"Well, that should be it for today," I commented, glancing at Jesse who was leaning against the wall in the garage, guzzling a bottle of water.

A voice called over from the other side of the truck. "I don't know, Donovan, did you check the bearings over here?"

The voice in question belonged to Emily Lane. She was our station employee who basically did everything.

"Sure did, took care of it before you got here," I returned, and Jesse grinned.

All of us around the station treated Emily like our little sister. Jesse was about to marry Emily's aunt, who had adopted Emily after her mother passed away. I pushed away from the truck and rounded to the other side. Emily was leaning over, scrubbing furiously at one of the tire rims.

Her short dark hair was dyed with purple all over the tips. She looked up and grinned. "I knew they were done."

Her latest focus was learning about all things related to

vehicle maintenance. Between Jesse, myself, and a few of the other guys on the crew, we'd taught her how to change the oil and a ton of other basic maintenance. She wanted to be a hotshot firefighter. She certainly had the personality for it, but she was too young at fifteen. As it was, Jesse already had to hold her back from begging to go out on local runs with us now.

I shook my head with a laugh as she straightened and rested a hand on her hip.

"Even if the bearings weren't done, I'm done for the day. We've been dealing with equipment all day long," I stated.

"Same here. Come on. Charlie's making dinner, so let's get home on time," Jesse said, as he rounded the fire truck. Charlie was his fiancée and one of the town's doctors. She had him wrapped around her finger, but he seemed to love it.

In between fires in the summer, we did all kinds of maintenance around the station. At Emily's laugh, I turned away, snagging a water bottle off the bumper where I'd left it earlier and heading into the showers, the low hum of whatever she was saying to Jesse fading as I moved down the hallway.

I was grimy and greasy. With the steaming water pounding over me, my mind spun in the direction of Jasmine Phillips. The delectable Jasmine had been dancing through my thoughts far more than I would've preferred today.

I wondered what had brought her home to Willow Brook because Levi sure as hell seemed surprised to see her last night. While Levi and I were friends, prying for information about his little sister who had kissed me last night didn't seem like the wisest plan.

I shook my thoughts away from Jasmine, turned off the water, and headed to the lockers to get dressed. As I walked down the hall on my way out, someone called my name. Glancing around, I poked my head in the closest door, which happened to be Beck Steele's office. He was leaning back in a chair with Levi sitting across from him.

"Hey man," Beck called.

"Hey," I replied, then stopped short.

Jasmine, the very woman I'd been trying to kick out of my thoughts was sitting in a chair beside Levi. Lucy, Levi's badass wife, was sitting beside him, laughing at something he'd said, Levi's arm loosely draped over her shoulders.

Beck caught my eyes. "Jasmine was just asking us where you were."

"Oh?" I countered, keeping my expression calm as I looked over at her.

Just like last night, the first time I'd ever laid eyes on her, my body tightened in response. Today, she wore a baggy T-shirt and sweatpants with tennis shoes. Her hair fell in loose waves around her shoulders. The moment I saw it, all I could think was how badly I wanted to wind my hand around it and kiss her.

Needless to say, with her older brother and Beck, one of the superintendents on another crew, as an audience, those thoughts would not be appreciated. When my eyes met hers, it felt as if a live wire came to life between us.

I wondered if she even remembered kissing me last night. I sure as hell hadn't forgotten. My lips burned now, just thinking about it. I nodded in her direction. You found me."

"I just wanted to thank you for giving me a ride to Levi's last night," she said, a pink flush cresting on her cheeks.

"No problem."

Lucy looked up, casting a slight smile in my direction. I'd gotten to know her through my friendship with Levi, but damn, if the woman didn't intimidate me. She wasn't the friendliest sort and didn't hesitate to tell anyone what she thought about anything. Just now though, she seemed relaxed and friendly.

"Yes," she said firmly. "Thank you. For that and then some."

I wondered if she knew a bit about Jasmine's fight with the guy who'd grabbed her ass.

Levi cast a quizzical glance Lucy's way, but she ignored him. Rather than waiting around, I decided it was better to keep on moving for now. The longer I stayed in close proximity to Jasmine, the more my body responded. I lifted my hand in a wave. "Well, I'm headed out. If you ever need a ride again, just ask."

At that, I left. I was almost to my truck when I heard the door to the back of the station open and close. Turning around, I saw Jasmine walking briskly in my direction.

She didn't have a lick of makeup on and hadn't done a thing to her hair. Yet, she was so fucking beautiful, she stole my breath for a beat. I stopped where I was, turning and resting my hips on the back bumper of my truck.

"Donovan," she called, when she was about halfway across the parking lot.

"Yes?"

She stopped in front of me, glancing up. "I wanted to thank you. Not just for the ride but ..." Her cheeks flushed again. "Well, thanks for helping me out after I, uh, hit that guy. Sometimes I have a temper."

"Oh, I think he deserved that punch."

She grinned at that, and my heart thudded hard in response.

"He did, didn't he?"

I chuckled. "I thought so. So did the bartender."

Her smile widened and then faded quickly. Even though I told myself it wasn't smart, my curiosity about her kept expanding. "You make a habit of getting in bar fights?" I asked, a grin tugging at the corners of my mouth.

Her cheeks flushed an even deeper shade of pink, and she rolled her eyes, catching the corner of her bottom lip in her teeth. The sight of her white teeth digging into the plump surface sent a hot jolt of need through me.

"Um, I can't say I make a habit of it. That's the first time

I actually hit somebody. I've definitely told people off. I had a little too much to drink."

"Right," I said, my mind flashing to the feel of her lips against mine and that fingertip of fire tracing my mouth.

We stood there, just looking at each other. I sensed she wanted to say more, but she didn't. After a beat, and after a damn hard nudge in my mind, ordering my body to behave, I pushed away from my truck. "Well, I gotta go. I'm sure I'll see you around if you're staying in Willow Brook."

Jasmine nodded, stepping back and smiling slightly. "Thank you again."

I drove away, thinking I needed to steer clear of Jasmine. I wasn't so sure Levi would appreciate just what my body thought of his little sister.

There was that, and the fact I didn't do relationships. I tried it once, and it had blown up in my face, rather spectacularly.

Once was enough. That rule had worked well for me. Yet with Jasmine, somehow, I was tempted to break my rule.

Chapter Five

JASMINE

Later that night, I looked across the table at Levi and rolled my eyes. "Oh, for God's sake, Levi. So I *kind* of made a scene. But the guy grabbed my ass, like full-on. It pissed me off. If you don't believe me, ask Donovan or the bartender. They both saw the whole thing."

Levi was standing at the stove, cooking. In their household, he was the cook. According to Levi, it was questionable if Lucy could even heat up soup properly.

At the moment, she was glancing between us, but letting it play out. I took a sip of my wine and glared at him. "Who cares if I hit him? He's obviously fine. I called the bartender today to ask."

"If somebody grabs your ass, they're fair game. I just want to know why the hell you showed up, without telling anybody, and got three sheets to the wind," Levi replied.

I'd been dancing around this one with my brother because it was embarrassing as hell. I'd just walked back into Levi and Lucy's house a few minutes ago after spending the afternoon with our parents. I'd already had to tell them what happened, and now, here I was, having to repeat it for the third time today.

In our family, I tended to feel like the flaky loser. Levi was rock solid. He'd known what he wanted to do since he was in high school, and he'd done it. After being a bit of a flirt for a while, he'd settled down so thoroughly with Lucy, I was still sometimes kind of surprised by the whole thing.

As I sat there, contemplating if I wanted to tell him the whole sordid story, Ham came scurrying into the kitchen. He paused and looked around at the kitchen, first scampering over to Levi. Ham was officially the most spoiled hamster in the universe, according to Lucy. I'd given Ham to Levi a few years ago, telling him he needed the company. It turned out to be a good call for Ham. He ran loose in the house, and Levi loved him. Case in point, the moment Ham started sniffing Levi's bare foot, Levi leaned over and offered him a carrot slice from a bowl of chopped veggies he kept on the counter for this express purpose. As Ham chowed down, Levi looked over at me, waiting.

"Fine," I huffed. *Third time today, it is.*

As I summarized the events, Levi straightened, his eyes narrowing, while he waited for me to finish. "Then, of course, I had to go back to work. I got fired because I called Lisa out for screwing Glen, in front of some customers."

Lucy chimed in. "Totally the best move on your part. She deserved the public humiliation."

Levi returned to the stir-fry he was making on the stove. "That fucking asshole. I always thought he was jerk. I'm sorry that it happened, but better to have it happen now than later," he said flatly.

Looking over at Levi, I bit back my retort. He'd told me before he thought Glen was an idiot. Just now, my reflexive defensiveness rose sharply. But what was the point in defending Glen now? He certainly hadn't been considering my feelings when he was dick-deep in Lisa.

I'd always felt slightly out of place, both in my family and in Willow Brook. Not completely, but it was what it was. Art was my thing, and I'd wanted a chance to see the big, bad world. When I got accepted into the art program in San Francisco, it had been a dream come true. The thing Levi hadn't liked about Glen was that he was pretentious. I'd never admitted to Levi that I agreed with him. Glen *was* pretentious. I'd overlooked that annoying character flaw, thinking he would grow past it.

I took a gulp of my wine. "So you were right," I finally replied. "I hope you feel good about it."

Levi stopped stirring. "I don't feel good about it at all, Jazzy. It's a good thing he doesn't live here, or I'd kick his fucking ass. That's bullshit. Fucking around on you is not okay. Not that I would've been happy if he had broken up with you, because you seemed to care about him, but that would've been a much better option than this."

My heart ached, and my throat felt tight. I was still so angry, I couldn't think too clearly about Glen. Yet, I knew as much as it hurt, that I'd dodged a bullet.

"I didn't mean to snap at you," I said with a sigh. "It was just so shitty, and I'm tired."

"What's your plan?" Levi asked.

He was now the fourth person who'd asked me this question today—Lucy, both of my parents, and now Levi. It wasn't as if the question was a surprise. I just hated it because I didn't have an answer. I needed to have a plan to answer it.

Lucy must've picked up on something on my face because she looked over to Levi. "Hey, she's got some downtime. She just caught her fiancé screwing her friend, and she lost her job. I sure as hell wouldn't have a plan yet."

Levi's gaze cut to her. I didn't know what passed between them, but when he looked back at me, his gaze was softer. I adored my brother, but he could be overprotective and opinionated when it came to me.

Ham had left the kitchen, but he conveniently returned,

distracting Levi. Levi leaned over and gave him another carrot slice.

"I forgot how funny it is to see you with him," I commented with a laugh.

Lucy chuckled and rolled her eyes. "I know, right? I was thinking we could get a dog, but Levi's worried the dog won't like Ham."

Levi glanced over, his expression serious. "Hey, I didn't say we couldn't get a dog, just that we need to make sure we find a dog who likes Ham."

That made me laugh so hard, I almost cried. Lucy was right there with me. Levi, being the good sport he was, merely shrugged and took it in stride.

In a few minutes, he was serving us dinner, and conversation moved onto more lighthearted topics. I fell asleep later that night, thinking it was actually good to be home. I had friends in San Francisco, even good friends, but Willow Brook was where I felt most at home.

I was a small-town girl and probably always would be. I just had to figure out how to have the life I wanted here. As I fell asleep, my mind flashed to Donovan. In the clear light of day, he'd been even more handsome than my tipsy memories had recalled.

His piercing hazel eyes and that almost black hair, paired with his rock-hard body, were a potent combination. Lying in bed alone, a shiver raced through me. Even though it didn't make a lick of sense, I wanted to know more about him.

Chapter Six

DONOVAN

A few days had passed since I'd crossed paths with Jasmine. I'd seen her from a distance, stopping by a store on Main Street to get gas. Despite my passing connection to her, she'd burrowed into my damn brain.

I kept recalling the feel of her mouth under mine, and her fingertip blazing like fire on my lips. Since I'd moved to Willow Brook, I'd come to like the little town. I'd grown up a southern boy in the Appalachian Mountains in Georgia. I'd loved the mountains; the heat, not so much. I'd moved to Alaska from Northern California after completing my hotshot training there and spending a few years on a crew in that area. Things went south for personal reasons, and I'd been hunting for a job on a hotshot crew elsewhere. When the job opened up here, I jumped at the chance.

It was hard to beat the wilderness in Alaska, and I damn near loved it. Now that I'd been here a while, I'd come to a sort of peace. The truth was, I'd come here to get away. It might be a cliché, but sometimes you need a change of scenery, and I sure as hell had.

That evening, as I left the station, the sun was setting,

but there was still some light on the horizon. I swung by Wildlands because I often headed there after work. It was a go-to place for the guys on the crews from Willow Brook Fire & Rescue, and it was an easy place to kick back and forget.

I snagged a beer and a table in the corner. My eyes caught the back of a man's head as he turned, and for a flash, I thought it was my friend Bill. Wildlands was the kind of place Bill would've liked to frequent. But Bill wasn't here, and we hadn't spoken in over three years. He'd been my oldest friend and then he wasn't anymore.

Just that moment, nothing more than a flash of time, and there was a sharp burn on my heart. Loss was a strange thing. You got used to it. It was like something broke and healed a little crooked. Perhaps you could use it just the same, but it always felt a little off, and you had to work around it. The shape of it morphed and changed—smaller and larger at different points in time, but always there.

After the moment I thought of Bill and then managed to get past it, Jasmine came walking in the back. She wore jeans and those cowboy boots again, this time paired with a deep blue blouse. The dark amber fall of her hair contrasted against the blue.

Looking at her across the room, I realized why she unsettled me so. I could own that I thought she was damn beautiful and sexy as all hell. I could acknowledge the wrinkle of a complication that she was the little sister of a friend. But what threw me was there was only one other woman who'd called to me like her. The pull I felt to Jasmine was raw and elemental, under the surface and beyond my control. The power of it cast a long shadow over the only woman who'd hurt me.

That woman? Well, she not only stomped on my heart, but she tore my best friend and me apart. Bill and I had yet to mend the rupture in our friendship, although lately the pain of the betrayal had dulled enough I thought it might be possible.

I liked to think that the man I was now would've seen her for who she was back then. Yet, the physical attraction to her had been so strong, I couldn't see past it. In hindsight, I'd say it was mostly lust. But when you're young and you're a man, lust cracks the whip.

I told myself not to watch Jasmine, but that was damn impossible. There was something burning in her, a reckless edge. It worried me slightly and tugged at every protective instinct I had. She strode to the bar and the eyes of every man in the room tracked her. At least, every man that wasn't with another woman.

She ordered a beer and then turned, her elbow hooked on the edge of the bar. I sensed the moment she saw me. From across the room, our gazes locked. It felt as if there was a force between us, heat and electricity shimmering across the room.

For some reason, it surprised me when she pushed off the bar and walked across the room toward me. As she got closer, the force between us heated, my body tightening.

She slipped into the chair across from me without even asking. Only when she was seated did she look over and arch a brow. "Mind if I join you?"

"Of course not."

I couldn't say aloud what I actually thought. I didn't mind at all. In fact, I'd have liked to pull her into my lap, tangle my hand into her wild hair, and kiss her senseless. On the heels of that thought was the reality that I needed to stay sane and keep a friendly distance.

Striving to keep my tone casual, I teased, "As long as you don't get too drunk and start another fight. If I end up taking you home after that, your brother will assume it might have something to do with me."

Jasmine laughed softly, but something flickered in her eyes, and I didn't know quite what it was.

"So, Donovan, tell me how you like Willow Brook," she began conversationally.

"I like it quite a bit. What brings you back here?"

Her cheeks pinkened, and a flicker of anger and pain danced in the backs of her eyes. I wanted to know who put that pain there. She took a pull from her beer and then cocked her head to the side. "Well, I'll be blunt. I caught my fiancé fucking my friend. In our bed. So I left. But the friend was the assistant manager at the same place where I worked. I ended up saying something about it in front of some customers and got myself fired. It only took about twenty-four hours for my life to completely blow up. No job, no fiancé, no place to live. I decided I might as well come home."

I experienced a hot flash of anger at her words. I couldn't decide if I was more pissed at her ex, or her friend. And I couldn't fucking believe any man would be so stupid as to fuck around on her. I might not know her well, but I knew she was a prize; the kind of prize that didn't come along often in life.

Considering my words, I held her gaze. "He's a fucking idiot."

Her smile unfurled slowly, her eyes widening in surprise. Fuck. Jasmine smiling was dangerous. My cock twitched. Between her smile and the pink stain on her cheeks, she'd hit me like a bolt of lightning.

"I think so too," she said, her smile fading as quickly as it appeared. "But it still sucks." She picked at the edge of the label on her beer bottle.

"Want me to kick his ass?"

I heard my question and couldn't believe I'd said it. But right now, if she had said yes, I would've found out where the guy was and done it.

A startled laugh escaped as she looked at me. "You *would* kick his ass for me, wouldn't you?" she asked, her tone wondering.

"Yes. Although I'm sure Levi would do the honors as well," I offered.

Saying Levi's name reminded me that Jasmine was his little sister.

And so what? She's a grown woman, she can make her own decisions.

I ignored that line of thinking.

"Oh, I'm sure he would. But somehow, I'd rather you do it," she said with another laugh. The flash of pain had faded from her eyes, and for that, I was relieved.

We fell into a comfortable silence for a moment, with Jasmine pausing to look around, her eyes scanning the room. When her gaze made its way back to me, she caught a lock of her hair around her finger, twirling it idly. "Where are you from?"

"Most recently, Northern California, but I grew up in Georgia."

That earned me a smile, and my heart gave a hard kick.

"Ah, you have a bit of your southern accent left."

"Yes ma'am," I replied with a wink.

"How'd you end up in Alaska?"

"Hotshot training in Cali, a few years there, and then I needed a change. The job opened up here, and I took it."

I left a lot of blanks in that story, but I didn't care to fill those in. Not now.

It was fair to say I had some experience with friends screwing around with someone I loved. Bill fucked my fiancée. But that was another story for another time.

I'd always loved the mountains and the wilderness. That was what drew me to becoming a hotshot firefighter, and what drew me to Alaska. My job kept my mind occupied, and I could be in the wilderness I loved.

Jasmine nodded slowly. She took another pull on her beer and stood as if to leave. "I think I'll go play some pool," she said.

That protectiveness flashed inside of me again as I

glanced over at the men currently clustered in that area. The same guy who had grabbed her ass was over there, along with a few of his jackass buddies.

I bit back the urge to tell her not to, but it definitely wasn't my place. With a wave, she turned away. Her cowboy boots struck with a distinct echo on the floor as she walked away. My eyes tracked the swing of her hips.

I forced myself to look away, telling myself I'd finish my beer and leave. Because if there was one thing I was coming to understand, proximity to Jasmine might not be the best thing for my sanity. She tugged at me. The electricity that sizzled in the air whenever she was near was hard to ignore. Layered into that was that flicker of vulnerability and that reckless edge I saw in her eyes.

I was getting up to leave not much later when I heard her voice ring out again. What the fuck was she up to now?

Spinning back, I surveyed the far corner where she was playing pool. Hand on her hip, she pointed her pool stick like a weapon, her eyes laser focused on the same idiot who'd grabbed her ass the other night.

Without thinking, I threaded my way through the crowd. Reaching her side, I didn't even wait. I caught the eyes of the asshole who was looking her up and down like she was a piece of meat just for him.

"Jasmine," I murmured, my voice low as I curled my hand around her arm. "Let's get the hell out of here."

Her eyes flashed as she looked up at me. For a beat, I thought she was going to argue, but she didn't. She set her pool stick down on the table and spun away, holding her middle finger up in a salute. She let me lead her away, but I was under no illusions that I was in control at the moment. She was walking away with me because *she* decided she was.

For the second time in a week, I walked down the narrow hallway out to the parking lot with Jasmine Phillips at my side. Unlike the other night, she was sober; she hadn't even finished her beer.

Once we were outside, she tugged her elbow free from my hand before spinning back to face me, her gorgeous blue eyes flashing. "I can take care of myself, you know," she hissed.

I kept walking past her. I wasn't going to have this scene right in front of the door. Whether she chose to follow me would also be up to her. I wasn't thinking clearly. At all. Need thrashed inside of me, that hum of electricity at her nearness burning hot.

I stopped at the back of my truck, turning to see her still approaching from behind. She stalked right up to me. "Don't walk away from me," she demanded.

Her amber hair glinted under the single light in the parking lot. Damn, she was glorious when she was angry.

"Sugar, I don't know why you're pissed off at me. The guy's a fucking asshole, and I can guarantee idiots like him are like a broken record. You get near him, and he's gonna look at you like a piece of meat, and treat you like one. Every damn time. Unless that's what you want, I'd suggest you steer clear."

Jasmine was quiet, her eyes still flashing. She rested a hand on her hip and rolled her eyes. "I'll do whatever the hell I want."

"Of course you will. You certainly didn't need to come out here with me. I figured you probably didn't want a repeat of the other night. Not that it's any of my damn business ..."

My words trailed off because none of this *was* my damn business. I didn't need to spend any more time with Jasmine this close to me because the longer I did, the more my brain fuzzed. As it was, all I wanted was her legs wrapped around my waist and her blouse torn open, so I could see the curves I knew were hidden behind it.

Shackling my need, I pushed my hips off the back of my bumper. "Well, I'll be going then."

I started to turn and then her hand caught my sleeve, her

fingers curling around my forearm, her touch like fire on my skin.

"What's it to you?" she demanded.

As I caught her gaze, I was in an all-out war with my body. I didn't say anything, simply arched a brow.

After a beat, she spoke again. "I know you want me," she said, her words a dare.

I didn't know what game she was playing, but it was definitely testing my limits.

Just when I thought she was going let go of my arm, just as I told myself sternly to remember to steer clear of her, her hand slid down my forearm, leaving a blaze of heat in its wake. She caught my hand in hers, pulling me toward her as she closed the distance between us.

Once again, her mouth was on mine. I couldn't resist it. I was certainly taller than her and could have leaned away. Yet, when she leaned up, her free hand sliding around to cup my nape, her fingers teasing along the edge of my hair, I just couldn't. It was like a match dropped into a vat of gasoline. I caught on fire. This time, I tangled my hand in the glorious fall of her hair, cupped her cheek, and devoured her mouth.

Our kiss went wild, almost instantly. Her tongue tangled with mine, and she moaned into my mouth. I was flat out oblivious to anything else around us. When she flexed into me, her breasts pressing against my chest, my knee slid between her thighs, and I could feel the damp heat there. All I wanted was her. A soft sound escaped from her throat. It was like cracking a whip through the air, electrifying me, every point of contact lighting sparks under my skin.

The sound of a raven calling sharply through the falling darkness punctured the haze. With an act of will that took everything within me, I tore my lips free from her kiss almost violently and took a step back. My breath came in heaves, as did hers. The air had started to chill. Stars winked in the gloaming, bright as the night claimed the day.

"We can't do this," I murmured.

As she stared at me, her tongue swiped across her bottom lip, and my cock swelled even more.

"Why not?"

I wanted her like mad, and yet I needed to pump the brakes because I could feel her starting to get to me. There was desire, and then there was this—a desire so intense it threatened to overtake all my restraint. She was my friend's little sister, so it couldn't just be sex. Levi would kick my fucking ass, and rightfully so.

I'd like to believe I was that honorable, but Levi wasn't the reason I was trying to put a stop to this madness. There was an emotional tug. She caught at the edges of the binding I'd wrapped around my heart and threatened to unwind it.

The vulnerability I sensed under the surface with her only served to threaten my control even more. I didn't know what she saw in my eyes, but a flash of pain flickered in hers before she closed them quickly.

Without a word, she spun away. I watched as she walked across the parking lot, her footsteps on the gravel distinct in the quiet. Only after she drove away did it occur to me she hadn't waited for me to answer her question. *Why not?*

I supposed that was a good thing because I had no good answer.

Returning home that night, there was no choice but to find release at my own hands. With Jasmine dancing through my thoughts, my mechanical release came at the vision of her tongue swiping across her lip and the feel of her body against mine.

Chapter Seven

JASMINE

My phone chimed on my nightstand. It was late, and I still couldn't sleep.

Sliding up against the headboard, I tucked the covers around my hips as I looked out the window. The moon was high in the sky, casting a silvery glow across the field behind Levi's house, the spruce trees shimmering under the light. The jagged line of the mountain ridge in the distance was a dark silhouette. With a sigh, I leaned over to snag my phone off the nightstand, swiping my finger across the screen.

It was a text from Glen.

I know I fucked up, but you could at least tell me where you are. This doesn't have to mean things are over. I blew it, and I know it. Please just give me a chance to talk.

I might've had all kinds of feelings about Glen and what had happened, but I knew without any doubt that there was no chance for us. Every time I thought of him, my mind conjured up the sight of Lisa on his lap, fucking the hell out of him.

I contemplated whether to even grace him with a reply. I finally decided the only reason it was worth it was because he would probably keep pestering me. Picking up my phone, I typed out a reply.

It's none of your business where I am. As far as us, it's over. That's final.

I hit send and then tossed the phone back on the nightstand. I felt so small, so unwanted. Even though I could tell myself Glen had been a cheating asshole, it didn't take the sting away from knowing what he'd done. My self-esteem when it came to my desirability had taken a major hit.

My mind flashed to Donovan, and I wanted to cry all over again. Even he didn't want me. To clarify, I thought he wanted me. Just not enough to see past whatever barriers he thought existed. I didn't know why this mattered so much. But it did. I wasn't being rational.

Hot tears rolled down my cheeks, and I curled my knees to my chest, letting my forehead fall to my knees as I cried. I'd been reckless in the bar the other night and again tonight, and I knew it. I just felt all out of sorts. Donovan did funny things to me. Aside from the fact that he was hot as hell—because he was—there was something else, this lure to wrap myself in him and his strength.

Yet, that was twice now he'd made it perfectly clear he wasn't looking for anything like that, certainly not with me.

I let myself cry for a few minutes, then wiped my cheeks on the sheets and tried to go back to sleep.

———

A week passed while I was at loose ends trying to figure out what the hell I was going to do. Levi and Lucy had made it clear I was welcome to stay as long as I wanted. Much as I loved them both, it didn't feel right to stay there indefinitely. I needed to find my own place and get my feet back under me.

With that in mind, I headed into town one afternoon to visit Janet James at Firehouse Café. My mother had mentioned in passing that she thought Janet was renting out the space above her B&B in downtown Willow Brook. As I drove into town, I rolled down my window, inhaling a deep breath of the fresh air. I didn't know if it was all in my head or not, but I was convinced even the air in Alaska was special.

Crisp and fresh, the summer air was scented with spruce and the rich greenery that grew in abundance during the short, light-filled summers. The lupine was in full bloom, the lovely purple flowers scattered amongst the tall grasses. Fireweed would bloom soon, and the landscape would be awash in fields of fuchsia, the wild weed creating an explosion of color.

As I drove into downtown, a smile tugged at the corners of my mouth. When I'd graduated from high school, I couldn't wait to get away from here. I'd loved Alaska, yet I'd been convinced I needed to spread my wings and fly away to see the world.

I'd done some traveling during college, crisscrossing the United States whenever I had time off between classes, visiting a number of cities and sort of falling in love with San Francisco. Yet, no place quite felt like home. Now that I had seen more of the world, Willow Brook no longer felt so limiting.

I paused after I climbed out of my car, spinning in a slow circle. Downtown Willow Brook was both familiar and strange at once. The aptly named Main Street ran right through the center of town. The police station and fire station were at one end. Main Street intersected another street on the opposite end that led to the small hospital where it was situated in a tiny valley just outside the main part of Willow Brook.

In between those two anchor points for downtown, Main Street had a run of retail stores mingling with restaurants and coffee shops. Swan Lake Road ran parallel to Main Street. The sprawling lake itself was named after the

Trumpeter Swans, the elegant and stunning swans that migrated here every summer. Swan Lake was visible from anywhere in downtown unless a building was in your way. Fishing lodges and hotels encircled it with the far side open wilderness as the forest gave way to the mountains in the distance.

As I spun around, my eyes arced over the familiar storefronts before my gaze landed on Firehouse Café, a local favorite hangout, and busier than ever in the summer.

Firehouse Café was in the town's original firehouse, a square brick building and cute as ever now. Since I'd moved away, a mural I'd painted on the corner of the building had faded away. That had been in my earliest phase of rebellion. Without anyone's permission, I'd painted giant sunflowers on the building late one night. I couldn't have said why, or maybe I could, but I had a slightly wild streak that emerged every so often, spurring me to do stupid things. I'd been lucky. Janet had liked the sunflowers and had only made me work as a penance.

I took a deep breath and let it out slowly. Coming home was grounding for me. The sting of Glen's betrayal was like a scratch over the surface of my heart; it stung and tore open. I told myself—and valiantly kept trying to convince myself of the point—that it was all for the best, but it still hurt. I struggled to feel worthy when it came to relationships.

For a moment, as I looked at Firehouse Café, the place beckoning me, my heart flinched and emotion lodged in my throat.

So, we're right back to that? You just can't let old habits die.

Oh, for God's sake, do you have to beat yourself up over beating yourself up?

If there was one thing I was an absolute expert at, it was giving myself a hard time. I metaphorically kicked myself in the ass to knock off that line of thinking.

With a deep breath and a flick of my hair over my shoulder, I forced myself to walk forward, pushing through the door, the sound of the cheerful bell above the door lifting my spirits slightly.

When I glanced up, I saw Janet at the counter, smiling at whoever was standing in front of her. Even though she wasn't smiling at me, my heart eased. I didn't know what Willow Brook would do without Janet. She was the heartbeat of the town.

Since I'd last seen her, her dark hair had a few more streaks of silver in it. Her smile was still wide, and I could see the warmth of her brown eyes from here. It was midday, so the place wasn't completely packed. I imagined it would be shortly, when the workday ended and people filtered in.

The café looked just as I remembered. It wasn't as if I hadn't been here at all since I'd been away; it just felt like a long time. My eyes scanned the space, taking in the stained blue concrete flooring, the cheerful curtains, the bright pink windowsills, the artwork hanging on the walls, and the fire-weed flowers painted on the old fire pole. The area that had once served as the garage for the fire trucks was now seating for customers. The back of the space held an open kitchen with a deli counter and then a bakery through a door behind it.

The warm scent of baked goods and fresh coffee filled the space. Although I was here for a very specific reason, there was no way I was walking out of here without a cup of coffee. I strode to the counter as Janet finished ringing up the customer there.

She looked to me, her eyes widening with another smile, and she paused in whatever she was saying. "Jasmine! So glad you're here."

Without missing a beat, her focus returned to the customer as she handed them some change. When they moved away, she gave me her full attention as I stepped up to the counter, curling my hands over the edge.

"Oh my goodness! Get back here," she said, waving me around the counter.

It was impossible to say no to Janet, not that I wanted to. As soon as I rounded the counter, she tugged me into her embrace. She smelled like cinnamon cookies and coffee.

When she stepped back, she gave my shoulders a squeeze. "How are you, dear?"

"I'm good." I paused, twisting my mouth. "I think."

Janet was, of course, a friend of my parents. I assumed she heard what happened with Glen, what had spurred me to finally come home. But now certainly wasn't the time to cover that topic. She lifted her chin. "I know you're glad to be home, and we're glad you're here," she said firmly. "Come on, let's go next door."

She must've picked up on my confusion and continued, "I'm in the process of renovating the place, so I'm not renting it out this summer as a B&B like I usually do. I've got several people interested in the suites upstairs. There's no construction going on up there, but it's loud downstairs, so I didn't want to rent to tourists. When your mother mentioned you were looking for a place, I wanted to give you the first shot. Do you want to go take a look?"

At my nod, Janet called into the back bakery. "Daniel!" A young man poked his head above the swinging half-door.

"Need me?" he asked.

Like myself back when I was in high school, plenty of kids still worked here when they could catch a few hours. Janet was a good boss and the tips were great.

"Yes, please. I'm taking Jasmine next door. Give me ten minutes and I'll be back, okay?"

He pushed through the door and stepped up to the counter, throwing a smile in my direction. He was tall and lanky with brown hair and blue eyes.

"Before we go, can I grab a coffee?" I asked, as Janet hooked her hand through my elbow.

Janet grinned. "Of course. Hang on." Within a minute, she was handing me a cup of the house coffee with a dash of cream.

With her hand tucked back into my elbow, she tugged me outside. The B&B she rented in the summers occupied a house next door to the café. Back when the original firehouse was built, the home was where the Fire Chief lived. Janet and her husband had bought both buildings when the town built the new fire station. After her husband died in a car accident on an icy highway up north, Janet had weathered her way through the grief and was a mainstay in Willow Brook, running the businesses on her own since then.

We hurried next door because Janet was perpetually in a state of rush. She led me through the downstairs, which was definitely under construction. Framing was exposed, sheetrock was torn out, and it looked as if all the cabinets had been removed.

"Wow, you weren't kidding when you said you were renovating down here," I commented.

She flashed a grin over her shoulder. "If you remember when you were in high school, I renovated the upstairs. I meant to get around to taking care of the downstairs sooner, but one thing after another delayed it. Then last winter, there were some frozen pipes down here, which burst and made a mess. I figured if I was going to have to pay for all the repair work, I might as well do the whole project. Well, *I'm* not doing the project but I'm paying for it," she said with a laugh.

She opened the door to the stairwell, gesturing for me to follow. A set of glossy hardwood stairs led upstairs where there was a short hallway with two guest suites. Even though I'd seen the outside of this place many times, I'd never actually been in here.

Opening the door on one side of the hallway, we stepped into a lovely suite. It opened into a shared living room and kitchen area with a tall ceiling and two skylights. Sun filled the space. The living room windows looked beyond the buildings across the street to Swan Lake. The kitchen was tucked in the corner with two counters running along two walls and a small circular dining table. It might have been small, but it had everything I needed.

There was a large bedroom suite with a bathroom to the side, which included a luxurious soaking tub.

"Wow," I said as I turned to glance at Janet, "this is really nice."

Janet grinned. "Of course it is. I make people pay me a fortune to stay here in the summer."

I bit my lip, wondering if I could even afford what she would be charging for rent here. "How much is it?"

She waved her hand dismissively. "For you, nothing."

"Janet, I have to pay something," I protested.

"Hon, you're like family to me. I know that once you get a job and you've got some money coming in, you'll be able to pay rent. I don't want you to drain whatever savings you have right now, just to pay me rent. Don't even argue with me about it," she said firmly. "Just let me know if you want it. If you do, it's yours until next summer, or until you make other plans."

I wanted to argue, but she was more stubborn than I was, and I knew that look in her eyes.

"Well, of course I'll take it. I'd be crazy not to. It's beautiful. I promise you'll be getting some rent within a few months."

"Perfect," she said, spinning around and striding out of the room quickly. "I've got to get back to the café. Oh, and your neighbor ..."

She paused when her phone blared out in song, specifically Prince's "1999." She glanced down. "I need to take this, this is one of our suppliers. Hang on, let me get the key."

Before I could reply, she answered her phone, tucking it between her ear and her shoulder as she fished in her pocket and handed over a key. Already deep in conversation, she hurried off before I had a chance to say anything else.

I stepped back into the small suite, looking around again. It was perfect. It would give me time to get my bearings without feeling like I was underfoot at Lucy and Levi's. Aside from not wanting to mooch off anyone, the freshness of my blown-up engagement stung being around Lucy and Levi so much. As much as I loved them, it was almost painful to see them together. Levi so clearly adored Lucy, and there was absolutely no question she returned the feeling.

It made me wonder if I would ever find someone who loved me like that and illuminated how wrong I'd been about Glen. Even before I'd walked in on him being ridden like a horse by my friend-slash-sort-of-boss, he'd never looked at me the way Levi and Lucy looked at each other. They were, simply put, crazy for each other.

With a swift mental shake and metaphorical kick in my ass, I forced my thoughts away from that line of thinking. I closed the door behind me and headed back out to Lucy and Levi's, intending to pack up and let them know where I'd be staying for now.

Despite all my worries and not really knowing my plan, it felt like I had a little island for myself right now.

Chapter Eight

JASMINE

Later that night, after a game of cards at Wildlands with the girls—the girls being Lucy and her friends, Amelia, Susannah, Maisie, Ella, and Charlie—I walked along Main Street, relieved I'd only had a few glasses of wine. I wasn't much for drinking. In fact, I was such a lightweight that I was tipsy even from that. I let myself into Janet's B&B and headed up the stairs.

When I got upstairs, I dropped the key as I tried to fit it into the lock. I accidentally put it in upside down next. When I wiggled it out, it flew loose from my fingers and clattered to the hardwood floor. The door across the hallway swung open. I jumped and spun around. I'd completely forgotten that anyone other than me could be in the building.

Donovan Ryan stood before me, in all his glory. Glory didn't quite capture what he looked like. The man was obscenely handsome. He wasn't wearing a shirt, for starters. Which meant I was staring at a wall of muscle. His chest was all hard planes with a dusting of black hair that narrowed to a point and disappeared behind the waistband of his jeans. My eyes—naughty, disobedient eyes that ignored my brain's warnings—followed that trail of hair down, wishing I could see further south. His jeans hung low on his hips, so I had a perfectly good view of the deep V of his muscles as they disappeared behind his jeans.

My mouth watered while heat bloomed through me and my channel clenched. Dear God. This man took the concept of *hot* to new levels. I was surprised I didn't simply melt into a puddle at his feet. I forced my eyes up to his face, feeling the heat on my cheeks.

I was hot and bothered all over.

His eyes darkened when my gaze met his. I swallowed, trying to will my pulse to slow down. After a weighted silence, a brow rose in a dark slash, his gaze skimming down my body and back up again, searing me everywhere his eyes landed.

"What are you doing here?" he asked.

Only then did I realize my mouth had dropped open slightly. I snapped it shut and gestured over my shoulder. "I'm staying here. What are you doing here?"

His eyes narrowed and then closed as he shook his head side to side. When he opened them, his expression was slightly pained. "Ah, I see. I'm staying here too. I guess we're neighbors then."

"Don't you have your own place?" I asked.

His mouth curled at the corner in a lazy grin. Damn, his grins were dangerous for my sanity.

"It's just temporary. I'm in the middle of getting a new house built, so Janet offered to let me stay here. I'm helping her out with the renovations downstairs. You're not staying at Levi's?"

I shook my head. "No, I wanted my own place. Janet offered and, well, it's a really nice place." I paused, uncertain what else to say and feeling restless. My body's response to him made me feel half crazy. "Anyway, I should go," I said quickly. "Good night." I shoved the key into the lock, breathing a silent sigh of relief when it slid in easily this time.

I hurried through the door, slamming it shut behind me and then leaning against it. I gulped in air, my heart thudding wildly in my chest.

Oh hell. I didn't know how I was going to do this with the unholy temptation of Donovan right across the hallway.

Chapter Nine

DONOVAN

The following day, I woke after a shitty night's sleep. The last person I'd expected to see last night was Jasmine. Having her mere feet away was going to be torture.

I'd taken Janet up on her offer to stay here for the summer in the midst of the construction on my house. I'd started building my place last summer, but this year, I'd hired on a crew to finish it. Janet had offered for me to stay here at no cost in exchange for handling the renovations downstairs. It worked out for both of us. My house was a major project, more than I could handle and get done in any decent time in between fires. Yet, the renovations Janet needed were small and manageable. I could easily fit them in when I was in town and save the money on trying to find a rental.

I'd known Janet might rent out the space across the hallway, yet it never occurred to me to even worry about who it was. Laying eyes on Jasmine had sent me into a cold shower last night. A mechanical release had done little to slake my need.

I did not need to lust after Levi's little sister. Nor did I need her living across the hall from me.

I vividly remembered the sight of her long amber hair cascading down her back, her sapphire blue eyes flashing, and the sweet curve of her breasts.

Fuck me.

I woke up, my cock hard, after she'd spent the night sashaying through my dreams. I usually had better control than this. I'd convinced myself I could forget the feel of her lips on mine. Perhaps I could have, yet chances were I'd see her often now. For all intents and purposes, we were practically living together.

With a groan, I kicked the sheets back and headed for another cold shower. Yet again, my hand didn't do justice to what I imagined it would feel like to sink inside of Jasmine.

For no rational reason, I was annoyed with Janet. Why the hell did she have to rent that space out to Jasmine? Of all people. Even though she had no clue the two of us knew each other. *And now I feel ridiculous for being irritated with Janet.* It wasn't like she'd done anything wrong.

After my cold shower, I tugged on a pair of jeans and a T-shirt and headed over to Firehouse Café. I couldn't give Janet a piece of my mind, but I *could* see if she had any clue how long Jasmine would be staying there.

I was here at least through autumn. That left a few months of torture in store for me if Jasmine was here the entire time.

Pushing through the door into Firehouse Café, the scent of fresh coffee and baked goods assailed me. As usual, the café was busy, a low hum of conversation mingling with the music playing in the background. Most of the tables were full. As I glanced around, my eyes landed on Jasmine, sitting at a table by herself in the corner.

Her hair was tied up this morning in a ponytail. It swung about halfway down her back. She was looking out the window, her thumb tracing circles on the top of her coffee mug.

The moment I laid eyes on her, my body tightened again. Damn. If this kept up, I'd be becoming best friends with my hand. Forcing my gaze away from her, I stepped to the back of the line. Within minutes, I was at the counter with Janet smiling at me.

"Good morning, Donovan," she said. "I was next door the other day, and it looks like it's coming along. Thank you so much for your help."

"Not a problem," I replied. I was considering whether to ask her about Jasmine staying there when she answered my question for me.

"I meant to give you a call, but it just got away from me. Jasmine"—she paused, her eyes flicking over to where Jasmine sat in the corner—"she'll be staying across the hallway for now. I'm sure you won't mind, right?"

Janet couldn't know that the mere sight of Jasmine sent lust jolting through me. I didn't mind Jasmine living across the hall, except for the fact she might make me crazy. I kicked those thoughts to the curb.

"Of course not," I lied. "How long will she be there?"

Janet shrugged. "As long as she needs for now. As it is, I won't be renting out those suites to tourists until next summer. I'm not worried about it. I'm sure you two will be good neighbors," she said with a satisfied nod.

I bit back a laugh. As long as Jasmine stopped being such an unholy temptation to me, I was sure it would be fine.

"I'm sure we will. Anyway, I could use a Shot in the Dark," I said, referencing my preferred house coffee with a shot of espresso, and handed over a five-dollar bill.

"You got it," Janet said, whirling away to get my coffee started. I stepped to the side, waiting until she slid it over to me. She attempted to hand me some change, but I tossed it in the tip jar.

As I turned away from the counter, coffee in hand, it so happened Jasmine looked up, her eyes catching mine from across the room. That same jolt of electricity I felt whenever I looked at her flared up and before I knew it, my feet were walking in her direction.

What the fuck are you doing, dude? Just being a friendly neighbor. It's not like I can ignore her.

I kicked those thoughts away as I reached her table, glancing down.

Her thick lashes curled against her cheeks as she glanced up at me.

"Good morning."

"Morning," I replied, my voice coming out gruff.

Standing close to her did not help matters. Unfortunately, or fortunately, depending on how I looked at it, I had an excellent view of the sweet curve of her breasts from above. She was wearing a blouse, and though it was loose, I could see into the valley between them. Her blouse was a deep blue, and my eyes landed on the navy-blue lace teasing me along the edge. I'd have given just about anything to flick those buttons undone and cup her breasts.

The air felt electric around us as I stared at her, noticing her nipples were pressing against the thin cotton of her blouse.

Fuck me.

I forced my eyes up, keeping them trained on her face. That should've helped, but it didn't. Her lips were slightly crooked, plump and full. She caught the bottom corner in her teeth, quiet for a beat. "So, I guess we're neighbors."

"I guess so," I replied, ignoring the thud of my heart against my ribs and the swell of my cock. "If you need anything, just let me know."

"How long are you staying?"

"Another few months, at least. I'm doing renovations downstairs in between jobs. I'm there because I'm also finishing up building my own place."

Jasmine sipped her coffee, and I was jealous of her lips

when she swiped her tongue across the bottom, catching a drop of coffee.

"We'll be neighbors for a little while then. I think I'll be there at least for the summer. You won't even notice I'm there. I promise I'm a good neighbor," she said with a subtle grin.

She had no idea the effect she had on me. I managed to nod and took a gulp of my coffee, needing the rich, bitter flavor. "I'm on my way to the station. I'll catch you later," I said as I turned away, literally forcing my feet to walk away.

Heading into the station, I told myself that the need that lashed at me whenever I was near Jasmine would fade. It had to.

Later that afternoon, I turned to look at the flames licking at the sky. We were in the middle of handling a controlled burn just outside of Willow Brook. The owners of the property had given us permission to burn here. It would benefit them because we'd burn off clusters of dead spruce while also giving our crews an opportunity for training.

It was a clear, cloudless day, and the wind was down. Half of our crew was just finishing up, with the rest rolling in to help manage the burn as it died down. I watched the flames flicker and listened to the sound of the trees burning for a moment. As I turned to walk away, I heard my name. Glancing up, I saw Levi walking toward me.

The moment I saw him, Jasmine sashayed through my thoughts. Fuck me. I did not need to be this obsessed with his sister. He approached, flashing a half-grin. "Hey, so you guys got it nice and hot for us," he said with a chuckle.

"It's not too bad. Y'all should be busy for a bit, but it's already slowing down."

Levi nodded, his gaze sobering. "By the way, thanks again for taking care of Jasmine the other night."

"Of course. I'd do it for any friend."

I almost commented that she was now my neighbor—my

way-too-close-for-comfort neighbor. But I didn't. The last thing I needed to do was chat with Levi about his sexy as hell sister, who tempted me day in and day out.

The less I thought about Jasmine, the better.

Chapter Ten

JASMINE

Sitting at the round table in my parents' kitchen, I looked out over the field behind the house. It was late, and the sun was only now starting to set. The kitchen offered a lovely view of a field with a stream at the far end winding into trees with the mountains in the distance. I didn't suppose there was anywhere I could look in Alaska without ending the sentence "with the mountains in the distance."

Levi's voice brought my focus back. Glancing across the table, I caught his grin as he rubbed Lucy's round belly.

Lucy rolled her eyes. "Are you going to do this every day for the rest of my pregnancy?" she asked with a smile. She was only a few months along, and Levi was already getting on her last nerve, although she was good-natured about it. My mother glanced between them, smiling indulgently. Levi and I had inherited our blue eyes from her, while my hair was darker than the blonde hair they shared.

"I'm sure he will. Maybe humor him a little," she suggested.

Lucy laughed again, casting a smile in Levi's direction. "I am."

Levi dipped his head, dropping a kiss on the side of her neck, and Lucy's cheeks flushed pink. My heart gave a hard thump. There was something so adorable about them. My older brother, who had once been nothing but a player, had fallen so hard for Lucy, it was hard to imagine that he'd ever been anything other than madly in love with her.

As for Lucy, well, she was on the prickly side, not exactly a warm and fuzzy type of person. Yet with Levi, it was obvious he cut right through her defenses.

Emotion hit me with a flash. I wouldn't say I missed Glen, I was still so angry and so hurt, but for a while there, I thought I'd finally gotten something right. I'd pieced together a life that offered an outlet for my art and was going to marry someone responsible and upstanding.

My record with men before Glen, well, it wasn't too stable. I seemed to have a knack for finding guys who wanted nothing more than another notch on their bedpost, while I was busy searching high and low for, well, something else. Glen seemed to want more, or so I'd been fooled into thinking.

I leaned my elbows on the table, reaching for my water and taking a sip. My mother glanced my way. "So, dear, any ideas on what your plans are?"

I bit back a sigh. I was averaging some variation of this question about five times a day right now. It had occurred to me this morning when I'd seen Donovan that he was about the only person who didn't ask me "what next?"

I forced a smile and tried to keep my tone casual. "I don't know yet, Mom. I've got a place to stay, thanks to Janet, so I'm going to hunker down there. Amelia mentioned that Quinn is friends with a woman in Diamond Creek, who runs a gallery there and manages a few others. You remember Quinn Haynes, right?"

"Of course I do!" my mother exclaimed. "I'm friends with his mother. Good grief. So proud of Quinn. He runs the family medical clinic in Diamond Creek now and has another baby on the way."

Levi chuckled, casting a glance my way. "Don't you dare imply Mom might forget someone."

"Ha ha, I know. Anyway, I'm going to give Quinn's friend a call. It's a definite possibility. Even if she's not interested in selling any of my pottery, maybe she'll have some suggestions for me. Then, I need to find a place where I can set up my kiln and throwing wheel."

"I was thinking about that, by the way," Lucy interjected. "Whenever you figure out where, if you want, Amelia and I can help out in between jobs."

A flash of excitement zapped through me. It felt as if my entire life was off balance and had been ever since I'd walked in on Glen and Lisa. Throwing pottery grounded me and made me feel sane. Perhaps it had only been a few weeks, but I missed it. With my entire life turned upside down, it would help to have that.

"Well, let me see about where first. Then I'll see what I need to do. Once I get some money coming in, I can pay you."

Lucy shook her head firmly. She and her best friend Amelia ran a construction company. "You're not paying me. I can't imagine it would be much work for us, maybe a day or two at the most."

I could feel the eyes of my mother, my father, and Levi on me. Somehow, I always felt like the one who needed to be taken care of in our family.

"That would be great," I finally said. "But I'll still pay you back, one way or another."

My dad, who was definitely the quietest in our family, winked at me. "As far as I'm concerned, anything that'll keep you here works for me. If you need my help, all you have to do is ask."

Levi rested his arm across the back of Lucy's chair, his fingers sifting through the ends of her hair. He glanced down, the pride in his eyes evident. "Lucy and Amelia do the best construction work in town."

The tension bundled inside of me started to loosen slightly. I was still all over the place, both mentally and emotionally. With everything that had happened in the past week, I didn't know which end was up anymore.

Conversation moved on, and a while later, I walked out with Levi and Lucy. Pausing at the foot of the stairs leading to the deck, Levi caught my eyes. "You know, you didn't have to move out."

We'd had some variation of this conversation every time I saw him in the days since I'd moved into the suite. Clearly, I'd hurt his feelings. Yet, he didn't understand why I needed some space. In the fading light, I bit back another sigh.

"I know, Levi. This way, I won't feel like I'm underfoot."

Lucy spoke, nudging Levi with her elbow. "Babe, I told her plenty of times she was welcome to stay. I think maybe, just maybe, she doesn't want her older brother breathing down her neck."

Lucy never failed to surprise me with her sharp percep-tion. I hadn't said a word to her about it, but obviously she understood. A flash of annoyance rose in Levi's expression, his rich blue eyes narrowing.

"I wasn't breathing down her neck." His eyes flicked back to me. "If you're not planning on staying too long, don't get Mom and Dad's hopes up."

Now I was angry. I felt my cheeks heat, a mixture of hurt and anger tangling inside as I stared at Levi. My fun-loving, funny brother was a deeply caring person, and like so many siblings, we rubbed each other the wrong way sometimes. We also had some history that had only served to reinforce his tendency to be overprotective of me.

The past was the past, but sometimes it left scars. I knew how foolish I felt, so I could only imagine how foolish I looked. I'd managed to get engaged to an asshole who screwed around on me, and lost both my temper and my job in the same afternoon. Here I was, back home, relying on family and friends to float me through this situation.

As I stared at him, whatever he saw in my eyes, he closed his, giving his head a hard shake. Lucy stayed quiet, her own eyes wide as she glanced between us.

Her uncertainty was unusual. If there was one thing I could count on with Lucy, it was for her to speak her mind.

I swallowed through the tightness gathering in my throat and chest. When Levi's eyes opened, I saw nothing but regret contained there.

"I'm sorry, Jasmine," he said, his voice low and his eyes pained. "I didn't mean it the way that came out."

"It's okay. It's not like I don't understand why you said it. I get it. Maybe I'm not sure of everything I'm doing, but I'm here and I'm not planning on going anywhere. I have to go," I said, spinning and hurrying away.

"Jasmine," Lucy called from behind me.

I felt her soft, yet steely presence as she caught up to me. "Do you need anything?" she asked softly.

"I'm okay. I just need to go." I looked beyond her as Levi approached.

I waved and climbed into my car before the conversation could continue. Driving back into town toward Janet's B&B —my temporary home—I felt restless and edgy. Buried underneath a scar, Levi's words had torn at an old, painful truth. It hurt.

I didn't want to think. A few minutes later, I pulled up, swung my purse over my shoulder, and strode across the parking lot. I stepped into the downstairs, closing the door behind me. The rhythmic sound of somebody hammering something echoed through the downstairs. I figured Donovan must be working on something. The moment I turned to look into one of the rooms he was renovating, my mouth went dry.

There was Donovan fully clothed, and then there was Donovan wearing nothing but a pair of faded black jeans and no shirt. The man was dangerous for my sanity, yet now, it was all I could do not to simply melt to the floor. He hadn't heard me come in, so my eyes took full advantage of the free moment. He was holding a two-by-four in place at the top of what I assumed would be a new wall. His back was on display for me. It was nothing but muscle. My eyes tracked the hard planes, glistening with a sheen of sweat.

A sweet ache built between my thighs, and my pulse lunged to a gallop.

I was just standing there, staring at him, when he turned. His eyes widened slightly when he saw me. Yet, he appeared far more in control in this moment while I took "hot and bothered" to an entirely new level.

I didn't doubt for a second that my cheeks were on fire. I might as well have handed over my ovaries on the spot. That was how needy I felt.

Hopefully oblivious to my internal state, Donovan slowly lowered his arm, his hand curled loosely around the grip of the hammer. Even at rest, he was glorious. Sweet hell, I wanted him. He was positively lickable. My eyes followed the dusting of dark hair narrowing to disappear behind his waistband. My fingers literally itched to touch him.

Before I knew it, I was walking toward him as if drawn by a powerful tug. I didn't even bother to resist. I wanted Donovan, and I wanted him *now*.

Chapter Eleven

DONOVAN

Jasmine walked across the room, her hair falling in tousled waves around her shoulders and her sapphire eyes darkening as she approached me. She'd caught me off guard. I'd come home after what should've been a tiring day, still wrestling with a sense of restlessness. I'd thrown myself into working downstairs. Unfortunately, that hadn't taken the edge off.

The moment I sensed Jasmine's presence behind me, it was as if a whip snapped through the air, the sensation akin to lightning on a stormy day, electrifying everything.

She wore her cowboy boots with a skirt—a stretchy, cotton skirt that hugged her hips and flared just below her knees. Atop that, she wore a loose blouse with a scoop neck, the tiny buttons marching down the valley between her breasts—the sheer cream-colored silk serving to convince my eyes I could see the silky lace of her bra behind it. I had no idea if I actually could, yet my body thought so. All she had to do was exist, and she was a tease.

I dragged my eyes up to her face just as she came within a few feet of me. Her cheeks were flushed, and her eyes wide. I didn't know how to read her expression. Hell, I didn't know why I thought I should. I needed to keep a clear distance between Jasmine and me. I did *not* need to be lusting after my friend's little sister.

But there was need, and then there was the need I felt for her, which shorted out every circuit in my brain.

I knew I saw desire flickering in her eyes. The moment our eyes collided, that whip cracked again, sizzling the air with electricity. My cock swelled, and I curled my hand tighter around the hammer, as if gripping that would help me maintain control.

As she stared at me for a beat, the hard look in her eyes fell away, and I glimpsed vulnerability in the depths. Somehow, that only made me want her more. An intense sense of protectiveness rolled through me. The protectiveness only served to feed into the need I already felt for her.

We stood in silence for several moments, our eyes locked together. I tried to tell myself I couldn't act on my feelings. Yet, raw desire hijacked all rational thought. I told myself nothing would happen unless she made the first move.

She took two more steps, closing the distance between us. I could feel the heat of her body as her scent drifted to me—a subtle musky scent mingled with strawberries. I distantly wondered if that was her shampoo.

She reached for the hammer in my hand, taking it from me.

"You don't need this," she said, her husky voice wrapping like smoke around me, heating the air and sending another hot jolt of lust through my body.

I barely heard the hammer fall to the floor. She wasn't very tall, her head just coming to my shoulder, as she lifted her hand to trace the stubble along my jawline. Just like that first night I met her, her touch was like fire on my skin.

Even though I told myself she had to make the first move, the moment she touched me, I slid my hand into her hair, cupping the nape of her neck. I held still for a beat, almost as if I were testing myself to see if I could hold back.

I couldn't. In a flash, my mouth was on hers. That point of contact—when our lips collided—was like a match being thrown into gasoline. It flashed hot and high around us. I couldn't have told you if I meant to go slow because that was impossible. The moment her lips softened and she sighed into my mouth, I swept my tongue into hers and our kiss went wild.

Her tongue tangled with mine, and she stepped closer as my hand moved from her hair down her spine to cup her sweet ass. I growled into her mouth, and she arched against me, her soft breasts pressing against my chest. I could feel the tight little points of her nipples through the thin silk of her blouse.

Fuck me.

I had known the moment I saw her, before I ever knew who she was, that it would be like this. There was my mind and then there was my body. My body recognized her as a touchstone to mine.

Her hand traveled across my chest, tracing along its planes. Everywhere she touched sent streaks of fire under the surface of my skin. To think I once thought I could hold back, that I could be sensible, that I wouldn't give into this burning, yearning white-hot desire for her. My restraint— what little there had been—burned to ashes in the searing heat of our kiss.

In a very distant corner of my mind, reason knocked its fist loudly on the door, just barely puncturing the haze of need.

Hanging onto the thinnest thread of control, I tore my mouth free, instantly missing the feel of her lips under mine, and almost dragging my tongue along the side of her neck. I could see the wild flutter of her pulse in her neck, her scent wrapping around me like a drug.

That distant voice forced me to speak.

"Are you sure you want this?" I asked.

I couldn't have told you if I was asking myself that question, or Jasmine. Perhaps both.

Her eyes stared back, hazed with desire. Her lips were swollen and red from our kiss and her cheeks flushed. She didn't move, every inch of her front pressed against me. Somewhere in the midst of the madness of our kiss, my knee had slid between her thighs. I could feel the damp heat of her pussy through the layers of fabric between us. I knew, without even touching her, that she was hot and slick. I couldn't wait to test that theory.

She stared at me, completely silent. The only sound in the room was our breathing, hers coming in little pants and my own in ragged gasps. My heartbeat thundered in my ears.

"I'm sure," she finally replied, her husky voice wrapping around me, tightening the ropes of need twining around us.

I was so fucking out of it that, for a second, I forgot my question. Her mouth curled at the corner in a half-grin. "Are *you* sure?"

That voice of reason, still not quite completely drowned out, spoke. "Your brother's my friend," I murmured.

Oh, she didn't like that answer.

Her eyes narrowed, darkening further. "Levi's not my keeper. He sure as hell doesn't have a say in my sex life," she said flatly, lifting her chin, almost as if she were daring me.

We stood there, the air heavy as if a storm were impending—weighted, powerful, and restless to be unleashed.

My defenses were down, my control nothing more than a frayed thread. If I could've mustered up the strength to walk away from Jasmine before now, I couldn't the moment she flicked her eyes to me again and dipped her head, dusting kisses across the surface of my chest.

Having her lips on me was like being dipped in lava. A groan escaped and then her head lifted, and her lips were on mine again. We spiraled right back to where we'd been before, lips and tongues tangling in nips and kisses—hot, wet, and deep.

Her foot curled around my calf as her hand stroked down my back, her nails scoring my skin lightly, just enough to stoke the fire inside. I lifted her against me, growling as I tore my lips free to finally taste her skin. Blazing a wet path down the side of her neck, she tasted sweet and salty and smelled like heaven. I wanted to eat her up.

Her legs curled easily around my hips, her skirt riding up. I took several steps and slid her hips onto a counter against the wall. Drawing back, I took a moment to simply absorb the sight of her. Her breath was coming in soft pants, her nipples pressing against my chest with each inhalation. With her cheeks pink, her lips swollen, and the heat of her core pressing against my cock, I could barely think, need beating inside me like a drum and drowning out everything.

She lifted her hands, reaching between her breasts. In a matter of seconds, she unbuttoned her blouse. I didn't know what was driving her, but I sensed a wildness under the surface. Not that I could've stopped myself, I was far past that point. The moment her blouse fell open and my eyes flicked down, I was so lost, I couldn't see my way out.

She wore a cream lace bra, the taut beads of her nipples pressing pink against the lace, teasing me. Her breasts swelled up and over the small cups. Reaching out, I dragged the backs of my fingers over her belly, satisfaction rolling through me when her breath hissed through her teeth. I held her gaze as I trailed my fingers under the soft curves of her breasts and cupped one in my palm. Rolling my thumb back and forth over her tight nipple, I watched as her eyes flashed. Her lips parted, and I could feel her heartbeat against my palm, beating hard and fast. Like mine.

"What do you want?" My question slipped out without thought.

Because even though I was tied up inside and wanted her

more fiercely than I could recall wanting anyone, there was a hint of vulnerability to her, softness that gave me pause.

"You. Now," she said flatly.

I dipped my head, dragging my tongue along the side of her neck, breathing in her scent and savoring the salty tang of her skin. I traced my tongue over the line of her collarbone and down between the valley of her breasts. Swirling my tongue over the lace, I circled one of her tight little nipples, sucking and nipping lightly, savoring her cry as she buried her hands in my hair. The subtle sting of pain when she gripped my hair was a lash to the need burning me up and offered a relief at the same time.

Lifting my head, I stepped back, curling my palms around her calves and sliding them up her legs, easing her knees apart. Her skin was like honey, light amber all over, her bright blue eyes standing out.

I needed to touch her, all of her. With her cowboy boots on and her feet dangling from the table, her skirt pooled at her waist, just looking at her nearly did me in. She looked wanton and wild, and I wanted her so fiercely, I ached.

When my palms reached her thighs, I slid them over to grip her hips and tug her to the edge of the counter. Glancing down, I saw that she wore practical blue cotton panties. Somehow that was even more of a turn-on. I gritted my teeth and hung onto my control. No matter how much I wanted her—and fuck, I wanted her so badly, I ached—it wasn't about my need tonight.

I needed to taste her, but I wanted more than one wild night, so I was going to wait because it all felt too rushed. Tonight was about her.

When my thumbs reached the apex of her thighs, I traced along the crease at her hips, the silky soft skin its own tease. She shivered under my touch, goose bumps forming on her skin. I dragged my fingers over the damp cotton between her thighs. Hooking a finger over the edge, I pushed her panties aside, almost groaning aloud at the sight of her pink, swollen pussy, glistening and slick with need.

I didn't live like a monk, yet it had been a while. Jasmine was going to push me to my limit. Flicking my eyes up, I trailed my fingers through her folds. She was soaked, dripping wet, the insides of her thighs damp from her juices.

"Look at me," I murmured.

I needed to see her when she came. Her breasts rose and fell rapidly with her short, sharp pants. Her eyes locked to mine, her tongue darting out to trail over her bottom lip. My cock swelled even further.

I sank a finger into her channel, knuckle deep, watching as she moaned, her lids falling. Another finger joined the first. Teasing my thumb over her clit, I watched her, stretching her channel gently before drawing my fingers out and sinking back in.

For all of my control, I needed to taste her more. Dipping my head, I traced my tongue around her folds as I pumped in and out of her with my fingers, savoring the clench of her channel, so slick and wet around me. I knew what it would feel like to be buried inside of her. Fucking heaven.

Little sounds came from the back of her throat as her hips rocked into me. Slowly finger fucking her, I was almost drunk on the salty sweet taste of her and the way she cried out, gripping my hair. I used my free hand to hold her hips fast, my fingers digging into her. I loved her generous curves —she was so fucking beautiful she took my breath away.

When I felt her body tightening, I swirled my tongue over her clit, sucking it lightly into my mouth. She cried out, her channel clamping down around my fingers. With a last lick, I drew back, watching as she arched back, her plump breasts jutting forward. She was glorious.

Chapter Twelve

JASMINE

Pleasure rocked me, to the core. It slammed through me so hard, all I knew was this moment—with fire capturing me in its flame and scattering through me. The only thing anchoring me was the feel of Donovan's hand on my hip and his fingers buried inside of me.

As I slowly came back into my body, I dragged my eyes open to find his gaze waiting. My heart was thudding, hard and fast, inside my chest. I had no idea what to say. He'd just given me the most intense orgasm of my life.

What I'd wanted—to lose myself, to forget myself, to burn off the restlessness inside—had happened. If only because it was impossible for me not to completely lose myself in sensation the moment Donovan's lips met mine.

I hadn't expected this—this burning, yearning need, spinning me wildly until I was dizzy with him, drunk on him.

Stunned, I stared at him, the haze inside my mind starting to clear. There he stood, in all his glory, his muscled chest, the tease of dark hair narrowing over his rigid abs. I wasn't done yet though. Reaching between us, I caught the buttons on his fly, quickly flicking them open and curling my hand over the hard, hot ridge of his cock.

Oh, I was so screwed. Of course Donovan Ryan went commando. The hot, velvety skin came alive under my touch. He was already hard as hell, but when his cock sprang free and I curled my palm around it, giving it a little squeeze, his breath hissed between his teeth and a low growl came from his throat.

Even his cock was beautiful. Thick and long, it filled my hand as I flicked my eyes up to his face. He stepped back, gently shoving my hand away.

"Not yet," he murmured, gripping himself in his fist.

Sensation spun inside of me, the walls of my channel clenching at the sight of him fisting his own cock. I wanted him. Inside of me. It didn't matter that I'd just nearly lost my mind with pleasure. The sight of him sent need spinning through me, sliding through my veins.

"Not yet, what?"

His hazel gaze held mine, his eyes narrowing. "Some things are better saved for later."

I wanted to argue the point, but before I could even open my mouth, he stepped between my knees, his eyes flicking down. Somewhere in the heat of the madness, he'd tugged my hips close to the edge of the counter. My legs were dangling over the side and my pussy was right there, swollen, slick, and wet.

He stepped closer, dragging the thick head of his cock through my folds and teasing my clit. With my senses on fire, I cried out.

I distantly heard myself begging, "Please ..."

"Later," he murmured.

He stepped closer yet again, sliding the underside of his cock over my pussy. My juices soaked him. I was so slippery wet, he slid back and forth easily.

Instantly, I was needy—panting and chasing after another sweet release. I looked down between us. He cupped one of my breasts in his palm, teasing my nipple as his cock slid back and forth, driving me to madness. I watched a drop of pre-cum roll off the tip of his cock, mingling with my juices.

I was frantic as my hips flexed into him. Then, pleasure snapped through me again, my sex clenching and spasming. I watched as he slid over me once more, before letting out a low groan as he came, spurting onto my belly with his fingers pinching my nipple, the subtle pain an anchor point as I spun loose inside, flying to pieces.

Consciousness gradually filtered back in through the thick haze around me. I felt as if I were coming out of a coma of pleasure.

I was suddenly uncomfortable, almost afraid to look into his eyes. I was usually more in control, more able to orchestrate what happened. With him, I couldn't control anything. I was teetering far too close to the edge of vulnerability.

I sternly ordered myself not to be a coward and gradually lifted my eyes. His gaze seared into me.

It almost hurt to look at him. I felt stripped bare, naked inside and out. My entire body flushed. As he looked at me, I didn't know how to read what I saw in his eyes. It felt as if he rang a chord inside of me—with nothing more than a look—that I didn't even know existed.

His hand slowly eased its grip on my hip, and he stepped back, muttering something under his breath as he glanced around. He reached over for something, my eyes immediately following the flex of his abs as he stretched. He snagged what I presumed to be his T-shirt off the corner of the counter. He quickly wiped my belly and his cock before buttoning his jeans. I was still sitting there, my panties shifted to the side and my skirt in a rumple around my waist.

I felt downright dirty. I had a wild side, not that I acted on it very much. That was the crazy thing about this situation. I hadn't been with anybody other than Glen in three years.

I forced myself to move, shifting my hips off the counter and slipping to the floor. My boots hit the floor with a loud *thud* in the unfinished room as my skirt fell down around my hips, and I adjusted my panties. What I wanted in this moment was to crawl into bed beside Donovan, wrapped in his strong, sheltering embrace. But that didn't make a lick of sense.

Well, this was awkward.

When I glanced up, his eyes snagged mine. I suddenly toppled over that edge of vulnerability—naked and raw, inside and out. Everything in me was leaning toward him, yet I willed myself to step back, and summoned a bright smile.

"I have to go. I'm sure I'll see you around," I said quickly before spinning away.

As I opened the door, I realized that I must have looked like an idiot. Calling upon every ounce of bravado inside of me, I turned back as I tried to button my blouse when I realized it was still hanging open.

Donovan stood before me, his hand resting on the edge of the counter where he had just driven me absolutely wild. His skin was damp with a sheen of sweat. My eyes flicked down to the deep cut of his muscles as they disappeared beneath his waistband.

In a flash, he stole my breath—again.

My cheeks were hot by the time my eyes made their way back to his. I had no idea what he was thinking. His gaze was inscrutable.

I managed a shallow breath and then flashed another smile. "That was more than I bargained for," I said, trying to keep my tone light and flirtatious. Little did he know that he'd just given me the two most amazing orgasms in my life.

That was about all I could manage. The veneer of courage I'd swung over my shoulders as I buttoned my blouse was already slipping.

With a wave, I spun away again, closing the door behind me and hurrying up the stairs, my boots loud as they struck each stair tread. I rushed into my suite, almost slamming the door. I caught it at the last moment, closing and locking it quietly. Not because I was worried he would come in. It was more that I needed some kind of barrier between myself and my need to seek him out.

Because I was already on fire inside. Again.

What was supposed to take me away in my mind had done so quite thoroughly. Yet, now I was spinning as if I'd been flung into the ocean, desire running through me so fiercely I was caught in its undertow, barely able to keep my head above water.

I leaned against the door, my breath coming in short pants, only belatedly realizing I'd left my purse downstairs.

Fuck, fuck, fuck. My head thumped against the door. *What an idiot.*

I wasn't usually a coward, but right now, I couldn't bring myself to go back downstairs and face Donovan. I pushed away from the door, deciding I would wait until I heard him come upstairs before I tiptoed downstairs to fetch my purse.

Slipping out of my boots, I walked across the room to look out the window. Janet's B&B offered a view of Main Street, which was the prettiest part of downtown Willow Brook. There were cute storefronts, bright flowers, and cheerful colors, all in celebration of the tourists pouring into town. The upper floor of the B&B had enough elevation to look out past the buildings across the street to Swan Lake.

The sky was awash in the sun's lingering wake. Streaks of tangerine and violet shimmered on the surface of the lake. It was late, and I should've been tired, but I wasn't.

I'd turned myself inside and out emotionally. Unsettled after Levi unintentionally hit a sore spot, I'd come home, taken one look at Donovan, and figured I could lose myself in him.

I'd been quite right on that account. Yet, I hadn't calculated the true cost. But then, how could I have known what it would feel like to be that intimate with him?

I took a deep breath, trying to slow the residual echoes of my climax. My pulse was still running along at a high idle, humming in the aftermath of my body shattering with pleasure. Twice.

I heard Donovan's footsteps on the stairs. Each step on the hardwood surface echoed. My heart started thundering again, speeding up as I waited to hear his door open and close.

I figured I would give him a few minutes before I snuck downstairs to find my purse. The footsteps kept coming, right to my door. A soft knock followed.

I considered not answering because I guessed he had my purse. I wasn't quite ready to face him, but I figured I'd best. I needed to learn to steel myself against him and the effect he had on me. On the heels of a deep breath, I strode back across the room and swung the door open. He loomed larger than I recalled, even from a few moments ago. I didn't have the added height of my cowboy boots.

I stood there in my half-buttoned blouse, my rumpled skirt, and my socks. Donovan met my gaze, the barest hint of a smile kicking up the corner of his lips and promptly sending my belly into a free fall.

His eyes flicked down, his smile widening when his gaze returned to mine. Glancing down, I realized I had on a pair of mismatched socks—one bright pink with stars all over it and the other neon green with lightning bolts.

I liked to have fun with my socks. When I looked back to him, I shrugged sheepishly. "My socks don't match," I said, stating the obvious.

"Not so much," he replied, that hint of a southern drawl catching at the edge of my heart. God, I could listen to him talk all day. He conveniently continued for me. "You left your purse downstairs."

He lifted it, and I reached out to take it from him, my fingertips brushing his knuckles as I did. Even that little point of contact sent a sizzle through me.

Staring into his eyes, I was nearly mesmerized by the swirl of color—green and amber with flecks of gold, darkening as I held his gaze.

"We're not done yet." He reached out and brushed a loose lock of hair off my cheek, tucking it behind my ear. "Good night, sugar."

His hand fell, and he turned away. I simply stood there, stunned into silence as he stepped across the hall and through the door to his suite, closing it quietly behind him.

Oh. My. God.

Chapter Thirteen

DONOVAN

Looking ahead, smoke drifted across the sky in the distance. Fred, our pilot for the afternoon, spoke into his microphone headset, and then glanced over to Levi.

"Almost there," I heard Fred say over the steady *thwack* of the helicopter blades.

We were headed out to a fire in the western part of Alaska. Much of Alaska was considered the Interior. The area we were headed for was on the edge of the Interior, but not quite on the coast either—where the mostly spruce forest gradually transitioned to tundra and wind whipped across the dry land. We were landing north of Willow Brook by about an hour or so as the crow flew.

We were having a rough fire season this year, but then, it seemed we'd had a rough fire season every year I'd been here so far. Fire season everywhere out West was getting progressively worse. I'd worked a few years on a crew in Northern California before I came here, and it was just as bad there. Longer, hotter, dryer summers led to more fires.

The slender advantage Alaska had was we had far fewer areas where you were dealing with actual people and homes that needed protection. That said, fires could whip out of control fast without anyone around to notice them. With small planes crisscrossing the skies of Alaska all year, fires were usually noticed from the air in unsettled areas. This area was mostly forest—thousands upon thousands of acres, primarily undeveloped, with nothing but hunting cabins and lodges scattered here and there. We needed to get this fire under control before it ballooned much larger and threatened a few nearby communities.

Within minutes, Fred was bringing the helicopter down at the main fire camp. Willow Brook Fire & Rescue was the base for two hotshot crews and a local crew. I shared foreman duties with Levi on this crew. Cade Masters was our crew's superintendent. He'd already flown out the day before.

All told, there were twenty-five of us on the way. Needless to say, we weren't all arriving at the same time. Half the crew came out yesterday with the rest of us today. There were several fire camps on the outskirts of this blaze. I helped Fred unload the gear from underneath the helicopter. He flashed me a grin and a wink as I turned away. Fred often shuttled our crews around Alaska. His weathered face usually greeted us after a few weeks of grueling work.

We checked in at the staging area where a crew from Fairbanks was just finishing up a rotation. Cade was busy conferring with their superintendent. I caught Levi's eyes as he nudged his chin toward the pile of equipment on the ground. With a few calls to round up the crew, we got organized.

I rested a hand on my hip as I drained a bottle of water a few minutes later, looking into the distance to where flames flickered high in the sky, trees tumbling in their path. We were about to split apart into two groups where we would tackle different areas, creating firebreaks and using the landscape to our advantage.

I was looking forward to the work, if only because I'd

been damn distracted the last few days. The moment I'd realized Jasmine was staying across the hall from me, any mental peace and quiet went up in smoke. I was definitely the moth, while she was the flame. I could easily get burned, and I didn't give a damn.

Last night, it had taken every ounce of my discipline not to bury myself inside of her. Yet, for some damn reason, I'd been determined to save that. I couldn't stop thinking about the feel of her channel clenching around my fingers and the look on her face as she flew apart.

I was fucking crazy to be pursuing anything with her. Levi would have my head if he knew the thoughts I was having about his sister. Well, they weren't just thoughts anymore. And just like I had said last night, we weren't done. I didn't want us to be.

I recalled the flush on her cheeks when she opened the door, her hair a wild tangle around her shoulders. Her shirt had been only half buttoned, the sweet curve of one of her breasts visible.

I told myself it was just lust—raw, primitive lust. Yet, in a corner of my mind, I couldn't forget that look of vulnerability in her eyes. It made me want to wrap her tight in my arms and make sure she knew she was mine.

See, that was the problem. When it came to Jasmine, I thought crazy thoughts.

Someone called my name, and I glanced over to see Levi gesturing for me. With a hard mental shake, I jogged over to his side.

"We ready?" I asked.

"Yup. Like we discussed, you take half the crew over to that side," he replied, gesturing toward the trees.

Glancing over, I scanned the area. The trees were still a mix of green, not yet burned up. The land angled up to a rocky bluff. Reportedly, there was a stream over on the other side of the bluff. I'd take half the crew to create a wide firebreak, all the way to the stream, and then use that to our advantage.

Meanwhile, Levi would take the other half of the crew and follow a ravine over on the other side of the fire to create another firebreak. We were following the work begun by the Fairbanks crew. They'd been out here for two weeks and were just leaving, looking exhausted and weary. This fire was fierce in the center, which was miles away from here for now.

"Got it," I replied.

Levi ran a hand through his hair with a sigh. "Let's hope we can beat the wind," he said as he turned away.

When you were a firefighter, the wind was usually your enemy. Oxygen was fuel for fires. No matter which way the wind was blowing, it fanned the flames.

This afternoon and the next few days were supposed to be calm, but then the weather forecast had a few storms blowing through. Storms would bring needed rain, but we hoped not much wind.

Jasmine was temporarily dismissed from my thoughts, a welcome relief for the moment. I gathered up my half of the crew and we headed out, gear on our backs, hiking into rugged terrain.

Creating the firebreak was grueling work, and I'd take anything to keep my mind occupied. Jasmine had knocked loose a few stones in the wall I'd built around my heart. She'd shaken loose old memories, memories I preferred to keep in the past.

Even as I threw myself into the heavy work, at night under the stars, Jasmine feathered through my thoughts.

I kept trying to convince myself it was just because she was so fucking beautiful and the attraction burned so hot between us. Yet, the memories she'd kicked free told me another story. They told me that she was the only woman I'd met in years who made me long for more than a passing encounter.

Late one afternoon, into our second week of being out at this fire, I was working with the chainsaw to clear out some thick brush. We'd created a firebreak almost a half-mile wide running along the edge of the trees for miles. We were following along the stream where it widened and intersected with a river.

"Donovan!" Levi called.

Glancing over my shoulder, I released the clutch on the chainsaw and flipped the switch to turn it off. Setting it down carefully, I snagged a water bottle from the ground nearby, guzzling it quickly.

"What's up?" I called in return.

Levi and I walked toward each other, meeting halfway amongst the cluster of downed trees. The sound of axes whacking and chainsaws humming continued around us nearby. Levi look tired, precisely how I felt.

He dragged a sleeve across his face, removing his heavy work gloves and whacking them on the side of his leg. "Just got the radio call from Cade. Rain's coming in tomorrow, so we should be able to fly out. We've got a good handle on the fire on the far side," he explained.

I nodded, dragging my own sleeve over my forehead. Sweat ran in a trickle down my back. "Good deal. How far do we want to get today before we let the guys rest?"

Levi flashed a weary grin. "I'm so fucking tired, I'd like to call it quits now. But we've got hours of daylight. I say we get to the river. What do you think?"

"Exactly what I was thinking," I replied.

"Good. That'll give us time to have dinner and maybe hike about halfway back to the main camp," he replied.

We chatted for a few more minutes before separating again, checking in with the crew and spreading the orders for the afternoon. Whenever we knew we were about to finish up out in the field, everybody always worked harder. Being a hotshot firefighter was one of the most physically demanding jobs in the world. The men and women who did it gave a new name to dedication.

As I threw myself into the afternoon, my mind spun back to another time, only a few years before. I loved my crew here, loved the camaraderie, the honor, and the trust. I trusted every single person on this crew with my life.

Back in Georgia, my best buddy Bill and I grew up together. We both wanted the same thing when we started volunteering at the local fire department. We left Georgia for hotshot training together in California. Just like my crew now, I'd trusted Bill with my life. Just thinking about him brought a bitter taste in the back of my throat. There were different kinds of trust. I still assumed Bill would have my back in a life or death situation.

Yet, he'd torn my trust to shreds personally.

We'd gone to college together, like so many friends did. I didn't even know why I went to college, seeing as I knew exactly what I'd wanted to do. But I had because I thought I should. I'd fallen in love, or lust, or something like that, with Katie Sharp. She was everything I thought I'd wanted—ballsy as hell, beautiful, and smart. She didn't bat an eye out in the backcountry. She wasn't a firefighter, but then, that life was for few.

We were together for three years in college, and I asked her to marry me later. Because I was a fucking idiot and didn't see the writing on the wall, it wasn't until I came home one night, to the apartment I shared with her, that the truth slapped me in the face.

Bill and I both were firefighters. When we'd moved out to California, Katie had come with me. After our training, we took jobs on different crews just because that was what had been available. I'd gotten in a day early after a weeklong stint at a fire in Arizona. Coming home tired and wanting nothing more than a shower and a night tangled up with Katie, instead, I found her sucking Bill off in our kitchen.

To this day, I wasn't sure which was worse. The betrayal

was all tangled up. My best friend for years had been seeing my girl behind my back for months at that point. Or at least that was what I pieced together after asking around. I hadn't seen Katie since I'd seen her with her lips wrapped around Bill's cock. The second to last time I'd spoken to Bill had been when I'd hauled off and punched him while his jeans were hanging around his hips.

The kicker? It was bad enough that my best friend had been fucking around with my girl, but he tried to make it up to me, tried to call and *talk*. I guess he felt bad in the end. At the time, it didn't really fucking matter. Not to me. Friends didn't do that shit to each other. Yet lately, the anger and bitterness had faded. I missed Bill. I fucking missed the friend who'd betrayed me.

Since then, I hadn't been looking for love. In fact, I'd flat out decided I was better off without it. After years of being teased for wanting to settle down so young, I'd shifted gears entirely, and it worked out just fine. I'd yet to meet a woman who made me want anything other than a few nights between the sheets.

Jasmine was different. Maybe it was because she was so damn sexy, but just the sight of her made my cock ache. Sexy didn't make me think about my bitterness.

Restless and annoyed at the fact my thoughts were going in a direction they hadn't gone in years, I kicked away the sense of bitterness. Jasmine, beautiful sexy Jasmine, had unraveled the threads along the tattered edges of my heart.

I didn't even think she'd been trying. I knew from her comment about her ex that she was quite familiar with betrayal. All I knew was I wanted to never see that vulnerability flickering in the depths of her eyes again. I could take it because she shouldn't have to.

Hours later, I finally got my damn mind off Jasmine. It took a tree almost falling on my head to make it happen, but what the hell? Whatever worked.

That night in the endless sunset in Alaska, the guys and I

lounged on the ground. No campfires for us. Still, we had food and laughter. A while later, I lay on my back, staring at the sky. It was well past midnight, and darkness was finally falling. Stars winked against the sky, the moon rising over to one side with the smell of smoke in the distance.

Jasmine, once again, nudged into my thoughts. I fell asleep, restless for the feel of her against me.

Chapter Fourteen

JASMINE

Rolling my car to a stop, I scanned the area. Midnight Sun Arts gallery was on a boardwalk on the rocky beach, along with a cluster of other shops. Kachemak Bay sparkled under the sun just beyond the boardwalk. Mountains rose tall across the bay with a glacier glowing that otherworldly blue in the distance. Mount Augustine, a volcano that sat sentry beyond the bay, anchored the view. Climbing out of my car, a salty breeze gusted, ruffling the surface of the water. Taking a deep breath, I marshaled my courage and walked up the steps to the boardwalk.

Diamond Creek was a few hours south of Willow Brook on the shores of Kachemak Bay. Like Willow Brook, the small town was a tourist draw in the summers. I looked around the gallery as I stepped inside, taking in the high ceiling, the bright light, and the soft cream walls. Artwork hung on every available surface with displays scattered throughout the gallery.

I meandered through the space, taking a deep breath and letting it out with a sigh. I loved being surrounded by art.

"Hello," a voice called as the sound of footsteps echoed on the hardwood flooring. "Can I help you?"

A woman rounded one of the display cases, coming into my line of sight. She had short dark hair that fell across her forehead. It was cut in shaggy layers with a streak of pink on one side and purple on the other. She was about medium height with a curvy build. She wore a loose cotton purple blouse over a fitted black skirt that fell to her knees. Cowboy boots and chunky silver jewelry completed her ensemble. She was beautiful.

The moment she saw me, she smiled. "Oh, are you Jasmine?"

"Are you Risa?" I asked in return with a smile. Because if she knew who I was, I figured she must be Risa.

"I'm definitely Risa. So nice to meet you," she said, striding quickly to me and holding her hand out.

Her handshake was firm. She stepped back, her smile warm and her eyes bright. "I'm so glad you could make it, and if you've been here for a few minutes, I'm sorry. I was tied up with a phone call in the back."

There were other customers milling about. She leaned closer, lowering her voice. "Mind if I check in with a few customers? We can chat behind the counter after I do. Someone else will be here in just a few minutes to cover the front."

"Of course. I'll take a look around."

"You do that," she said with a little wave before striding across the room.

Risa Thomas was part owner of Midnight Sun Arts in Diamond Creek. Amelia, Lucy's best friend, had connected her with me through her friendship with Amelia's older brother, Quinn, who happened to live here in Diamond Creek. I knew Quinn, but I hadn't seen him in years. He was a few years ahead of me when I was in high school, just old enough that I didn't really know him well.

. . .

While I'd been obsessing about calling Risa, she beat me to it. She emailed me the other day and asked me to stop by the gallery. She was looking for more pottery for this gallery as well as a few other galleries she managed with her partners.

Midnight Sun Arts in Anchorage was one of the busiest galleries there. I wouldn't have had the nerve to approach them. Even though I'd been involved in the art world in San Francisco, which should've been more intimidating, I'd had a few connections there since I'd attended one of the local art programs.

In Alaska, I had no such connections, and confidence wasn't my strong suit when it came to this part of trying to be an artist. I walked slowly through the gallery. Risa had an excellent selection with paintings, photographs, pottery, jewelry, woodcarvings, and more. The prices were higher than I would have expected in this area, but I didn't really have any sense of the local art market.

I'd emailed Risa a link to my website, which had photos of pottery I'd sold at shows and galleries in San Francisco. I was nervous, and I hated the feeling. Just when I was starting to think the art she had here was too classy for my work, I came around the corner and found an utterly charming and whimsical collection of painted furniture. This was right up my alley. My pottery tended to be on the playful side.

Risa's voice reached me again as she came around the corner. "There you are!" I turned to find her warm smile waiting. "Come on. We can actually go in the back now. My afternoon help just showed up."

I followed her through the displays to the back. She paused and introduced me to a friendly girl named Kayla before leading me around the counter and through a back door into a hallway. We stepped into a small office, my eyes immediately drawn to the window, which offered a stunning view of the bay.

Her gallery was right along the shore near Otter Cove

Harbor. Aside from being surrounded by artwork all day, she had a simply spectacular view. Kachemak Bay stretched out in front of us. Gulls were swooping and calling along the edge of the water.

"Have a seat," Risa said, gesturing to a small round table. "You want some coffee?"

"Sure," I said.

She stepped to a small counter at the back and quickly filled two mugs. I heard the distant hum of some sort of tool, but I didn't know what it was. Returning to the table, she took a sip and stretched her legs out. She brushed her hair off her forehead and then cocked her head to the side.

"So, like I said in my email, I've already seen your work online. I would love to carry it in our galleries. We've got this one and then others in Anchorage, Juneau, and Fairbanks. We sell a lot. I know you're probably thinking I'm crazy, but between all of our galleries, I would imagine we would need an order every other week from you. My only concern at this point is whether you have somewhere you're going to be able to work. I know you were living in San Francisco and just returned to Alaska."

I was so busy trying to scramble for purchase in my brain and get my feet under me, I could hardly absorb what she was saying. If she meant what she said, I would basically have a full-time job throwing pottery and selling it. It would be more than enough to keep me in business.

She must've sensed my surprise because she laughed softly. "I told you, we stay busy. It's different here than in the cities. I mean, I'm sure, dollar for dollar, San Francisco sells more art in a day than we do here. But tourists love buying things, just so they can say they got it here. Local artists are preferred, and it's a different kind of customer base. You were born and raised in Alaska. Your work is beautiful, fun, and practical. Trust me, I can sell the hell out of it."

I met Risa's warm gaze and felt myself nodding. I couldn't quite believe her offer and was entirely prepared for it not to work out. She seemed confident but, well, I had a knack for things not working out. I wasn't stupid though, and I wanted this. So much. I knew I would need to figure out exactly how and where I was going to set up a studio, but come hell or high water, I'd make it happen.

When I nodded, she clapped her hands together. "Perfect. We really need more pottery. People love it because, aside from the fact that it's beautiful, it's useful. That furniture you were looking at out there?" At my nod, she continued, "We sell it like crazy. It's wild and funky, and just like pottery, it's practical. When I saw your stuff online, I thought of that furniture. It's a totally different type of art, but it has that same whimsical vibe."

"I thought the same thing when I saw it," I added, a smile tugging at the corners of my mouth. Joy buzzed inside of me. With everything that had happened in the last month, I felt knocked back in life. This was something positive, something I could hold onto.

"Come on," Risa said. "Let me take you upstairs. You can meet Jessa. She's the one who does all that furniture. She lives here in Diamond Creek and rents a space upstairs. I like to paint, but I'm not too artsy. I do signs and things for all of our galleries. It's just Jessa and me up there right now. I'm having the other two rooms renovated."

I followed her down the hallway and up the stairs into another hallway with two doors on either side. The distant humming sound I'd heard earlier became stronger, and I assumed this was the renovation work she'd mentioned.

Risa quickly showed me her space, which had a worktable with paint and posters everywhere. She quickly checked next door, only to discover that Jessa wasn't there. Just looking into the space made my heart squeeze. Paint was dripped all over the heavy cloth draped on the floor, with unfinished pieces of furniture scattered around.

"Well, maybe if you're down here again, you can meet her," Risa said as she turned away.

As she spoke, the humming sound slowed in a room across the hall. She paused by the door to open it, calling in, "Hey, how's it going in here?"

As soon as the door opened, sheet rock dust blew into the hallway in a thick gust, hitting me right in the face.

"Oh!"

I sneezed, and then again and again and again as I tried to catch my breath. It was too much. In a matter of seconds, I was in the midst of an asthma attack.

Risa appeared to quickly assess what was happening and slammed the door closed, apologizing profusely as she hurried me down the hall. Gasping and wheezing, I could hardly breathe, so she was basically dragging me. She got me down the stairs and into her office. I dimly heard her asking if I had an inhaler. I tried to fumble with my purse, but she took it from me, quickly producing the inhaler and handing it to me.

A few minutes later, I had my breath back.

"I'm so sorry. I wasn't even thinking. That much dust usually sets me off."

"You don't need to apologize," Risa said, giving my hand a squeeze. "I'm the idiot who decided to open the door while they were sanding the sheetrock."

"You couldn't have known I have asthma," I said, as I took a slow, steadying breath. It was hard to put to words how good it felt to breathe when you knew what it felt like when you couldn't.

"Do you need more of that?" she asked, gesturing to the inhaler curled in my fist.

After another hit of the inhaler, my lungs felt clear. I leaned back in the chair with a sigh. "Asthma's a pain in the ass."

"How do you deal with it with your pottery?" she asked.

"Well, there's not too much dust if I manage it. I love it. I had my studio in San Francisco set up with an air filtering system. I'm sure I can get that set up in Willow Brook."

The moment I made that comment, my mind flashed to the sight of Donovan bare-chested and working downstairs at Janet's B&B. That was how bad off I was when it came to Donovan. A passing comment sent my thoughts spinning in his direction. I forcibly turned my focus away.

There was a knock at the door. Glancing over, Risa called out, "Come in."

A police officer stepped through the door. The moment Risa's eyes landed on him, her smile widened. She stood and walked to his side. The police officer leaned down and caught her lips in a quick kiss.

"Had a call out this way, so I thought I'd stop in and see you before I went back to the station," the police officer said.

Risa looped her elbow through his and caught my eyes. "This is my husband, Darren. Hon," she said, gesturing between us, "this is Jasmine Phillips. Quinn's sister called me about her. I'm hounding her into turning all her pottery over to me."

Darren flashed a grin in my direction. "Nice to meet you. Don't let her push you too hard, or she actually will take all of your pottery. She wouldn't shut up about it the other night."

Risa nudged him with her elbow. "I love finding new stuff," she said with a sheepish grin.

They were well-matched. Risa was beautiful, and Darren was handsome with his dark brown hair and eyes.

"I gotta go, babe," he said. "Just had a minute to stop by."

Risa turned with him to the door. He dipped his head again, dropping a kiss on the side of her neck. It was rather innocent, yet the intimacy between them was so powerful, I felt as if I were interrupting. They clearly loved each other. That was what I wanted. Emotion tightened my chest out of the blue. I forced my eyes away from them and stood to walk to the window.

"Isn't that view just ridiculous?" Risa asked over my shoulder.

Turning back, I smiled, forcing myself not to dwell on the personal mess of my life. Somehow my asthma attack had knocked me off kilter and reminded me of how uncertain everything was for me. "It is. My parents used to bring us down here in the summer sometimes. It's so pretty. Anyway, I should go. I want to get back to Willow Brook before it's too late."

"You'll call me as soon as you think you can start supplying us, right?" Risa asked in return.

It still didn't feel quite real that she planned to sell my pottery. "Are you sure?" I asked.

"Of course I'm sure! Once you have some inventory, let me know and we'll sort out how much we need on a week-to-week basis. My partners in Anchorage can meet with you at any time as well. I won't be up there for another couple of months, which is why I was hoping you could come down here. Thank you for making the drive," she said with another warm smile.

The tension that had quickly bundled inside eased slightly. "I'm glad I came. I have to say, your enthusiasm is a little surprising. I like my work but ..." My words trailed off because I wasn't sure what I meant to say.

"I can't even imagine what it's like to try to sell art somewhere like San Francisco," she offered. "We opened a gallery in Seattle, and I go down maybe once a year. It's totally different. I love art, but I don't love the pretentiousness that comes with it sometimes."

"That's one way to put it," I said with a laugh. "Anyway, I'll email or call. My goal is to hopefully sort out a studio space in the next few weeks."

"You sure you're okay to drive?" she asked as I put my inhaler back in my purse and hooked my purse over my shoulder.

"Oh, I'm fine. Trust me. By no means was that the worst asthma attack I've ever had. It just took me off guard."

Risa stepped to me and gave me a quick hug. "We're going to be friends. I just know it. You might not be down here in Diamond Creek, but with your pottery, we'll be in touch a lot. If you need anything, just let me know."

Chapter Fifteen

JASMINE

As I drove home late that afternoon, I felt a little out of whack. Between Risa dropping this absolutely amazing opportunity in my lap and my unexpected asthma attack, I just felt off.

Asthma had been a part of my life since I was a little girl. I hated it. When I was little, I'd had a few too many bad asthma attacks. I didn't like to think about it much, but my asthma has been part of what drove a wedge between Levi and I when we were younger. Levi was four years older than me and only occasionally let me tag along with him.

I forgot to bring my inhaler once when we were out hiking nearby, not long after we moved to Willow Brook. It was an average summer day in Alaska. We were at Swan Lake, but on the far side. When I realized I didn't have my inhaler, I knew I should've told Levi we needed to go back. But we were with a few other friends, just wild kids running free.

When you're young and you don't quite grasp the seriousness of certain things, you think you can will them away. I had an awful asthma attack that afternoon, and Levi carried me back to Wildlands where our parents were having lunch.

I remember being so scared, more frightened than I'd ever been. I'd had asthma attacks before, yet that had been the first and only time in my life when I didn't have my inhaler with me. I'd been almost blue by the time he got me to Wildlands, and it had terrified my parents. For good reason.

Levi had always been an overprotective brother before then. Not in the annoying bossy way, but just taking care of me. Since that day, well, it had been worse. By nature, Levi was an easygoing, teasing kind of guy. Yet, when it came to me after that, let's just say adolescence wasn't too fun for me with him around the house.

As an adult, I could look back and realize he must have been scared to death that day. He'd been aware enough to see the terror in my parents' faces. I barely remembered that afternoon, although I vividly recalled not being able to breathe and how scary that was.

Just now, as I drove north along the highway, flanked by the ocean and the mountains, I took a deep breath of air and let it out. Air was such a gift, and it was easy not to appreciate it unless you'd experienced times when you couldn't get your lungs to work.

I knew a part of me was defensive. I'd fought so hard to show that I could do things on my own, that I didn't need to have anyone hover over me. The hovering and the background worry from my parents and Levi had been part of what spurred me to leave Willow Brook. Yet, somehow, I spun right back like a boomerang.

Life had sent me careening back. I wanted to show them I could take care of myself, yet all I'd shown them was how much I needed them.

As I drove home, I considered my options for finding a place to set up a studio. I needed space for my pottery wheel, my kiln, a worktable, a glazing area, and storage. I thanked the stars my old kiln and wheel from high school were still stored in my parents' garage. The studio where I'd worked in San Francisco included rented equipment. Though I had the more costly items, I still needed to find a space and have it set up. I either needed to call in a big favor from Lucy and Amelia ... or I could ask Donovan. I couldn't even believe I was considering asking for his help.

I didn't know why, but that seemed the easier of the two. Even though Lucy had already offered to help, relying on her meant Levi would be involved. I hated this old sore spot between us.

Sometimes, when I was being honest with myself, I knew part of my desire to spread my wings and fly away from Willow Brook went all the way back to the afternoon he'd likely saved my life. It was odd how events could shift the course of a life.

It was just an asthma attack. Asthma was something so many people had. Yet, I'd been careless, and I had almost died as a result of it. That had profoundly shifted the dynamics in my relationship with Levi, who I adored and still did, and my parents.

It was unspoken in our family, but I'd been trying ever since to make up for my carelessness and show that I was someone else. Instead, I'd had the poor judgment to get engaged to an asshole who screwed around on me. Then, I'd let my temper get the best of me and lost my job as a result of it.

Now, here I was, back in Alaska, the place that held my heart all along. It was hard to miss a place, and yet try so hard to prove yourself away from it.

I hated depending on people.

The landscape rolled by as I drove north from Diamond Creek. Sterling Highway wound along the coast. Here and there, the highway angled further inland, yet Cook Inlet was visible most of the way. The mountains rose tall on the far side. Even now, at the height of summer, there was still a little snow left on some of the tallest peaks. An icy blue glacier glittered under the bright sun. It was late afternoon, and the sun wouldn't set for hours yet.

Eventually, I turned onto Seward Highway, the highway that would bring me through Anchorage before I traveled west to Willow Brook. Seward Highway went through the Chugach Mountains. For a little while, the ocean disappeared from view as I passed through trees and along Trail Creek. The scenery was so beautiful it almost brought me to tears.

Beyond the mountain pass, I traveled along Turnagain Arm, the portion of highway that hugged the feet of the mountains as they kissed the salty ocean waters of Cook Inlet. I remembered thinking the mountains were so close on the far side when I was a little girl that if I could stretch far enough, I could touch them.

Traffic crawled for a stretch, with vehicles slowing down to view the Beluga whales traveling through the inlet, their white forms flashing as they undulated through the surface of the water. A raven flew past the side of my car, its call distinct and clear.

Hours after I left Diamond Creek, I turned onto the side highway that would lead me to Willow Brook. As I rolled into town, my heart thudded, and I resolved to myself that I would somehow soon, once and for all, try to clear the air over that afternoon long ago when Levi saved my life.

The oddest thing about all of it was there was nothing dramatic about it. I didn't have an exciting story to tell about almost dying. My near-death story was an asthma attack. All I'd done was forget to bring my inhaler. I'd been too damn stubborn to go back and get it.

By the time I pulled up in front of Janet's little B&B, I was feeling raw and vulnerable. Despite the great news from Risa, somehow this day had rubbed against old wounds—striking at that feeling as if I could never quite stand on my own two feet, that feeling of vulnerability. As awesome as

Risa's offer was—and believe me, it was *way* more than awesome—it struck a nerve. She was so confident it would all work out. What if it didn't?

I gave my head a shake as I parked my car outside the B&B. It had been a full two weeks since I'd seen Donovan.

When I saw his truck parked out front, it was like a bell ringing inside, the vibration humming through my body. I didn't know what was worse—to see him, or not to see him. I hadn't laid eyes on him since that night when what had passed between us was so intimate that every time I thought about it, I blushed straight through.

Taking a deep breath, and telling myself I wouldn't see him because that would be the easiest thing, I quietly let myself in downstairs. I hated admitting it, but ever since I'd come in and found him shirtless working down here, I wondered every night if I'd find him here again. I didn't have the nerve to try to ask around and find out when he might be back from the fire. He was on Levi's crew, so they were out there together. I was too anxious about my feelings for Donovan to even dare ask Lucy when Levi would be back.

That was a cue to how ridiculous I was feeling. Tonight, it was dead quiet downstairs. Just the hallway light was on. Walking through, feeling slightly bruised inside over my own messed up head, I made my way upstairs.

Cresting the landing, I almost jumped out of my skin when I saw Donovan at the far end of the hallway, shirtless and fiddling with the window. He didn't appear to have heard me come in, so I took a moment to enjoy the sight of his back. If you'd told me before I'd met Donovan that a man's back would turn me on, I would've laughed. But this was now the second time I'd encountered Donovan's shirtless back and gotten hot all over.

He had an arm stretched up, the muscles in his shoulder bunching as he gave the window a hard push.

"For fuck's sake," he mumbled to himself. "Just open."

My question slipped out before I thought about it, more of a reflex than anything. "Do you need some help?"

He froze. Before he even turned, the air felt charged. The hum of electricity started at the floor and lifted, filling the space in the hallway. He brought his arm down and slowly turned. My mouth went dry. His chest was a work of art—all hard planes. I itched to touch him, to trace every ridge.

I managed to meet his eyes and not look away, although I knew my cheeks were bright pink. I felt on fire, inside and out.

His eyes held mine, his gaze assessing, measuring. It felt as if he could look right through me. All a jumble inside as it was, I suddenly felt even more vulnerable.

He looked tired with a hint of weariness contained in his eyes.

"Did you just get back?" I asked.

"I did. Just about an hour ago."

All I could seem to do was stand there with need spinning through my veins.

"I could use some help," he added after a pause.

For a moment, I forgot I had asked him a question. Then, I remembered.

"Oh! Okay."

He was at the end of the hall, perhaps twenty feet away from me. I walked toward him, pausing by my door to set down my purse. As I approached him, I felt the burn of his gaze on me with every step. I was wearing my favorite cowboy boots. I wore them so often, they were almost like a friend. The leather was soft and worn, hugging my calves and fitting me perfectly. I wore a twirly skirt that fell just to my knees with a loose blouse over a navy silk camisole.

I hadn't thought much about how I looked until his eyes swept up and down my body as I approached. My nipples tightened to little points, so tight they ached.

If nipples could talk, I was fairly certain mine would cry

out Donovan's name and ask him for a lick, and maybe a nip of his teeth. Slick need coiled between my thighs. I told myself that right about now would be a good time to tell him I couldn't help with whatever he was doing with the window. Because it was dangerous to get that close to him when I felt this vulnerable and needy.

But the desire inside of me was far more powerful and drowned out everything else. It was bossy, snapping at me, cracking like a whip, and driving every step forward. I reached him, nearly shuddering inside.

"Are you trying to open the window?" I asked inanely.

Of course he's trying to open it. Idiot.

My critical voice had plenty of practice and always knew when to chime in.

I ignored it and tried to catch my breath and function like a normal human being. This was a friendly neighbor who needed help with the window in the hallway.

The slightest hint of a grin kicked his mouth up at one corner, and butterflies took flight inside my belly, spinning and twirling madly.

"Yes, I'm trying to open it. I thought we could use the fresh air up here," he finally said. "If you push on this corner, I'll push up top."

I watched as his hand curled over the edge of the window frame. Dear God, just looking at his hand made my channel clench. My panties were a lost cause. His hands looked rugged and strong, his fingers were long and thick. I vividly remembered the feel of them inside me.

I tried to force my thoughts from that. Dear God, I was helping him open a window, and I was so turned on I could hardly think straight. I doubted he was even remotely as bothered by me as I was by him.

After a moment, with both of us giving it a little push, the window nudged loose, sliding open and bringing a gust of fresh air into the hallway. The cool, late evening air hit my skin, and my nipples tightened even further.

Chapter Sixteen

DONOVAN

I kept my hand on the side of the window frame, gripping tightly. I needed something to hold onto, to keep me from reaching over and cupping the lush curve of Jasmine's sweet ass. I wanted to taste her tight little nipples, pressed against the navy silk camisole she wore.

I hadn't really needed her help to open the window. I just wanted her a lot closer to me. Now, no more than a foot separated us. Need cracked in the air, the lash of it stinging inside of me and sending a shot of blood straight to my already aching cock.

I was tired as hell after two weeks out in the backcountry. Most of the time when I came home, the last thing on my mind was sex. Usually I grabbed a beer and dinner at Wildlands, came home, and collapsed into bed.

Tonight, I'd been restless, so I picked up pizza and came straight here to shower. I tried to ignore my disappointment when I arrived to find no sign of Jasmine.

Yet, now she was here, right beside me. Her hair fell in messy waves around her shoulders. She wore her cowboy boots and flirty little skirt. All I could think about when I saw it was flipping it up and bending her over, so I could see her sweet ass.

As if her skirt wasn't enough temptation, she wore an open blouse over her silky camisole, the fabric outlining the curves of her breasts. I'd watched her nipples pressed against the silk as she approached me in the hallway, hoping like hell she wanted me as much as I wanted her.

Because, crazy as it was, there was no way we were done with each other. Not even close.

I finally let go of the windowsill, angling to face her. I half-expected her to take a step back, but she didn't. She stayed right there, her hip resting against the bottom frame of the window with her hand curled over it. I could see the flutter of her pulse in her neck and I beat back the urge to dip my head and drag my tongue over it. I hadn't forgotten how she tasted. Hell, I hadn't forgotten a single second of the last time I'd seen her.

It had been a long two weeks away. The only thing that kept my mind off Jasmine was working like a wild man. Fortunately, my job demanded it. I should've been too damn tired to want her this much.

Yet, with her nearby, my body was nearly on fire at the scent and heat of her. All the reasons why I told myself I shouldn't let anything more happen with her went up in smoke.

With the cool air gusting through the window, I lifted a hand and brushed her hair away from her face. I had to touch her. Tucking a lock behind her ear, I trailed my fingertip down the side of her neck, savoring the hitch in her breath and the goose bumps rising in the wake of my touch.

I kept expecting her to step away. But she didn't.

"How are you?" I asked.

I was caught in her gaze, so rich and so blue. I brushed my thumb across the wild beat of her pulse in her neck.

"I'm fine," she whispered, her voice husky and rough

around the edges. The sound of it alone was like flint to my stone.

Her tongue darted out, swiping across from bottom up. Her breath hitched again. "How are you?" she asked in return.

The scent of her had a hint of strawberry. It was like a drug, fuzzing my thoughts.

"I'm fine. Tired," I added with a shrug.

"Oh, I didn't mean to keep you. I bet you are. Two weeks in the backcountry is exhausting."

She started to step back. It was then that I realized she was interpreting my comment as a lead in to end this moment between us.

Oh, hell no.

I wanted Jasmine. Now.

I didn't give a damn about the depth of my response to her and the way she slipped through my defenses like smoke through the crack of a window. I had to have her.

Stepping even closer as she began to move away, I slid my free hand around her waist, dragging it down to cup her ass.

"Where are you going?"

I murmured my question as I dusted kisses along the soft skin of her neck.

She gasped. "I thought you were tired."

"I am, but I want you."

When I shifted my knee between her thighs, she moaned.

I drew back because I might be crazy and half out of my mind with raw lust for her, but I needed to make sure we were on the same page.

"If you don't want this, it's okay. Maybe ..."

I started to say that maybe I was reading her wrong. But she shook her head, so I let my words trail off.

"I want this," she said, her words almost forceful.

"Okay then," I murmured.

I tightened my grip on her ass, savoring the soft give of

her flesh as I rocked my hips into hers. Her breath hissed, and she caught her bottom lip with her teeth, the sight of them digging into that plump pink sent a hot jolt of lust through me.

I was usually in control, but when it came to Jasmine, I was always hanging onto the thinnest thread.

Dipping my head, I caught her sweet, fucking sexy-as-hell mouth in a kiss. The moment our lips met, it was like a bolt of lightning struck right between us, electrifying my entire body. Our kiss became hot, wet, and deep, almost instantly. I dove into the warm sweetness of her mouth and her tongue met mine stroke for stroke. When she moaned into my mouth as I rocked my arousal to the cradle of her hips, it was all I could do not to take her right there in the hallway. Her hips rocked over my knee, and I knew she was chasing her own pleasure.

The next few minutes were a tumbling blur. Her hands were as greedy as mine. She mapped my chest and back, her nails scoring my skin. Tearing my lips free, I tugged at her camisole. The stretchy, silky fabric had just enough give I could pull it down underneath her breasts.

I drew back to see them plumping over it in a black lacy bra. Her nipples were taut against the lace. Flicking my eyes up, I found hers wide, hazy and unfocused. Her head rolled against the wall. She was practically climbing my body as I held her in the cage of my arms, pinning her to the wall.

We stared at each other, the air heavy around us, thick with desire. I wasn't thinking, not at all. Later, this moment would be seared into my brain. The force of my need for her was so ferocious, I couldn't stop. Tangling with the need was the tightening in my heart when I looked into her eyes. The vulnerability flickering in their depths made me feel like a fucking caveman.

Trailing my hand up over the soft curve of her belly, I cupped one of her breasts, its weight heavy in my palm. I dragged my thumb back and forth across the lace, over the tight bead of her nipple, watching as her eyelids drooped and her breath came out on a low moan.

With Jasmine, I experienced something I'd never experienced before. A collision of this driving, fierce need that made me want to claim her and take her so hard and fast we both got lost in it. That need was a wave crashing into another—the need to absolutely soak up her response, to drag everything out as long as I could because it could never be better than this. Not that I'd ever imagined.

I dipped my head and dragged my tongue over the lace, smiling against her skin when she groaned and arched into me. Rolling a nipple between my fingers and teasing the other with my lips, teeth, and tongue, I savored the sounds of her gasps as she murmured my name on a little cry.

I needed more. *Now*.

Reluctantly lifting my head, I curled my hands under her hips and lifted her high against me. Her skirt pooled around her hips as she curled her legs around my waist, arching and flexing.

I could feel the damp heat of her core as she rocked her hips against my arousal.

"Fuck, Jasmine," I murmured as I spun away from the wall, holding her tight against me. Her lips were nibbling their way down my neck, teasing and sending a searing jolt of lust through me, the flame catching hold.

Walking swiftly down the hall, I fumbled with my door. In a few seconds, we were inside. I headed straight for my bedroom at the back. Easing her down on the bed, I straightened and looked at her.

Her skirt was in a rumple around her hips, the black silk between her thighs teasing me. Her hair was a wild mess and her lips were swollen from our kisses. My stubble had scraped along the sensitive skin at the tops of her breasts, leaving it reddened.

With her cheeks flushed and her eyes dark, her breasts plumped over the top of her bra and her clothes in disarray, she was the sexiest woman I'd ever seen. She pushed up on her elbows, reaching for my fly.

"Too many clothes," she muttered.

"Same goes for you," I bit out.

She rose, standing from the bed. Kicking her boots free, she shimmied out of her skirt and flung her blouse and camisole aside. Then, she stood before me in nothing but her black silk panties and black lace bra.

All I could do was stare. Hell, I could've come just looking at her. She circled her hand in the air before resting it on her hip and cocking her head to the side.

"Get on with it, Donovan," she teased, her eyes glittering.

I chucked my jeans off and snagged a condom from the nightstand. When I turned back, she was bare naked. One look stole my breath. She put a knee on the bed and crawled onto it. Moving swiftly, I was behind her, gripping her hips before she turned over.

"Not just yet," I murmured. "I need to taste you, and I fucking love your ass."

She giggled, the sound of it like a ribbon of silk spinning around my heart.

I trailed my palm down her spine, watching as her body reacted—her waist dipping on a gasp when I delved between her thighs. She was drenched, slick with desire.

I sank two fingers into her, knuckle deep, my eyes locked to hers as her hips arched back into my touch. She gasped my name when I drew my fingers out and buried them inside again, her channel clenching around me.

I needed to see her face. Spinning her over, I roughly pushed her knees apart before burying my face at her core. She tasted salty and sweet, pure heaven. Teasing her, I fucked her slowly with my fingers as I tasted and explored her. With her cries raining down around me and as her body began to tighten, I sucked her clit between my teeth, looking up as I stroked my fingers inside of her once more.

She gasped my name in a ragged shout, her entire body going taut as she clamped down tightly around my fingers. I was at the end of a frayed thread of control. It snapped loose, and I drew back swiftly, rolling a condom on like lightning and positioning myself between her thighs.

"Jasmine."

Her hair was a tangle on my pillows, her eyes a rich sapphire when she dragged them open. I held still, the tip of my cock at her entrance.

"Donovan, please," she murmured.

The thread snapped, and I surged into her slick heat, watching as her eyes went wide.

Chapter Seventeen

JASMINE

"Jasmine," Donovan murmured, his voice deep and gruff.

Dragging my eyes open, I looked up at him. He was above me, one hand fisting his cock and the other curled over the side of my hip.

My body was still quaking from the intense orgasm that had just crashed over me. But I already needed more. I needed the feel of him filling me.

"Donovan, please."

I heard the pleading in my voice. But I was beyond caring, beyond shame. I was caught in this web of madness. All I knew was what my body needed. His body was a work of art—all hard planes with a few scars scattered over him. There was no polish to Donovan—he was all raw, rugged man, a pure masculinity so intense he encompassed me with his mere existence.

My hips arched toward him, and he finally sank inside of me. It felt so good, so intense, that I was barely conscious at this point, spinning in a haze of need and vibration. He filled me completely—every thick inch of him.

He held still for a beat as my body adjusted to him. I

didn't want this to be slow. I wanted it hard and fast. I almost wanted it to be painful because I didn't know what else would slake the wild need inside of me. Opening my eyes, I flexed into him, curling my legs around his hips, my heels spurring the hard muscles of his ass.

Then he was moving, drawing back and sinking in. He started slow as he stretched over me. His hardness pressed against my softness with his lips on my neck as I went wild underneath him—crying out, my nails scoring his skin as he began to drum his hips into me, every stroke deeper. He murmured hot, dirty words while I spun tighter and tighter inside, chasing after another sweet release.

He rose slightly, reaching between us, his fingers teasing over my clit. I flew apart again, my sex pulsing and throbbing as I shattered from head to toe, this orgasm more intense than the last. With one last deep stroke, he shuddered, a rough cry raining down over me.

As I slowly came to, I felt him spin over, bringing me on top of him. I collapsed against him, boneless and sated.

Resting against Donovan's muscled chest, I listened to the sound of his heartbeat against my ear—hard and fast at first and then gradually slowing, mirroring my own.

Eventually, I lifted my head, resting my chin on my fist. As though he felt my gaze on him, his eyes opened—his green and gold gaze colliding with mine. Even though he was still inside of me, and I'd just had two explosive orgasms, at the look in his eyes, the languid heat contained there, my belly was a flutter again, a mix of heat and electricity spinning through my body.

I wasn't quite sure what to say. He saved me from worrying about my words, his palm sliding down my back in a soothing stroke. "Well, that was a nice way to come home," he said, his voice raspy.

When his mouth hitched at the corner in a slow smile, a giggle bubbled up. I wasn't shy when it came to sex, but I also wasn't accustomed to this intensity, this rushing feeling inside. I didn't want to think too hard about it because I didn't know what the hell to think. He rose and easily lifted me with him as he stood from the bed. I giggled—again—feeling light and bubbly inside.

"Well, that was easy," I murmured.

His low chuckle by my ear sent a hot shiver through me.

"Where are we going?" I asked.

"Shower," he said simply.

Within a few steps, we were inside the bathroom off the side of the bedroom. His suite was a mirror of mine. The bathroom was almost precisely the same with everything in reverse. He set me down once we were in there, quickly disposing of his condom with one hand and turning on the shower with the other. Then, we were in the shower with steam billowing around us. Before I knew it, he was wrapping me in a towel and we were tumbling into bed.

It didn't even occur to me to leave and go across the hallway to my own bed. Because, you see, it felt so damn good to be wrapped in his strength. He tucked me against his hard muscled body where I rested my head against his shoulder and fell sound asleep, too sated, too relaxed to do anything else.

Sometime during the night, I woke to the feel of Donovan's hands mapping my body, his breath teasing my skin, and his fingers sliding into my slick channel. He was curled around me from behind, and I could feel the hard, hot velvety skin of his cock against my bottom.

I dimly heard the sound of him tearing a condom open before he lifted my thigh, his thick head nudging my entrance. His teeth nipped my neck as I gasped, crying out when he sheathed himself inside of me.

In a sleepy, sensual haze, he fucked me slowly from behind. I flew apart, pleasure fracturing me from the inside out. I savored the feel of him going taut and the low growl of my name murmured in my ear as he found his own release.

I was caged in his arms, content in his embrace. I felt

sensual, sleepy, and so connected to him, my heart stuttered for a few beats before finding its rhythm again. I remembered nothing other than falling back asleep held tight in his arms. I had no idea how much time passed.

I awoke sometime later, muddled. After a beat, I felt the mattress shift as his weight left it. "Is everything okay?" I asked.

"Call out to a fire," he replied, his voice gravelly with sleep.

I was completely awake then, and sat up. "You mean you have to go back out?"

Donovan turned toward me. In the wispy light of dawn, he was so handsome, my breath caught. He stood there with the early morning sunlight cast through the shades, shadows and light playing over his muscled form. Unabashedly naked, his eyes met mine, darkening as his eyes flicked down.

I hadn't even paid attention to the fact that I was naked and the sheet had fallen to my waist. My nipples perked up, practically waving to him the moment his eyes drifted across them, his hot gaze a flame.

"No, it's not that kind of fire," he said. His eyes made their way back to my face. "It's a fire in a town nearby. Our crew's on call for backup."

He stepped back toward the bed, his hand threading into my hair. He caught my lips in a fierce, swift kiss, his tongue diving in, as if to lay claim, before he drew away.

"I'd love to stay, but I have to go," he said as he turned and strode quickly into the bathroom.

As the sound of the shower running filtered in, I sat there on the bed, my pussy throbbing and my nipples tight. I knew now was absolutely not the time to be coy. I swung my legs out of the bed, glancing around for my clothes. I didn't even bother getting dressed, just scooped up my clothes from the floor, and hurried across the hallway, grabbing my forgotten purse on the way.

In a matter of minutes, I'd tossed on a T-shirt and sweatpants, brewed a pot of coffee, and returned over to Donovan's place, not even bothering to knock. I stepped through the door just as he came out of the bedroom. He smiled slowly when he saw the travel mug of coffee in my hand.

"Here," I said, handing over the coffee and a blueberry scone. "It's not much, but it's something."

He tugged his T-shirt over his head as he stepped toward me, hiding his glorious chest from my eyes. It was quite a disappointment really. Dressed or not, Donovan just might be the sexiest man I'd ever known.

"Thank you," he said gruffly, accepting the travel mug from me and taking a quick sip. "Oh, that's good."

"Maybe not as good as Janet's, but I make a mean cup of coffee. If you like it dark, that is."

"I do," he said, his low voice sending a ripple through me. "I've gotta go."

He stepped into his boots by the door, snagging his jacket with his free hand. Turning back, his eyes coasted over me.

"Be safe," I called as I followed him out into the hallway.

He flashed a grin and a wink over his shoulder. "Always."

I listened to the sound of his footsteps as he jogged down the stairs and outside. Only then did I return to my suite.

As I soaped my body in the shower a few minutes later, I noticed the soreness between my thighs. Donovan was—no surprise—well-endowed. He'd fucked me more thoroughly last night than I'd ever been fucked in my life. I leaned my head back into the water, thinking that I was starting to like him an awful lot. I didn't know if that was such a smart plan. In fact, it might be flat-out crazy. After all, it had only been a matter of weeks since I'd driven away from San Francisco in a bit of a fit, leaving behind my cheating fiancé.

JASMINE

That morning, I went out to my parents' place for breakfast. My mother, Gloria Phillips, met me on the porch, her hair pulled back into a ponytail and her gaze warm as she smiled at me. Her blonde hair was streaked with gray now, but her blue eyes were as bright as ever. She was the kind of beauty that looked better with wrinkles. They simply gave her a quality of timelessness.

She wore a pair of royal blue, swingy cotton pants and a heather gray T-shirt. As soon as I stepped onto the porch, she tugged me into a hug, dropping a kiss on my cheek and then looping her elbow through mine. I walked beside her into the kitchen.

"Your father's out and about, so it's a perfect day for breakfast. I'm making omelets, and I've already started coffee."

I slipped onto a stool at the counter. My parents' home was a farmhouse-style house with two stories and a wrap-around porch. The kitchen was large and airy with a table by the windows that looked out over the field behind the house.

Three counters lined the kitchen walls with an island with a stovetop in the center. It was comfortable to sit across from her and watch her cook. I knew she would wave me away if I offered to help, so I let her cook. I loved to cook as well. The kitchen was one of my favorite places to be, mostly because it was where we spent the most time as a family. It didn't matter where we lived, the kitchen was the heartbeat of the home. My mother puttered about as she whisked eggs, chopped vegetables, and shredded cheese. Meanwhile, I sipped on my coffee as we chatted casually.

Once the omelets were ready, I carried the plates over to the table. She sat at an angle across from me. It was still fairly early. I'd been up since just past dawn when Donovan got the call out to the fire. I figured Levi was out there with him, but was careful not to comment on that.

Levi's job, day in and day out, was responding to fires. If I implied, at this time of day, that I knew he was already out at a fire, my mother might wonder why.

After a few bites, I decided to share my best news. "So, Amelia connected me with the woman who runs the Midnight Sun Arts galleries."

My mother smiled slowly. "I know. Lucy mentioned that Amelia told her about you. So, are you going to call her?"

For once, I had news my mother didn't have before me. "Well, she already called me. I took the day yesterday to go down to Diamond Creek. She wasn't going to be up in Anchorage for a while, and I had the time. Anyway, once I get a space set up so I can start producing pottery here, she wants to display my work in all of the galleries. They have a gallery in Fairbanks, Juneau, one in Anchorage, the one in Diamond Creek, and they even have one in Seattle."

"Oh sweetie! That is the best news. I'm thrilled!"

Emotion tightened in my chest. I'd moved away to pursue some sort of career in what I loved, but all I'd done thus far was cobble it together. I hadn't thought I could make my living in Willow Brook with art as a viable option, but Risa was leading me to believe I could.

"I know, right?"

My mother grinned, pausing to take a sip of coffee. "Speaking of your kiln, I talked to Janet about that too," she said.

"Mom! You know I can take care of things myself."

"I know you can. You've been taking care of everything yourself for years. There's nothing wrong with someone trying to help."

"I know, I know. It's just ..." My words trailed off when my mother shook her head.

"Hon, it's okay to have friends and family to help. We all take care of each other."

Not wanting to argue and realizing I did need some ideas about where I could set up a workspace, I took a sip of coffee and cocked my head to the side. "Okay, what did you talk to Janet about?"

"I just mentioned to her that if you were going to stay around, you would probably be looking to find a place for your studio. I don't know exactly what you need, although I do know you need enough room to work and set up your kiln. Right?"

"Of course. So, what did Janet say?"

"Well, you know the café's in the old fire station?"

"Of course I know that, Mom," I said with a laugh.

She shrugged. "Well, there's a whole storage section in the back that she doesn't even use. It's just empty. There were two garages originally—the main one where the café is now and then the one off the back. She said you can do whatever you want with the space back there. She even said that she figured you'd want to pay rent for it, so once you're set up, you can work something out with her."

My mother was clearly quite satisfied with herself as evidenced by her grin. Her grin widened when I replied,

"That sounds like it might work. I'll go talk to her." Pausing to take a sip of coffee, I added, "And thank you."

She winked. "I'm trying not to pressure you, but I'm also trying to make it easy for you to stay. You know your father and I would love for you to be here. You know how much we miss you."

"I know, Mom. I've missed you too."

One thing I loved about my mother was she didn't tend to dwell on things. As soon as we finished that conversation, she moved on. She chatted about her work, a few projects my father was working on, and how excited she was to be expecting her first grandchild.

It *was* good to be home. I always enjoyed coming to visit, but it felt different to plan to stay. I felt like I could relax and not try so hard to cram everything in.

After we finished breakfast, I got another big hug from my mother and then left, driving straight into town to Firehouse Café. With Risa's offer dangling in front of me, I needed a plan sooner rather than later.

When I stepped into the café, it was bustling as usual, but Janet wasn't at the counter. The young man named Daniel was standing there, his hands flying as he prepped coffees for customers. A cluster of tourists was gathered at the counter. He glanced up, smiling at me. "Are you here for Janet? Or something else?"

"Both." I could always use more coffee, so I ordered a Shot in the Dark.

After I paid, and he handed over my coffee, he gestured me into the bakery in the back where Janet was working. I found her at the wide stainless steel table in the center of the room. She had on an apron dusted with flour, and she was busy kneading dough.

"Hey, Janet," I called as the door swung closed behind me.

She looked up with a smile, using her elbow to nudge a loose lock a hair out of her eyes. "Hi, Jasmine, so good to see you. Have a seat," she said, lifting her chin in the direction of the stool beside the counter directly across from where she was working.

I slipped onto the stool, letting my purse slide to the floor. I watched her knead for a few minutes as I sipped my coffee.

"My mom mentioned she talked to you about a space for me for work," I finally said, not sure why I was so nervous to ask.

Janet was like family to me. I supposed my anxiety was all tangled up in how much it meant to me. Now that I was staring down a potential deadline if I didn't find a place to start throwing pottery soon, I was even more anxious.

In the back of my mind, I figured, in a pinch, I could make some calls around Anchorage and see if anyone would let me use a shared studio. But I didn't have connections there and that might take as much time as this.

Janet looked up with a warm smile. "Of course I did. That space is just sitting there. Back when Dan was alive, he used it for his own personal garage. That's where he would take care of things on his car, and had all of his tools and what not. For a long time, I just left all of his stuff there. A few years ago, I finally got around to giving it all away and now the space is just empty. I think it would be perfect for what you need. I already told your mother you can do what-ever you need to get it ready. Then, when you can afford rent, we'll work something out."

A smile bloomed from the inside out as I looked over at Janet. "That could definitely work," I finally said.

I was almost giddy with excitement. All this time, I'd been scraping by with odd jobs and working in galleries, and somehow trying to reach a point where I could do pottery mostly full-time. All along, I'd pretty much convinced myself I could only make it happen away from Willow Brook. Strangely, the universe was quite politely showing the oppo-site to be true. I just might be able to have it all right here.

Janet continued kneading the dough, rolling it into a tidy ball before setting it in an oiled bowl. She wiped her hands on her apron, resting them both on her hips as she smiled over at me.

"Perfect," she said. She turned to wash her hands in a sink behind her. Glancing over her shoulder, she pointed to a door at the back of the kitchen beside the massive walk-in freezer.

"I need to keep at this. I've got a few more things to get ready here, but you can go take a look. As far as I'm concerned, you just do what you need to do back there. I'll get you a key, so you can enter through the outside. I'm assuming you'll need to take care of a few things to set up the space. Just let me know if you need anything."

Standing, I rounded the table and pulled Janet into a quick hug. She squeezed me tight as I stepped back, snagging a towel to dry her hands. "We're glad you're home, honey."

Someone called her name. "Duty calls," she said over her shoulder as she hurried away. "Take a look and let me know what you need."

The swinging door whooshed as she pushed through it. Snagging my purse off the floor, I walked into the back, coffee in hand.

I vaguely remembered coming back here when Janet's husband was alive. There had been a bunch of tools stored back here, and he always had some kind of project happening. Now, it was just a big empty space. The concrete floor was stained the same soft blue as the front. I chuckled softly, wondering when Janet had done that. The walls were bare and had shelving on two sides. It felt like a garage because it *was* a garage. The big door was closed, and there was a single door beside it. Windows on either side allowed light in. Dust motes floated in the air, catching the rays of sun angling through.

I meandered around the empty space, trying to envision

the best way to set it up. I figured I would have my kiln in one corner with a worktable in the center and my throwing wheel in another corner.

Taking a deep breath, I let myself out the back, wondering who to ask to help me get everything set up. Lucy had offered, yet I knew she and Amelia were very busy this time of year. Building season in Alaska was short and crazy. Levi or my father would be other options. My hesitancy to ask for help was a little rough patch, but I'd get past it. I had to.

To force myself over that speed bump, I slipped my phone out of my pocket, stopping to sit on a bench outside of Janet's B&B. I quickly pulled up Risa's number and dialed.

She picked up on the third ring. "Hello?"

"Hi Risa, it's Jasmine."

"Oh hey," she said, her voice warm. "Any updates for me?"

"That's why I was calling. I found a space for my studio. Give me another few weeks, and I should be able to talk to you about a timeline. Are you still sure about this?"

Risa laughed. "Of course I'm sure! I've already talked to Ethan and Jack, the owners of the other galleries. They're totally stoked. Just give us a heads-up on timing, so we can make sure we have display space everywhere."

Joy buzzed inside of me and tears pricked at the backs of my eyes. This was going to be perfect. The terrifying part, hoping people actually bought my work, would come later. For now, I needed to get there.

Chapter Nineteen

DONOVAN

I leaned back against a fallen tree on the ground, tipping my head to look up at the sky. A week had passed since my night with Jasmine. I hadn't seen her since, yet I could hardly stop thinking about her when I had a spare moment. After our crew was called out to a fire in a neighboring town, I returned home that night, but it had been late.

I had rolled out of bed before dawn the following morning when our crew was called out to another fire out in the Interior. These calls weren't unusual. We dealt with them all summer long.

Yet, it bothered me I hadn't had a chance to see Jasmine before leaving for this long again.

And what would you have done? You were the one who said nothing could happen with her. You blew that up.

My mind taunted me. Hell, I'd burned that promise to myself to ashes.

She was just too damn tempting, and it felt too damn good to be with her. Being with her was a little slice of heaven—a hot, burning, yearning kind of heaven.

For the first time in years, I actually wondered about a

woman. By no means had I been a monk since my engagement fell apart, but I had kept to a narrow path called "casual." Honestly, I'd yet to encounter a woman who tempted me otherwise. Jasmine had caught the ends of the threads stitched around my heart and unraveled them so rapidly, I didn't know what to think.

It was late, and we were hunkered down for the night. The smell of smoke drifted through the air, and the stars winked above as night claimed the sky. We were a good distance from the fire now. We'd worked damn hard to establish firebreaks around it and had gotten the fire contained at this point. We'd received word we would be heading back to Willow Brook tomorrow. Given that we were all tired and weary, we were ready for a break.

For the first time in years, I had something, or rather someone, to look forward to when I got home. A while later, I lay on top of my sleeping bag, my head propped on my hands as I stared at the sky, drifting to sleep with the thought of Jasmine and the look in her eyes when she flew apart passing through my mind.

The following day, I watched as the landscape passed by underneath the helicopter. We were flying over a section of the forest where the fire had started and had ravaged acres upon acres of spruce. Blackened trees were stark against the sky, the landscape looking desolate. Yet, with a glance to the side, I could see the firebreaks we'd created in the distance and a wide river holding back the fire.

Another hotshot crew from Fairbanks had flown in this morning to take care of the last section of that fire. Looking ahead, the mountains came into view. Denali, the centerpiece of the Alaskan Range and the tallest peak in North America, rose tall in the sky—a fortress of spectacular beauty. Its snow-tipped peak was bright against the blue sky.

The sight of Denali meant we were within a half hour of Willow Brook. Jasmine sashayed through my thoughts—the feel of her hair, soft and silky, and the feel of her channel, slick, snug, hot ... and home.

To me.

I was going fucking crazy. To think, for even a minute, that any woman could feel like home to me—that was crazy. And dangerous. Yet, my body wanted what it wanted, and the impossible appeared to be happening. Lust was tangled up in emotion when it came to Jasmine. I didn't know what the hell to think about that.

Levi said something, and I glanced over. "Yeah?"

Chatting in the helicopter wasn't easy, not with the hum of the blades circling overhead.

"Just saying it's going to be good to get home," Levi said.

Somehow, I'd boxed out the fact he was Jasmine's older brother. Just now, that fact came barreling at me. If he had any clue about how intimate I'd been with her, he'd kick my fucking ass. I chose to continue ignoring the ramifications of that for now.

"Always good to get home," I replied. "You stopping by Wildlands?"

We often grabbed dinner and a few drinks together when we got back. After we showered at the station, it was a fitting way to end a tough stint as a crew.

Levi shrugged. "Probably, but if Lucy wants me home, that's where I'll be," he said, flashing a quick grin.

"Of course. If I were you, I'd always stay on Lucy's good side," I offered.

Levi chuckled. "Oh, I do, trust me."

It was a joke around the station that Lucy had once been uniquely resistant to Levi's teasing and flirting. But Levi was nothing if not persistent, and he'd plain worn her down. Now, they were happily married and expecting their first baby.

Until Jasmine, I hadn't even given a second thought to the

idea of settling down with anyone. Right about now, the vision of Jasmine, her belly plump and swollen with our baby, drifted through my thoughts, sending a shot of blood straight to my cock.

If that didn't tell you how bad off I was, I didn't know what would.

Even worse, I was far past caring what Levi might think about the fact that I wanted his sister so fiercely I didn't intend to resist. I would go to Wildlands with the crew tonight, if only because I didn't have family at home and there might be questions if I made excuses. Yet, I didn't intend to stay late, and I would absolutely be knocking on Jasmine's door tonight.

Chapter Twenty

DONOVAN

A few hours later, I leaned back in my chair at the table we'd commandeered at Wildlands and glanced around the bar. The tables were crowded, and there were several pool games going on in the corner while a band was setting up at a stage in the back for a show later tonight.

Beck Steele laughed at something and then nudged me with his elbow. "Know what I mean?" he asked.

I didn't actually know what he meant because I didn't even know what he was talking about. My mind had largely been focused on Jasmine ever since we'd landed.

I glanced his way and shrugged. "Not really."

Beck threw his head back with a laugh. "You don't even know what the fuck I'm talking about, do you?"

I shook my head with a chuckle. "No, can't say I was paying much attention. What do you mean?"

"Ha. I was just talking about the option of a fire out in the Interior here, or getting sent down to Arizona. I prefer to work here. Wouldn't you?"

"Definitely. Fires in Arizona are fucking hot as hell. At

least here, when we're in our heavy gear, it's not boiling hot outside on top of it."

Beck glanced over to Remy Martin and nodded. "See. Exactly what I said."

Remy rolled his eyes and chuckled. "Dude, I wasn't disagreeing with you. I was just saying, no matter what, it's hard work." Remy had only recently joined one of the crews at Willow Brook Fire & Rescue and fit right in. He had no trouble volleying jokes with Beck.

Cade Masters was seated at an angle across from us. He was the superintendent for another crew at the station. He cast a glance at Beck and rolled his eyes.

"What?" Beck asked.

"You just like to find something to debate."

Beck's phone was on the table between us, and I felt the vibration of it before he noticed it. After a moment, he glanced down and snatched it up. "Hey babe," he said into the phone.

I tuned out his conversation, replying to Cade when he asked me if I was taking any leave this summer. "Nah. I'd rather stay here in between fires. Plus, I'm helping Janet to finish up those renovations."

"How's your house coming along?" he asked. "Amelia mentioned they're a little ahead of schedule."

Amelia, Cade's wife, and Lucy from Kick A** Construction were doing my renovations. I had hired them because they were good at what they did. It wasn't anything I couldn't do myself, but with my schedule in the summer, it didn't fit in well to do a big project like that. Not when I was coming and going all summer long.

Catching Cade's eyes, I nodded. "It's coming along faster than I thought. They do damn good work."

"Of course they do. Amelia's better at building than me," he replied with a chuckle.

"I bet," I offered. "I know my way around construction, and I'm pretty sure they do a better job than me too."

Levi called across the table, cutting in. "Right, but Amelia's not as bossy as Lucy. I guaran-damn-tee it."

Cade laughed again, running a hand through his shaggy brown curls. "Maybe, maybe not. Depends on the day. Not that I mind. Far as I can tell, you're so whipped by Lucy, you don't even give a shit if she runs your life."

Levi flashed a grin. "Absolutely. I know who's boss, and I don't give a damn."

Beck finished his call, standing from the table. "Gotta go, guys. Maisie's exhausted and Max just threw up all over the couch. I'm on dad duty, so I'll catch you guys later."

With a wave, he turned and left. Our gathering slowly broke apart after his departure.

On my way out, I paused in the back parking lot by Swan Lake. I had parked my truck at the B&B, so I was walking home. The sun was setting in the distance, casting a pink and purple shimmer over the surface of the lake. A pair of Trumpeter swans floated near the dock, their necks arched gracefully. They were almost ghostly, their silhouettes silvery in the smudgy light of dusk.

As I stood there, looking out over the lake, my old friend Bill passed through my thoughts again. Bill would love Willow Brook. We used to fish at lakes like this back in Georgia when we were growing up. Nothing was quite the same there, with summers hot and humid and the mosquitoes thick. Alaska had plenty of mosquitoes, just like Georgia, but the air was drier and crisper here, and the greenery not quite as thick and dense.

I hated how Bill had betrayed our friendship. Somehow, his betrayal had cut even deeper than Katie's because he'd been my friend. The old anger had faded to nothing more than a twinge, though. I still missed him and our friendship. One thing I'd learned was someone could hurt you deeply, and you could still miss them when they weren't a part of your life.

As for Katie, she tried calling me after they eventually

broke up, apologizing and sobbing, telling me she didn't know what she'd been thinking. With her, I didn't need closure. Or rather, I supposed I already had it. The moment I knew she'd been fucking around on me for months, it was over in my mind and in my heart.

I had many faults, but loyalty wasn't one of them. It never crossed my mind to fuck around on her. I'd had chances and I'd never even been tempted. It didn't mean I was an idiot. I could appreciate a beautiful woman any time, but not once had I considered more than that.

I didn't want to keep thinking about the past and what I couldn't change. I spun away from the lake and headed toward home, walking down Main Street. This time of evening in Alaska was a slow dance of twilight. Twilight in most places was brief, yet it lasted for hours here. That in between time, as day gave way to night, felt suspended, almost magical.

People were still walking along the street and perusing the shops. Voices drifted out from a few restaurants as I passed, and Firehouse Café was hopping. Two nights a week, Janet held open mic night. Tonight happened to be one of them, so the crowd spilled out to the tables on the sidewalk.

I kept on walking, Jasmine on my mind. I wanted to see her. Badly. I wasn't in the mood to reason with myself about it.

After too much time away after the hottest night of my life, my need for her was fierce. When I reached Janet's B&B, the tension I'd been holding inside eased when I saw Jasmine's car there. I had no reason to expect her to be there, and no reason to expect her to want me as much as I wanted her.

And yet, as I walked up the stairs, all I could think was how long I would have to wait to be buried inside of her. I stepped across the landing of the top step, my eyes swinging to the door to her suite.

There were no guardrails on the parameters of whatever

it was we had. My feet stopped at her door, which happened to be a little closer to this end of the hallway than mine. My hand lifted on its own, my knuckles rapping sharply against her door.

I heard her footsteps crossing the floor and then the door swung open. Every fiber of me tightened with anticipation at the sight of her.

Her hair was up in a lopsided ponytail, half falling down. Loose tendrils fell around her face, framing it. She wore a fitted T-shirt that hugged her breasts. As I looked down at her, I saw her nipples tighten under the cotton. Fuck me.

She wasn't wearing a bra. She was clearly dressed for comfort, just wearing that T-shirt and a pair of sweatpants that hung low on her hips. I could see a slender strip of skin peeking out from between her clothes.

I managed to drag my eyes up to her face, taking in the fine arch of her brow, her angled cheekbones, and her plump lips curling into a slow smile. She looked startled to see me.

"Donovan, I didn't know you were home," she said, by way of greeting.

"I just got home tonight."

We simply stood there, staring at each other. I was about to step through her doorway when I realized I should probably ask.

"Mind if I come in?"

"Of course not. Come on in," she said, gesturing as she stepped back, her cheeks flushing pink.

I stepped through the door, my eyes arcing about the room. Her suite was a mirror of mine—the same open style living room with a skylight above, a view across Main Street, and a small efficiency kitchen to the back.

I caught sight of a bright pink bra dangling off the back of the couch. I was suddenly jealous of it—jealous of a fucking bra. I surmised that silk had been able to hug her breasts all day.

I wasn't thinking too clearly. Or rather, I wasn't thinking at all.

When the door clicked shut behind me, she just stood there with her back to the door and her hand curled over the handle. The vision of her held close as I fucked her against the door passed through my mind.

I figured I might as well make that vision a reality.

Stepping to her, I lifted a hand, brushing one of those loose locks of hair away from her forehead. "Mind if I take this down?" I asked, as I caught hold of her ponytail.

Her tongue darted out, pretty and pink, swiping across her bottom lip. I knew right where I wanted it. I wanted everything all at once—my mouth buried between her thighs, her lips wrapped around my cock, while I somehow managed to bury myself in her hot slick heat at the same time.

I'd have to take it one step at a time. Somewhere in this hot mash-up of a fantasy, I had my hand wound around her hair.

"No, I don't mind," she finally murmured.

At her reply, I hooked my finger under the elastic and pulled it free, watching as her hair tumbled loose around her shoulders in rich amber waves.

"Mind if I kiss you?" I asked next.

Her skin was blooming pink, and her breath was coming in short little pants. I wanted to know if she was wet already.

She shook her head, whispering, "No."

So I stepped closer, coming flush against her soft body. She was such a contrast to me. I didn't think much about my body, unless I had an injury that kept me from using it. My body was a tool, and it was a big part of my work. I needed to be strong and unbreakable. She was soft where I was hard.

I dipped my head, needing to taste her skin first. Dropping a kiss right behind her ear, her skin pebbled under my lips. Then, I was dusting kisses along the column of her throat before I made my way to her mouth. Fuck. She tasted like heaven—sweet and salty, so warm.

She sighed into my mouth when I brought my lips to hers, her tongue slipping out to tease with mine. I felt drugged, languid and slow, with the heat of her body and the scent of her winding around me, ensnaring me in its web.

Our kiss was slow and hot, her hips rocking into the hard ridge of my cock.

I managed to break free because I had to know. "Are you wet?"

Jasmine stared at me, her pupils dilated, the blue of her eyes so dark it was almost navy. She nodded slowly, biting her lip. "Uh huh."

"For me?"

Her hips flexed into me, and she nodded again. Her hand slid between us when she released the door handle. She dipped it past the waistband of her sweatpants. Her touch brushed against my cock when she reached between her thighs.

I couldn't see, but I knew she was teasing her pussy. She drew her fingers out, and they were slick with her juices.

"See," she said, her mouth curling slightly at the corner.

I leaned over and caught her fingers in my mouth, swiping my tongue around them and savoring the salty flavor.

That was the sexiest thing I'd ever seen.

I stepped back, swiftly yanking her sweatpants to the floor and her panties right along with them. I was down on one knee when I glanced up at her. Her belly was shuddering with her ragged breaths as she looked at me.

"Do that again," I ordered.

I didn't need to explain. Her hand slid down over her belly again. Her thighs parted slightly, as she bared her pink, wet, glistening pussy for my eyes.

My cock was so hard, I wouldn't have been surprised if I came in my pants.

Her fingers dipped into her swollen folds, circling over her clit and sliding inside.

I had to taste her. Leaning forward, I dragged my tongue over her folds, swiping all the way up to her clit.

"Don't stop," I murmured.

With her fingers sliding in and out, I teased her with my tongue. She tasted so fucking good.

She was so responsive—her breath coming in little gasps and pants with her hips rocking into my mouth. Looking up from my angle, I could see her head fall back against the door with a loud thump. She murmured my name, her free hand threading into my hair.

"I need to feel you come," I murmured, sliding my fingers inside of her. She slapped her palm against the door and held on as I sank my fingers into her hot, slick channel. In a matter of seconds, she came in a noisy burst, her hips bucking against my mouth.

Any wish to see her lips wrapped around my cock burned to ashes in the fierce need to be buried deeply inside of her.

Slowly drawing my fingers out, I gave her one last lick because I needed the taste of her on my tongue. As I straightened slowly, she tore at the buttons on my fly, shoving my jeans and briefs down around my hips and sliding her hand around my cock. I groaned at the feel of her grip lightly stroking me.

"Donovan," she murmured, her voice a husky rasp.

Glancing to her, I found her dark gaze on me. Her cheeks were flushed and her breath came in short heaves. "Yes?"

"I need you. Now."

Sliding my palm under one of her knees, I lifted her leg as I grabbed my cock in my fist, sliding it back and forth through her slick wet pussy.

I wasn't even thinking. I was just about to drive into her when I realized I needed a condom. I froze. Because I didn't have one. I sure as hell didn't usually bring them with me when I went out to deal with a fire. I also didn't usually come home and fuck someone before I even walked in my door.

That was how crazy Jasmine made me.

"Fuck," I muttered. "I gotta ..."

My words trailed into a growl when she rocked her hips against me, her slick heat teasing my cock.

"What?" she asked.

"Condom," I bit out.

"I'm on the shot," she gasped. "And I'm clean. I promise. If there's another reason we need one, just tell me now."

The least sexy conversation in the world was sexy with Jasmine, every word husky with her lips pink and swollen from our kisses.

"No need. I haven't fucked anyone without a condom in years. I'm totally clean. Are you sure? It's your call." I couldn't quite believe I'd managed more than one full sentence, but I had.

She nodded, tightening her leg around my hip. I lifted her, cupping her ass with one hand, the door giving me an assist as I held her high against me. I didn't wait. Positioning my cock at her entrance, I sank inside of her, all the way to the hilt. Her head thumped against the door and she cried out.

Her channel was so slick, so wet, so snug around my cock, it was like coming home. Heaven.

I held still for a beat. She was so tight. Adjusting her against me, I held her by the hips. She rocked into me, spurring me on. I finally drew back and sank into her again. In a matter of seconds, we were rocking into each other. A slow dance of raw pleasure. It felt too good to make it last. I tumbled into a cauldron of heat, surrounded by her scent, the smoke of our desire spinning around us together. With every stroke, her pussy throbbed and clenched around me.

Chapter Twenty-One

JASMINE

Donovan's strength surrounded me as he held me against him with the wooden door cool against my back. He held me easily as he fucked me in a dizzying, maddening slow circle, driving inside me to the hilt—again and again and again.

He stretched me and filled me, the sensation so delicious, I felt drugged, nearly incoherent with need. Every time he drove in, he hit that sweet spot inside. With each rock of his hips, the pressure against my clit sent hot sparks through me as I chased another sweet release.

His fingers dug into my hips, and I heard myself murmuring his name, begging and pleading—frantic as pressure gathered inside me again, rolling into a wave.

"Look at me," he murmured, his voice a warm command that I couldn't deny.

Dragging my eyes open, I found his gaze on me, searing in its intensity. My heart thumped—hard. The intimacy coiling around us was so intense I could hardly catch my breath. All the while, the slick pull and slide of his cock drove me higher and higher.

"So fucking hot," he murmured. "I want to see you come, sugar."

His voice alone pushed me over the edge. One more stroke, and I flew apart, the wave cresting and breaking free as pleasure crashed over me.

His grip tightened on my hips and then he cried out my name—a raw shout in the room. I felt the heat of his release fill me as pleasure shuddered through my body.

His forehead fell to mine as we tried to catch our breath together.

Without missing a beat, Donovan lifted me against him, turning as he drew his head away.

"Shower," he murmured softly.

It wasn't quite a question, but it wasn't exactly a statement either. At my nod, he turned and walked to the bedroom. Seeing as my suite was a mirror of his, it wasn't like he didn't know where to go. He didn't let me down until we were in the shower with the hot water steaming over us.

Only then did he draw out of me and ease me to the tile floor. The moment felt so intimate with the steam cocooning us—as if we were the only two people in the world.

A mere week without seeing him, and the relief that washed over me when I found him outside my door was immense. I didn't quite know how I could miss someone as quickly as I had missed him.

I watched as he efficiently soaped up. The man was practically carved from stone, his body nothing but hard planes. As he turned to duck under the water when I stepped out of it, I noticed a few scars on his back and a long, jagged scar along the back of his bicep.

Before I even realized what I was doing, I lifted my arm and trailed my fingertips along the path of the scar.

Donovan turned, his eyes catching mine. "Cut my arm during a fire. A loose piece of bracing fell when I was carrying someone out," he explained, his tone matter-of-fact.

I looked up at him, my heart thudding hard and fast inside my chest. "Oh."

He was quiet for a beat, his eyes searching mine as he lifted a shoulder in a shrug. "Just a scar."

I managed to smile, though my heart tightened. Stepping out of the shower, I handed over a towel as I dried off. I wondered what it was about him that got to me.

I supposed I should've been grieving the fact my ex-fiancé had cheated on me. While it stung and I was annoyed with it, I didn't really miss Glen. That said it all.

Glen had never once looked at me with fierce heat in his eyes the way Donovan did. That very first night I'd seen Donovan—the way his gaze had scorched me had reached in and grabbed ahold of me. He made me feel like a woman in a way that no man ever had.

As we walked out of the bedroom after Donovan tugged on his clothes, and I pulled on sweatpants and a T-shirt, I was speaking before I'd thought about it.

"Have you had dinner?"

Donovan stood there in his bare feet, turning to look back at me. My breath hitched. With his damp hair and his skin flushed from the shower, he was so fucking handsome. All he wore was a pair of faded jeans and a black T-shirt, and I wanted to tear his clothes off all over again.

There was something about what it felt like to be in his arms, his attention nearly devouring me. He literally swept me up into his strength.

"I had a little something at Wildlands, but I'm hungry again," he replied, his voice low, his eyes searching my face.

"How about I make dinner?"

We stood there, just staring at each other. Somehow, the moment felt weighted now.

"I'd like that," he finally said.

My heart clenched, and a smile bloomed. "Okay. I love to cook."

The kitchen here, just like his, had a counter running on

the wall with a small fridge, an oven, and a stovetop. Opposite the counter was a small island.

"Let me see what I can whip up," I said, gesturing to the fridge. "I even have beer."

Donovan grinned. "I'll take whatever you have. I'm not picky."

"I actually have the good stuff, some beer from Diamond Creek Brewery. I was down there a few days ago."

I handed over a bottle as he settled onto a stool at the island counter. I leaned into the fridge, surveying my options. "How about lasagna?" I called over my shoulder.

"Won't that take a while? You don't need to do something special."

The low rumble of his voice sent a little shiver through me.

Dear God. I was so screwed. This man had just given me two intensely hot orgasms, and I was ready to jump his bones all over.

I straightened, turning back to face him. "It's quick. I have all the ingredients. I'll throw it together, and it'll be ready within the hour."

He chuckled, the sound sending a prickle down my spine. "I love lasagna, so if you want to make it, go for it." As I got started, he caught my eye. "So, you're not a vegetarian then?"

His southern drawl and the teasing tone of his voice made me laugh. I shook my head. "No."

He winked as he took a pull from his beer. "I thought maybe so, with you living in San Francisco. No offense."

"Are you kidding? I was born and raised in Alaska. I'm not saying there aren't a few vegetarians here, but definitely not me. My dad made me learn how to hunt when I was in high school. I have actually killed an animal and eaten it."

Donovan smiled wide. "Good to know, sugar. Me too."

Mostly because his smile sent butterflies spinning in my

belly and I got anxious, I reached for the remote from the corner of the kitchen counter and turned the television on.

As it turned out, I didn't need it to stay distracted. It was just background noise as I cooked. For the first time since I'd met Donovan, we simply relaxed. There was no tension. We were crazy hot for each other, but we managed to behave like two normal people having dinner. We just talked.

The man clearly had manners, asking me all kinds of questions about where I grew up and what it was like and so on. I learned a lot about him too. Now I knew he had that sexy drawl because he grew up in Georgia. He swore up and down that he'd lost most of it.

"Sugar," Donovan drawled with a slow wink. "Trust me, I've lost a bit of my accent."

He was the one and only man whose voice alone sent hot shivers through me. It didn't help matters to be aware of just how expertly he could play my body. Mind-blowing sex aside, it was more than nice to hang out with Donovan. True to my word, I had the lasagna ready within the hour.

He offered to help, but I shooed him away, although I did let him grate the cheese. After we finished eating, we lounged on the couch. I'd say we watched TV, but I don't remember what was on, and I certainly didn't pay attention.

I fell asleep, tucked in his arms. When he stood to go, it was me who stopped him. "Why don't you just stay here?"

He turned, his hazel gaze sweeping over my body and sending sparks scattering through me. He stayed.

Once again during the night, he sent me flying. I woke to the feel of his fingers teasing a nipple, his hips rocking into me from behind, a slow, languid tease.

My climax came over me slowly, flowing through me like molasses, heavy and intense, shattering me at the core. I cried out and shuddered at the feel of his release filling me. I drifted back to sleep, warm, safe, and sated in his arms.

Chapter Twenty-Two

DONOVAN

The sun filtering through the curtains woke me. Jasmine was warm and soft beside me, one of her legs thrown over mine and tucked between my calves. She was plastered against my side, her fucking tempting, perfect breasts pressed against me. As it was, I woke up with morning wood. Perhaps you'd think after fucking her against the door and then sometime in the dark hours of the night, I'd have been sated, my need slaked.

But no. I was beginning to wonder if burning out my need for Jasmine was even possible.

It was early, but then I woke early. Rolling over, I glanced at the clock on her nightstand. Six a.m. I needed to be at the station within the hour.

For the first time in years, I didn't want to get out of bed. In fact, I'd have been more than happy to stay here all day. Just maybe I could satisfy my need for her.

I'd pretty much written off getting serious again. It hadn't been a conscious decision, more that I felt cynical. I hadn't figured anyone would matter that much to me again.

Jasmine had already shimmied through every crack in my defenses. She mattered. A lot.

The sex was fucking amazing. She was so responsive, so raw, so pure. Even when I'd been at the height of being half in lust and love with Katie, sex had never been this amazing. But when you're in your twenties and you're a man, well, it doesn't take much.

When I found out Katie was fucking around on me with my best friend, it burned. Badly. Yet now, with a few years in between, the burn had faded. I suppose I had loved her in the only way I knew how at that time. I also knew that it hurt just as much for Bill to be a part of the betrayal. Hell, that had burned the worst.

I hadn't been able to avoid the news that Bill and Katie got engaged, and then later broke up. Bill and I grew up together. Our parents were best friends, so avoiding news about him was near to impossible.

Despite thinking I'd never trust a woman again, there was no doubt in my mind Jasmine would never betray anyone like that. It's simply wasn't in her nature. How I knew that, I didn't know.

As I lay there with her tangled up beside me, sifting my fingers through her hair, my thoughts spun back to the night before. The woman could cook. Now, my mama was a hell of a cook. She was a Southern woman and prided herself on blowing your socks off, no matter what she made. She wasn't fancy, but everything she cooked was amazing.

I'd be hard-pressed to say that Jasmine hadn't made the best lasagna I'd ever had. Because I was a loyal boy to my mama, I didn't even like thinking that. I knew my mama would love Jasmine. Somehow that got to me. Jasmine was like smoke, sliding through the cracks in my walls.

I'd learned a bit about her last night. Her family was tight, that much was clear. She teased that Levi fancied himself the best cook in her family. She'd grudgingly acknowledged that he was at least as good as she was.

While she clearly adored her older brother, there was a thread of tension there. But then, wasn't there a thread of tension in everyone's family? I knew my mama still had her opinions on the mistake I'd made in asking Katie to marry me. Angry as she was at Bill after what went down, I knew she wished I would forgive him.

That was a sore spot between us. Mama also hadn't been thrilled when I'd moved all the way to Alaska. I hadn't run to Alaska. It's just that hotshot firefighters were in much higher demand out West. I went where the job took me, and I'd fallen in love with Alaska. I went home every year, and my parents came here to visit every year.

I took a breath, reminding myself I needed to get up and get my ass in gear. The moment I shifted, intending to carefully slide out from underneath Jasmine, she came awake with a start.

She rose on her elbow, her eyes swinging to me.

Fuck me.

With her hair a tangle around her face, her cheeks flushed from her sleep, her lips puffy from too many kisses last night, and her eyes sleepy, she was so damn sexy, my cock got hard. Again.

"Oh," she said, as if surprised to find me here.

That made me laugh, a little chuckle rolling out.

Her cheeks pinkened and then she smiled, her smile a little ray of sunshine, warming me inside and out.

"Good morning," she said, her voice husky.

"Morning." I briefly considered whether I had time to take her again. Her legs shifted, her knee brushing against my cock, and then her cheeks flushed an even deeper shade of pink.

Another chuckle rumbled out. "I need to get to work," I murmured.

"I'll make coffee," she said quickly, hopping out of bed in a flash.

That didn't help the state of my cock. I had a perfect

view of her heart shaped ass, full and curvy. An image of her bent over while I sank inside of her from behind flashed through my thoughts.

I knew exactly what I would be doing tonight when I got home. I wanted her from behind, her ass in the air while I buried myself in her slick, wet pussy.

Kicking the sheets back, I willed my cock down. As I walked out of the bedroom, tugging my boxers on, I looked over to where she stood by the kitchen counter, getting coffee ready.

"I'm gonna grab a shower across the hall, and I need a change of clothes. Be back in a few."

She glanced over, casting a quick smile my way. "Okay, coffee'll be ready by the time you get back."

I did *not* want to go to work today. I wanted to lose myself in Jasmine. I was falling for her. Hard. I needed to keep myself in check and stay sane. She hadn't said another word about it, but I remembered the first night I met her and what she told me. Her ex had fucked around on her. I knew a bit about how that felt and knew that it burned. While I knew what I felt between us and knew it was real and deep, I sensed Jasmine might be skittish if I moved too far, too fast.

A quick shower later—a cold one at that—I yanked on my clothes and walked back across the hallway. As soon as I entered her apartment, I knew she'd been up to more than making coffee. Somehow, inside of the maybe ten minutes I'd been gone, she was making pancakes.

"I decided you needed breakfast," she said, as I closed the door behind me and walked toward her.

"Sugar, you're perfect." I slipped my arms around her from behind, dipping my head to breathe her in. She flipped two pancakes.

"Pretty sure I'm not perfect, but I figured you needed to eat." She paused, a coy gleam in her eyes. "Food."

And just like that, I was hard again.

The pancakes were delicious, as was the coffee. Because I was bordering on being late, I left without taking her against the wall on the way out.

I just had to figure out how slow to take this.

Chapter Twenty-Three

DONOVAN

The morning at the station was quiet. Our crew, having just returned from a rotation out in the backcountry, was responding to local calls. The local crew was handling a controlled burn nearby.

I did some work in the garage, walking Emily through how to change the oil on one of the trucks. She was a blast to have around the station with her purple hair and her attitude. When lunch rolled around, I offered to go to Firehouse Café for everyone and pick up pizza on the way back for the crew. Of course, no one said no. Within minutes, I pulled up in front of Firehouse Café.

Stepping into the café, I scanned the room, finding a lucky pause in the action. While the tables were full, there was no one waiting at the counter as Janet handed over a coffee to someone.

She immediately cast her smile my way as I approached, her warm brown eyes crinkling at the corners. Janet was one of the first people I'd met when I moved to Willow Brook. I'd arrived late one afternoon at the end of days and days of driving, starving and in desperate need of a cup of coffee.

With Firehouse Café smack in the middle of Main Street, I'd stopped and found her behind the counter. As soon as she heard I wasn't a tourist and I was actually moving to town, she'd insisted on giving me my coffee for free and proceeded to tell me essentially the entire history of Willow Brook inside of a half an hour.

Of course, she did this in between waiting on other customers and checking on me at my table. As a result of that free cup of coffee, she'd earned over a thousand dollars or more from me since then. I stopped by here almost every day that I wasn't out in the field.

"Donovan," she said, her voice containing a hint of laughter in it. "How are you?"

"Good, good. Just got back last night. You know I can't go a day without getting coffee when I'm in town, so here I am."

"I expected you this morning," she said with a wink.

My mind flashed to how I woke up this morning with Jasmine tucked beside me. Just that passing thought, and a jolt of need spun through me. Fuck. I didn't even have to see Jasmine to get hot for her.

In fact, I still knew precisely what I was hoping to see tonight — her sweet ass tilted up in the air as I fucked her from behind.

I gave myself a mental nudge, forcing my attention to Janet. I wasn't used to obsessing over a woman like this. I shrugged. "Busy morning, that's all. Anyway, I've got a bit of an order for you."

"What'll it be?"

"I'll take my usual Shot in the Dark, but I need ten house coffees. Just give me some cream on the side because I don't know who likes cream and who doesn't. We've got sugar at the station, so we can survive without that."

Janet chuckled. "Lunch run?"

"Of course."

She spun around and began to get our coffees ready. I

moved over to the side of the counter, and we chatted while she worked. She paused a few times to wait on other customers. At one point, she glanced over, her eyes taking on a gleam. "So, I have a question," she said.

"What's that?"

"Jasmine's going to use the empty garage in the back for her studio. I'm wondering if I could persuade you to help her get it set up. She's a bit stubborn, and I'm guessing she's not gonna want to ask anybody for help. I'll pay you."

Over my dead body.

No way in hell was I going to let Janet pay me to help Jasmine.

"Of course I'll help. I need to talk to her about it though. I don't see how I can do what she needs without making sure I know what she's looking for. And for God's sake, you don't need to pay me. The place is built. I'd guess she needs a few shelves, perhaps a table, something like that."

Janet beamed as she handed over the last coffee. "I knew you would say yes. I figure you're right next door as it is, so you can just add it in when you're working on stuff for my place."

"Did you forget you're not paying me because you let me stay for free? I can probably do what she needs in about a day or two, so consider it done."

"Well, I am paying for materials, and I'll do the same here. I'm gonna tell her I asked you to do the work because it's my space," Janet offered with a smile, seeming quite satisfied with herself about this.

"That big of a deal?"

"Well, I don't know how well you know Jasmine yet"— my mind flashed to the feel of Jasmine's channel around my cock as I fucked her against the door last night—"but she's kind of stubborn. I'm on Team Jasmine, and I want her to stay in Willow Brook. To make that happen, we all need to conspire to make sure she can do her pottery here."

"Oh? So that's what it's for?"

She quickly rang me up, and I handed over the money.

"Yes, she's amazing and her work is beautiful. She's all set up to sell to a chain of galleries here in Alaska. With Amelia and Lucy busy this summer, I figured I'd stick my nose in things and make sure she gets her studio in working order."

"You get all this info from her?" I asked, teasing but also curious.

Janet smiled slyly. "I got it from her mother. Jasmine's almost like a daughter to me."

"Happy to help. Let me know when I'm cleared to talk to her about it."

"Of course."

Dropping my change in the tip jar, I gave her a wave as I left and headed down to pick up the pizza. Alpenglow Pizza had opened within the year after another pizza place had closed. In a short time, they'd quickly become popular and were definitely the go-to place for everyone at Willow Brook Fire & Rescue when we wanted pizza. With a wood fired oven and a varying menu, their pizzas were delicious and their service prompt.

The armload of pizzas I'd called in on my way to get coffee was ready, and I was headed back down Main Street within minutes. My mind kept looping back to Jasmine. She was independent and had a fiery streak. I'd seen it that first night when she hauled off and punched the asshole who'd grabbed her ass.

I'd become well-acquainted with her fiery side. Every time we were close, she nearly burned me up. Just like Janet, I was on Team Jasmine. I'd do whatever she needed for her studio if that meant she'd be staying in Willow Brook.

The day was fortunately busy after I returned to the station, and we scarfed down the pizza. We got called out to a small local fire, and on my way home, I went to help get Herman out of one of his favorites trees. Herman was the beloved cat of Carrie Dodge, an elderly woman who lived alone. The rascally cat was prone to climbing high in trees and getting stuck. This occurred with such frequency that all the firefighters in Willow Brook had helped her at one point or another. We'd purchased Carrie's excavator from her after she tumbled into a ditch in it one year. Now, the rather pricey piece of equipment sat idle in her yard until Herman got stuck in a tree and we used the bucket to get him down. Ridiculous, I know. But it worked.

After handing Herman over and getting a wide smile from Carrie, I climbed into my truck. With every free moment, all I could think about was getting home to Jasmine.

———

As I stopped at the end of Carrie's driveway before turning onto the highway, my phone vibrated. When I glanced at the screen and saw my mother's number, I was surprised. Mama was a scheduled kind of person. She called me when I wasn't out dealing with a fire, usually on a Saturday morning. This was out of the ordinary for her. Answering, I knew from her tone right away that something was wrong.

"What is it, Mama?"

"Oh hon, I'm so sorry to call you like this. I'm not sure how you'll feel about it, but I thought you needed to know."

My gut churned, even though I had no idea what she was about to tell me. "Okay, what is it, Mama?"

"It's Bill. He got badly injured in a fire and he's in the hospital. He's not expected to make it."

I gripped the phone in my hand, silent long enough that my mother spoke again.

"Donovan, honey, are you with me?"

Her soft Southern drawl soothed me somehow. She was right. I needed to know about this. My hand tightened on the phone as my heart pounded, its beat rapid and erratic.

Bill and I hadn't spoken in almost three years. Oh, don't go thinking I was hung up on Katie. I'd moved on from her long ago. In hindsight, I could see all the reasons why she wasn't right for me, all the signs I'd missed. Yet, Bill had been my friend, my best friend. The kind of friend I hadn't had since.

As life rolled along, you learned you could remake parts of your life, have a do-over, so to speak. You could never change the past, but you could try to get it right the second time. Hearing that Bill might die sent my mind spinning back to my last phone call with him.

It was right after I'd moved up here, not long after the news reached me that he and Katie broke up. Not a shocker. It felt like she'd blown our friendship to pieces, and it killed him. She'd gone on to cheat on him too. He'd called to tell me how sorry he was and how much he'd fucked up. At the time, I figured it served him right to get screwed over.

As angry as I'd been then, over time, the anger faded and dissipated. Mostly, I missed Bill. Now, he might be dying.

"I'm here, Mama. Where is he?"

"His mama called me. They airlifted him to a hospital in Denver. I guess his crew was at a fire in the mountains nearby. His parents are flying out tonight."

I swallowed through the sudden knot of emotion in my chest and throat. In a flash, I knew the meaning of forgiveness. Just like that. In the end, Bill's betrayal was smaller than my friendship with him. I'd ignored his attempt to mend fences. I'd just wanted to move on.

"You'll call me if you get an update?"

"Yes, honey. I asked his mama to give me a call when they landed."

Another rub in Bill's betrayal had been the fact our parents were best friends. I was fairly certain his mama had ripped him a new one when everything went down. Somehow, our parents had stayed close.

Once Bill and Katie were over for good, every so often, my mama gently suggested maybe I should give Bill a call.

I took a deep breath and let it out, regret washing over

me. The kernel of bitterness was gone. I guessed it had been for some time, but I hadn't bothered to do anything about it.

"You call me when they get there. I'll see if I can take some time off."

"Of course, honey," my mama said.

After I ended the call, all I could think was I needed to see Jasmine.

Chapter Twenty-Four

JASMINE

I leaned on the counter while Lucy put some dishes in the dishwasher, and Levi fed Ham pieces of lettuce by the table. I'd stopped by to have dinner with them, still out of sorts inside. I rarely had asthma attacks any more. I was careful about always having an inhaler handy. Yet, something about that and being home had tripped a switch in my brain.

"Levi," I called as I turned to approach the table.

Levi feeding Ham was Levi at his absolute least intimidating, so I figured now was a good time to bring up a potentially difficult topic. I didn't really care about having this conversation in front of Lucy. Another mark in her favor as the best sister-in-law ever—she wasn't judgmental.

"Jazzy," he replied. He was one of the very few people who used that nickname with me occasionally.

I decided to just cut to the chase. Slipping into the chair across from him, I caught his eyes. "I need to say I'm sorry. I think it's about seventeen years overdue."

He looked confused for a beat, but then his gaze cleared. "For that?"

I knew precisely what he meant by *that*. My cheeks got

hot, and I nodded. I took a deep breath, letting it out with a sigh. "Ever since then, I always thought you were too overprotective."

Lucy called over. "I might agree with that."

Her levity was welcome because I'd seen the lines of tension start to tighten on Levi's face. His shoulders rose and fell with a deep breath.

"Anyway, I was thinking about things the other day, and I guess maybe I understand why."

"You almost died," he said softly, pausing to give Ham another piece of lettuce.

The sweet little brown and white hamster somehow made this moment all okay. The sound of the dishwasher closing was loud in the room. Glancing over to Lucy, I realized Levi had probably never told her the story, based on the look on her face.

Looking back to Levi, I replied, "I know. I can't change what happened, but I hate that there's this little thing between us where you get protective and then I get tense. You're an awesome brother. I know that, even if I get cranky about how much you worry sometimes."

Lucy quietly slipped into the chair between us. Levi hadn't replied, his throat moving as he swallowed.

I glanced to Lucy. "I'm guessing you didn't hear the story?"

She shook her head.

"You know I have asthma, right?" At her nod, I continued. "I'll give you the really short version. We were young, and it was summer. Summer in Alaska is weird because the greenery explodes all at once, you know?"

She smiled a little. I took a deep breath and looked to Levi. He was quiet, but listening. "Anyway, Levi was going to hike with some friends, and I wanted to tag along, so I begged him to let me come. He let me and my friends come with them. There was nothing unusual about the day. Our parents were having lunch at Wildlands." I paused to take another breath and a sip of wine. "I forgot my inhaler. I knew I forgot it, but I didn't want to go back. The pollen was awful, and we were walking through the grass. I had an asthma attack. Levi had to carry me all the way back. It was awful. Or at least I think it was. I don't remember much except I could hardly breathe. I remember how scared he looked and the look on my parents' faces when we got back to Wildlands. That might be why he's kind of opinionated about my life."

I traced a circle on the table and looked over at Levi, who was trailing his fingers over Ham's back. Maybe this wasn't much, but the tension had simmered between Levi and me for years ever since that happened.

"Oh. That explains a lot," Lucy said softly.

Levi's eyes cut to her. She reached over and squeezed his hand. "Babe, you're laidback and easygoing, most of the time. Not so much when it comes to your family, and even less so when it comes to Jasmine. That's all."

She looked at me, cocking her head to one side. "I never had an older brother, but I get not appreciating people worrying about you. I always thought you two were so lucky because you adore each other. But every so often things get tense, and it makes me sad."

Tears threatened, but I took a breath and pushed through the feeling. "Is it that obvious?"

"Actually, no. It's just every once in a while, like a flare-up."

I chewed on the corner of my mouth, catching Levi's eyes. "It's not like I think you're gonna stop worrying. I guess I can take it as a compliment."

Levi barked a laugh. "Yeah, that day was pretty scary. And you're stubborn as hell."

There was a lot left unsaid, but then words weren't what we really needed. I suppose I just needed to acknowledge that I understood how that day had affected us.

"I'm still gonna worry," he added.

"I know," I managed with a slow smile.

Somehow, that was enough to kick through the emotional dam between Levi and me. It wasn't huge, it wasn't earth-shattering, but it was enough. As Lucy had pointed out, we adored each other. That event had been like a pebble in a shoe. Every so often, the rub would hurt.

For me, it was more about recognizing how that event had affected us and acknowledging how terrifying it must've been for him. He would always be my older brother, and he would still be overprotective, but I might have more patience with it.

Conversation moved onto lighter matters. When I stood to leave, Levi pulled me into one of his bear hugs, lifting me off the floor. When he set me down, he grinned.

"Love you, sis," he said.

I leaned up, kissing him on the cheek. "Always love you."

Lucy walked me out to the car, pausing beside it as I climbed in. "Thank you," she said, when I glanced up.

"For what?"

"I think that meant a lot to Levi. He never mentioned what happened."

"I gathered. I suppose it was bigger in my mind than his."

Lucy shrugged and smiled. "Either way, I'm glad I know. You mean so much to him." Leaning over, she gave me a quick hug.

I needed that too. When she stepped back, she closed the door for me. With a wave, I backed up, watching through my rearview mirror as Levi met her outside, catching her hand in his.

As overdue as that conversation had been, it left my emotions right at the surface of my skin. I felt exposed and raw.

Donovan immediately filled my thoughts. With the texts from Glen, more and more, I was realizing how little Glen and I had had together.

I had settled for him, settled for someone who, on the surface, I thought was a good bet. It wasn't as if things had been God-awful. They hadn't. They'd just been okay.

With Donovan ... Well, it was far more than okay. The sex was beyond anything I could've imagined. With the way I felt tangled up with him, I was starting to worry my heart was already in far too deep.

As I drove home, I wondered if I would see him tonight. It was impossible not to wonder, not with him living right across the hallway. When I pulled up at the B&B and saw his truck, my heart immediately began pounding. Butterflies took flight in my belly, the wild flutter so sudden I felt dizzy.

This wasn't just desire, and I knew it. I couldn't even imagine letting myself get in too deep with Donovan. Yet, I was already tumbling hard and fast, free falling into him.

You don't know if you're going to see him. He's probably tired from work. Just go to bed. Don't have any expectations.

That was my little lecture as I let myself in. The downstairs was dark and quiet. The light was on in the hallway, casting a soft glow down the stairs, and my footsteps echoed as I made my way up. Cresting onto the landing, I felt Donovan's presence before I even saw him.

Looking ahead, I saw him standing in the hallway with his shoulder resting against the wall. One hand was tucked in his pocket, tugging his jeans down just enough that I could see a strip of skin between his T-shirt and the waistband of his jeans.

I didn't know what I saw in his eyes, but it was intense and solely focused on me. He didn't move as I approached him, my heartbeat running wild and heat spiraling through me, flushing me from head to toe.

When I stopped in front of him, the last strike of my heel was loud in the hallway. When I looked up, I sensed that he was hurting emotionally somehow. Flying blind, my reaction was automatic.

"Are you okay?" I asked, reaching out to catch his hand in mine.

He was still and quiet for a beat and then he shrugged. "I don't know."

"Is there anything I can do?"

His shoulder lifted in another half-shrug. Pushing off the wall, he slipped his hand out of his pocket, lifting it to catch the ends of my hair and twirl a lock of hair around his fingers.

"I need you," he murmured.

The gruff sound of his voice and the heated look in his eyes gripped me and sent a hot jolt of need through me. There was no way I could have resisted him. All I had to do was look at Donovan, and I practically melted at his feet.

With his eyes on me and his hand threading into my hair, he stole my breath as he fit his mouth over mine. Donovan wasn't a man to kiss with any hesitation. He devoured my mouth, and I loved every second of it. There was something delicious about surrendering to him, to the intensity of the desire.

I tumbled into the fire willingly, wanting it. It was almost frightening, yet it was so overpowering I loved every minute of it. We spun in the hallway until my shoulder blades landed against the wall. He broke free from our kiss, trailing a searing path down my neck, his lips, teeth, and tongue sending hot shivers racing through me.

I could feel the intensity of emotion, could sense that he was trying to lose himself in us, in me. When he rocked his hips against mine, I bit my lip to hold in the moan at the feel of his hard, hot length against me. I needed to taste him.

He was hurting and in pain. I didn't know why, and I didn't even know how I knew; I just did. I wanted to make him feel better, to help him lose himself in me the way he did the same for me.

Spinning quickly, I pushed him against the wall. Stepping back, I slid my palm over the hard ridge of his cock. With a few quick flicks, I unbuttoned his fly and slipped my hand down into his briefs, shimmying them down just enough for his cock to spring free.

His breath hissed through his teeth as I curled my fist around his shaft, looking up at him as his head fell back against the wall with a thud. His eyes met mine, his gaze dark. The look in his eyes sent a surge of power through me. It was a heady feeling, knowing that I affected him as powerfully as he affected me. With Donovan, I didn't ever get caught up in my head, worrying if what I was doing was enough.

Everything between us was give and take, push and pull. Giving was the same as taking. It was an elemental dance of need and release. Slipping my tongue out, I swiped the drop of pre-cum beading at the top of his cock.

"Jasmine," he murmured, his fingers tightening in my hair.

Shifting down onto my knees, I swirled my tongue around the thick head. Dragging my tongue on the underside of his cock, watching as his eyes fell closed, I savored the sound of his low groan. I swirled my tongue around the tip again and then sucked him into my mouth.

"Fuck, sugar, that feels so damn good," he growled.

I looked up as I tilted my head back, drawing my tongue along the underside of his cock again and gripping his balls lightly with my hand. His eyes opened, his gaze dark and heavy as he stared at me.

I tasted the salty tang of his pre-cum. It was like a little drug, a tiny hit of it to the back of my throat as it spun across my tongue. I sucked him in again, his cock wet and slick. My palm got wet as I stroked up and down, pumping him with my mouth and hand. His head slammed to the wall again, his fingers gripping my hair roughly.

Then, he was coming, his hot release filling my mouth as I swallowed it down.

I drew back slowly with a last swirl of my tongue around

the thick head of his cock. When I was standing, I opened my mouth to say something but before I could, he fit his mouth over mine in another deep, intense kiss. If I wondered if he cared at all that he'd just come in my mouth, his kiss erased any questions on that matter.

With one hand tangled in my hair and his other cupping my cheek, he kissed me as if the world was about to end. Then, we were spinning against the wall again, and fell through the first door we reached, which happened to be mine.

Chapter Twenty-Five

DONOVAN

The scent of Jasmine surrounded me, wrapping around me like a drug. My heart was tethered to her, and I didn't even care.

When I heard her come home tonight, all I knew was I needed her.

Now she was here, her plump lips against mine, her tongue dancing and teasing with mine after driving me insane with that hot little blowjob in the hallway. It didn't matter that I'd just come in her mouth, I was already hard again. For her. Only her.

I tore at her clothes, hearing a rip of fabric, a button pinging on the floor. Stepping back, she stumbled as she kicked her boots loose and shimmied out of her skirt while I threw my shirt to the floor. In a flash, she was bare naked. We were standing beside the couch, and I spun her around probably a little rougher than I should've.

She didn't miss a beat, her hands curling over the back of the couch as she leaned forward. The musky scent of her desire drifted to me. Reaching between her thighs, I found her hot, slick, and ready. I didn't even wait, gripping my cock in my fist, I buried myself to the hilt inside of her from behind. She tilted her ass up; the sweet curve of her spine was so damn sexy. I held still for a beat, emotion tightening in my throat while my heart thudded hard and fast against my ribcage.

I knew I wasn't thinking clearly, knew I was acting on emotion. But it felt as if Jasmine knew that somehow, as if she knew I needed to lose myself in her, inside this madness that beat like a drum between us.

On the heels of a ragged breath, I drew back and surged inside, my low growl loud in the quiet room. Her channel felt so good, so wet and clenching. Another few strokes, and I was already barreling toward my own release.

Sweet as the sight of her ass was, I needed to see her face. I drew back, spinning her around again. We tumbled over the back of the sofa in a tangle of limbs. She straddled my lap as I leaned back into the cushions. Looking up at her with her amber hair a tangle around her face and her skin flushed, my heart knew the truth. She had ruined me—slayed me. And I hadn't even seen it coming.

She rose up, sliding down over my cock and sheathing me inside of her. Dusting kisses along my temple and down my neck, she rocked her hips into me. She came almost instantly, her tight pussy squeezing and clenching around my cock. I felt her shudder and the sweet sound of her cry before I let myself go, my second release pouring into her long and deep.

Jasmine fell against me, tucking her head in the crook of my neck, her breath gusting across my skin. Having a lapful of her with my cock buried in her was the closest thing to true heaven I'd ever experienced.

My hand was tangled in her hair, and I slowly sifted my fingers through it as I tried to catch my own breath. It was a damn good thing I was sitting down. Only Jasmine had the capacity to take so much from me that I was spent when it was over.

In taking, though, she gave. While my body was utterly spent, my heart was full, emotion rushing through me. The depth of intensity I felt for her was unlike anything I'd experienced.

At the feel of her lifting her head, I opened my eyes. Just looking at her and my cock stirred. It didn't matter that I'd just spent myself twice with her. *This* woman. She sat there, her warm channel cradling me, and her blue eyes coasting over me. Fuck, she was beautiful—her plump breasts with her pink nipples taut and her hair a wild mess.

She eyed me, her gaze considering. Lifting a hand, she trailed it along my jawline.

"How are you?" she asked.

Such a simple question, and it made me smile. We hadn't bothered with any of the niceties, not tonight. In these few moments when I had lost myself in her, I had briefly forgotten the call with my mother.

Bill was in the hospital, my old best friend. He would probably die, or at least that was what they were saying.

I knew I was falling for Jasmine; hell, I was already in so deep, I couldn't imagine her, *this*, not becoming a permanent part of my life. I was just trying to sort out how fast to move with her.

Despite the depth of intimacy between us and despite how quickly she had made her way straight to my heart—she all but held my heart in her hands at this point—I wasn't quite sure how to go about talking about Bill.

My limited experience with serious relationships was years enough in the past that I was rusty. I wasn't accustomed to sharing my feelings, much less about something that hit an old sore spot.

I was long over Katie. If I hadn't known that before, I knew it with certainty now. Jasmine had firmly claimed a place in my heart, the way I felt for her casting a long shadow over what I'd once thought I had with Katie.

I sensed that Jasmine was picking up that I was hurting inside. But that didn't mean I knew how to talk about it, not just now.

I wasn't going to lie. So I shrugged, slipping my fingers through her hair and down her spine. My hands came to rest at the dip of her waist, my thumbs brushing across the soft curve of her belly.

"I had a long day," I finally said.

I could see the curiosity flash in her eyes. I sensed her hesitation colliding with mine. This thing between us had been forged in the heat of passion. Picking our way through the rubble of our pasts felt dicey just now. Everything was too fresh, too damn raw. I knew from the first night I met her that she had her own recent baggage.

"Well, if you want to talk about it, I'm here," she finally said.

I stared at her, my heart squeezing and an unfamiliar sense of uncertainty washing through me as I nodded. I suddenly worried that this would create distance between us, but she seemed to grasp now wasn't the time to push.

Her finger trailed down my neck and over the curve of my shoulder.

"Have you had dinner?" she asked.

I shook my head slowly just as my stomach growled. "You?"

She giggled and nodded. "I had dinner with Levi and Lucy tonight. I'll make you something. You can't go to bed hungry."

Then, she was climbing off my lap and untangling herself. I reluctantly let her go. I'd rather she stayed skin-to-skin with me, but I was starving.

Even though it was late, she tugged on a robe and started rummaging in the kitchen. I slipped my jeans on and watched while she whipped together a quick dinner for me.

Somehow inside of twenty minutes, she created a delicious dish of pasta with chicken, sesame oil, garlic, and vegetables.

Hours later, I woke in the darkness, spooned behind her and breathing in the scent of her. In that moment, everything was as it should be.

Chapter Twenty-Six

JASMINE

The next morning, I made Donovan breakfast. I slipped out of bed before he was awake, got coffee started, and settled on making omelets. He had declared he would eat anything, so I figured it was a safe bet.

I was whisking the eggs when I heard him padding out of the bedroom. Glancing over, my breath hitched at the sight of him. His dark curls were damp as he ran a hand through them. He'd tugged on his jeans, not even bothering to button them yet. He was bare-chested, and I instantly wanted to lick him.

Walking to me, he rounded the small island and slid his hands around my waist to drop a kiss on the side of my neck.

"You smell good," he murmured into my skin, sending a hot shiver straight through me and butterflies spinning in my belly. He straightened, watching over my shoulder as I finished whisking the eggs and tried to order my body to behave. My nipples had tightened to little points and my pussy clenched.

Donovan couldn't be near me without turning me on, or so it seemed.

"Coffee's ready," I commented, as I poured the egg mixture in the pan.

He chuckled, stepping back and sliding a palm down my spine, an easy pass that sent a wash of heat through me.

"I could get used to this," he said, as he poured a cup of coffee. He glanced over to me, his eyes narrowing. "You don't have any coffee yet." He reached up, fetching another mug from the cabinet and filling it for me. "Cream? Sugar?"

The moment he said *sugar*, I recalled the sound of his voice saying that word when he was referring to me.

Pay attention. You're making breakfast, I sternly ordered myself.

"Just a dash of cream," I replied.

He poured the requested amount in my coffee before handing it over.

"Do you need any help?" he asked, as he rounded the counter and slipped his hips onto a stool.

"Nope, just a few more minutes," I said as I added some cheese and hastily chopped mushrooms and peppers in the omelet before folding it over. "Are you headed to the station?"

His eyes flicked up to the clock above the door. "Not for an hour. Do you normally get up this early?" he asked in between sips of coffee.

"I'm an early riser. Doesn't even matter if I have an alarm, I'm up early."

Donovan nodded, his mouth kicking up at the corner with his smile. "Ah, sounds like me. I've given up on trying to sleep in. The only time that happens is when I've been out working, and I actually haven't slept for more than twenty-four hours."

As I cooked, we chatted about nothing important. His phone rang somewhere along the way, and when he spun his phone around on the counter to check the screen, his expression looked pained.

"Are you okay?" I asked reflexively, turning off the burner and using the spatula to slide his omelet onto a plate.

When he looked over, for a moment, I thought he might tell me what was bothering him. I recalled his reply to me last night when I'd asked the same question. *I don't know.* Honestly, it wasn't that I'd forgotten that moment, nor the pain I'd sensed radiating from him. But, as was *always* the case, I'd simply gotten swept into the riptide of pure need with him.

Just now, I wanted him to talk to me. And yet, I didn't want to push. After a long moment, he took a sip of his coffee and gave his head a little shake. "I'm fine."

Okay, so that was the deal. I gave myself a mental shakedown, reminding myself things were fresh; I was tumbling headlong into this and didn't need to start pinning hopes and dreams onto anything.

Blessedly, I didn't dwell. We shifted back into an easy banter while we ate. He left for work a little while later, pausing to kiss me at the door.

After he left, I was nearly giddy. I was falling for him. Way too fast. I felt decadent after last night. Sex with him was almost like a drug.

I wondered when he would get called out to another fire again. I should've been used to it. Levi had been a firefighter for years now. It wasn't as if I didn't worry about Levi when he was out, but with Donovan, it was different somehow. In a blink, Donovan had occupied a large space in my heart.

The only thing marring it was the knowledge that he was holding something back. Maybe it wasn't a big deal, but I wasn't stupid. I knew something heavy was weighing on him last night. Whoever had called this morning—the call he'd ignored—had brought back a glimmer of the same look in his eyes. Maybe I needed to remember not to turn this into more than it was. I wasn't in any state to be jumping into love. It's just that Donovan made it hard to remember that.

I gave my head a shake, turning and hurrying into the

shower. I needed to make some calls about some supplies and decide what the hell I was going to do about my studio space in the back of the café.

When I got out of the shower a little bit later, I glanced down at my phone to see a text from Glen. I had expected to miss him, I just didn't. That pretty much said it all. I suddenly wondered if Donovan was a rebound. For someone who was practically an expert at worrying and overthinking and over-analyzing to the point of disintegrating anything down to nothing, my heart knew the answer when it came to Donovan.

Perhaps due to timing, someone from the outside could say it was a rebound, but there was no way. Everything with him was far more than I'd had with anyone. *Ever.* Even the night Glen had asked me to marry him hadn't contained the depth of intensity I felt when I was with Donovan.

With a sigh, I stared down at Glen's texts.

It would be nice if you could at least let me explain.

I fucked up. I'm hoping you're planning to come home soon so we can talk.

Looking at Glen's words, I didn't even feel much betrayal. Rather, I felt a sense of relief. Thanks to him and Lisa, I'd conveniently dodged a bullet.

I almost laughed at the idea of considering San Francisco home. It was where I'd lived for the last seven years, yet it had never felt like home. Home was the place where your heart *felt* at home. Without a doubt, my heart knew Willow Brook as home.

I considered not even replying to his text, or calling. But I was a sucker for being polite, so I quickly called.

He answered almost immediately. "Jasmine, thank God you called."

He started talking, jumping to repeat everything he'd just texted to me.

I cut him off. "Glen."

He stopped talking. "What?"

"We're over. It sounds like you have all kinds of things you want to explain. But I'm only calling just to give you the respect you didn't give me. We're not meant to be together. I think you know that. Maybe you don't want to be with Lisa, but I think you should take some time to figure out what you actually want. I don't want to be with someone who would lie behind my back and fuck somebody else in my bed," I said flatly.

"Come on, Jasmine. Give me a chance to explain."

"Glen, it doesn't really matter. I hear that you're sorry and I appreciate that, but it's done. I'm not coming back to San Francisco. Even if I were, I wouldn't be getting back together with you."

Glen was dead silent. I didn't think he was too accustomed to anyone setting a boundary this clearly with him. He was accustomed to flirting, cajoling, and teasing until he got what he wanted.

"Are you sure?" he asked.

I heard the hint of condescension in his tone. There were ways I wasn't the most confident, and he used to play on that sometimes. Not now.

"I'm sure," I said firmly, without an ounce of doubt pervading my thoughts. "Good luck. I hope you find someone who really matters to you."

I tapped to end the call and set my phone on the counter, feeling a sense of freedom. In all honesty, Donovan had so quickly filled every corner of my body, heart, and mind that there was no room for anyone else. Yet, even without that, with Glen screwing around on me and just feeling like an idiot, I didn't need to cling to him. No matter what happened with Donovan in the future, I wasn't going back to Glen, and I wasn't going back to San Francisco.

Chapter Twenty-Seven

DONOVAN

A few days passed since I had heard about Bill. I had called my mother to check in a few times and had also been in touch with Bill's parents. I was beginning to feel hopeful that he might actually pull through.

Weighing in the back of my mind was whether or not to go see him. His mother wanted me to wait because she was hoping he was going to get better, and I could visit then. He had started to stabilize in the burn center.

Meanwhile, I spent every night with Jasmine and those silky ribbons she wound around my heart cinched tighter and tighter. I knew that she knew that something was weighing on me though, and I didn't quite know how to talk about it. I was a private person in general.

As close as I felt to her when we were intimate and skin-to-skin, I was in uncharted territory as far as learning how to be open about something like this. My skills were rusty since I hadn't had a serious relationship since Katie. Yet, even that relationship hadn't been like what I had with Jasmine. It hadn't come close to the depth and power.

Katie and I had been young and carefree. Neither of us

had experienced any great loss at that point in our lives. The shared betrayal by her and Bill had knocked me back, but then, you see a lot when you're a hotshot firefighter. You come face-to-face with death and near-death in ways that most people never do.

Emotions were something I was used to handling alone. For now, Jasmine seemed okay with letting me keep some distance. But I also knew there was a reckoning on the horizon.

Our crew got called out to a fire out of town for three days. I was starting to face the reality of Jasmine being Levi's little sister. I'd conveniently ignored it for weeks. But there was no going back. Jasmine was mine. I knew I needed to fess up to him about us, sooner rather than later. The longer I waited, the greater the chances were that he'd kick my ass.

That meant a conversation with Jasmine. Not for a minute did I forget that she had a fiery streak. That streak was what resulted in her hauling off and punching the guy who grabbed her ass weeks ago. That fiery streak also meant nights so hot it was a damn miracle I hadn't burned to ashes yet.

The thing was, at first, I figured ... Well, I hadn't figured anything. I'd simply been unable to resist the temptation of Jasmine.

It was so much more now. I knew she knew it too. Yet, all of it was just between us. It was entirely possible for us to keep it that way living across the hall from each other. We were practically moved in together at this point. I missed her when we were out at fires. The only time I didn't think about her was in the thick of the heat of whatever fire we were fighting.

Day three at a controlled burn that had skipped its firebreaks, and we had it back under control and were rotating back to Willow Brook. Our usual pilot Fred was tied up in Fairbanks, so they'd sent in a few small planes to fly us out.

We'd be landing in Anchorage rather than directly in

Willow Brook. Once we were in the air and I had reception, I powered on my phone. A message from my mother was waiting. What little progress Bill had made had been erased with an infection.

"Honey, I think you should come down here. It's not looking like he'll make it."

My heart seized and gave a hard thump of grief. The scrape of regret that had been lingering bloomed into a full-on gaping wound.

No matter what had happened, he was the friend I'd known all through childhood.

We landed in Anchorage, and I glanced over at Levi. I wanted him to pass on a message to Jasmine, but I knew that wasn't how to go about this. She would be expecting me back and damn, I wanted to see her. But I had to do this, and I was at the airport.

I strolled over to him. "Levi," I called.

He spun back in my direction from where he'd been walking to the car rental counter. Normally, we drove back to Willow Brook from here, but we had to snag a few car rentals because we'd actually helicoptered out directly from Willow Brook.

"What's up?" Levi asked.

"I need some time off, maybe three or four days. My old buddy from Georgia got injured in a fire. Doesn't sound like he's going to make it. I can catch a plane straight from here, so I thought I'd skip the trip home."

Levi was quiet, his eyes assessing. He knew this would hurt. I also knew Levi was the kind of friend who was loyal. He was there for his friends. Unlike me, he might've already been down to see Bill. All of this went unspoken because he didn't know the story.

He clapped me on the shoulder, his hand resting there. "You do whatever you need, man. Do you need anything from me?"

I shook my head because what I needed was Jasmine. He

couldn't give that to me. Not now, most certainly not when he didn't even know what lay between us.

"No, man. Just a few days off."

"You okay?" he asked.

That grief thudded in my heart, and I shrugged. "I'll be all right. It sucks, but it is what it is. He still might make it."

Levi pulled me in for a quick, thumping hug and then set me back. With a wave, I turned away, heading for the ticket counters upstairs. Once I snagged a ticket to Denver and was routed to the other gates, I slid my phone out and tried to call Jasmine.

I got her voicemail.

It's Jasmine. You know what to do.

"Jasmine, it's Donovan. I have to fly out, but I'll be back. My return ticket is for Friday. I'll try to call again."

I almost told her I missed her, but the words didn't come. Coming to grips with the reality that I might never get to tell Bill I forgave him, that we were good, was fucking with my head.

After I left a message, I texted her basically the same thing. For my text, I threw an *X* on the end.

Then, my flight was called, and I was headed to Denver. I landed and headed straight for the hospital once I rented a car. My mom had texted to tell me she and my father had already flown in. Bill's mother was her best friend, so I knew she'd want to be there. I fucking hoped like hell that he somehow pulled through.

In the jumble of it all, I barely had time to do anything, not to check my messages, not to take Jasmine's call. She didn't leave a return message. Her text was so vague as to make it impossible for me to read into it.

I hope everything's ok.

Chapter Twenty-Eight

JASMINE

I missed Donovan, and I was also pissed off at him. I knew I had no right to expect him to let me know what was going on. No matter how I felt and how deeply entwined my heart was with him, we hadn't talked about it. I sure as hell couldn't expect us to be something official.

Yet, it still stung that I didn't know why he left abruptly. A phone call would've been nice.

He did leave you a message. You just didn't answer because you were busy.

Yeah, but he didn't say why he left, or what was going on.

This was the mental volley in my brain. I'd known something was bothering him for a few days, but it was clear he didn't want to talk about it, so I'd left it alone.

You could've asked.

"Fuck, fuck, fuck," I muttered to myself as I yanked on my jeans.

I needed to figure out my studio situation. I didn't need to dwell on Donovan. He'd called one more time since he left, and I'd been in the shower, so I missed the call. He said he would be home tomorrow.

Reminding myself rather sternly that I shouldn't be counting on a man and that it was insane for me to be falling in love with Donovan when I'd just ended my engagement, I stepped into my cowboy boots and left. I was planning to grab a cup of coffee and a scone at Firehouse Café. After that, I'd get over myself and ask my dad for help with my studio.

A few minutes later, I pushed through the door to Firehouse Café. It was early, quite early actually—just past six a.m. Despite the early hour, the café was crowded. The weather was beautiful today. I presumed many of the tourists I saw were prepping to leave for their daily trips.

I waited in line, thinking how I missed waking up with Donovan. I needed to readjust and stop wishing for something that wasn't there. Him going away like this was a good wake-up call. I had no clue where we stood, and I didn't need to be moping over him.

It was like a little scratch on my heart, again and again, to think that he couldn't tell me what was going on. I had somehow convinced myself we were more intimate than that. Maybe it was just lust on his end, and I was reading far more into it.

When I got to the front of the line, Janet's wide smile greeted me. She flicked her braid behind her shoulder, drumming her fingertips on the counter. "So, what'll it be this morning?"

"The strongest coffee you've got, and a blueberry scone heated up a little. Mind if I take a look at the space afterwards?"

"Of course not. I've got a key for the back door for you anyway. Hang on, let me get this for you, and I'll have Daniel come up front. We can walk back together. Daniel!" she called over her shoulder.

She prepped my coffee and put a scone in the small oven up front. She got another coffee ready, while Daniel came out. After I paid him, she and I walked into the back together. She handed over a key that was hanging on a hook by the door.

"All yours, hon. I meant to talk to you anyway. I spoke to Donovan about it, and I'd like him to do the work you need back here. Since he's already working on the B&B for me, I can have him take care of a few things here, and he'll do whatever you need while he's at it."

My mouth must've fallen open because Janet grinned. "Surprised?"

I nodded slowly, wondering why he hadn't mentioned this to me. I didn't quite know what to think.

"Um, are you sure? I'll pay for whatever he does for the studio," I finally said.

Janet shrugged. "Hon, I don't think he's going to charge you."

I felt my cheeks get hot. "Why would you think that?"

"Because I think he likes you," Janet said bluntly.

By this point, my face felt like it was on fire.

Janet chuckled and reached over to squeeze my shoulder. "Hon, he hasn't said a word to me. It's just a feeling. Plus, I saw you two the other night."

I was suddenly worried about what she'd seen. Lord knows what showed on my face, but she threw her head back in a laugh.

"Well, I guess I was right. Don't worry, I didn't see anything exciting." She was quiet for a beat, her gaze considering. "Donovan is a good man, the best kind of man. You deserve nothing less."

I swallowed through the sudden emotion knotting in my throat. Taking a quick sip of coffee, my fingers tightened around the top of the little paper bag that held my scone.

"Maybe he is, but I don't think he thinks about me like that. I mean, he just left town without even telling me why."

I was suddenly feeling way too emotional for this conversation. I adored Janet, and she was like an aunt to me. But I sure as hell didn't want to break down in tears over Donovan in front of her.

I took another sip of coffee, forcing my mind to not think about him. Janet cocked her head to the side, taking a deep breath and letting it out with a sigh, her too perceptive gaze coasting over my face.

"Hon, I can't speak for Donovan, but he's not an asshole. No matter what, I don't think for a second he would screw around with you. Because he knows he'd have to deal with me, and I'll be a hell of lot worse than Levi about it. Levi's his friend, so he's got some explaining to do if he's being an ass to you. I don't know why he went out of town, but I know he's a mama's boy. She's been up to visit every year since he moved here. He's good to his family. I've seen it with my own eyes. Maybe it has something to do with that, and he just didn't have time to explain. But by the look on your face, it's obvious he means something to you."

I simply nodded, taking a gulp of my coffee before I said anything else stupid. "I guess when he gets back I'll talk to him about whatever I need back here. I need a few shelves and a worktable in the middle. Will that be okay?" I asked, completely shifting off topic. I just couldn't speculate about Donovan. I did *not* need to get my silly hopes up.

Janet squeezed my shoulder again. "I told you. Whatever you need to do is fine."

I pulled her into a hug. "Thank you. Once I've got some money coming in, we'll figure out the rent, okay?" I asked as I stepped back.

Right then, someone called Janet's name. She winked at me before spinning away. "Of course," she called over her shoulder just before pushing through the door, out to the front.

When the door swung shut behind her, I was alone in the back garage. It was quiet in the space, completely empty. Spinning around slowly, I didn't quite know what to think about having Donovan get the space ready for me. I'd thought of asking him, yet I wondered why he hadn't said anything to me about this. Maybe he wanted it to be a surprise, or maybe it just didn't mean very much.

My insecurities had been pretty chatty the last few days. I'd tricked myself into tumbling into the haze of hot sex and imagined intimacy between Donovan and me. I didn't know what was real, or what was all in my head. I didn't have a ton of confidence in my judgment when it came to men and reading the tea leaves.

With a sigh, I turned away, letting myself out the back and locking the door behind me.

Chapter Twenty-Nine

DONOVAN

Standing beside Bill's hospital bed, I looked down at him. He was unconscious, of course. He was hooked up to a breathing tube and God knows what else with the hum of the breathing machine and occasional beeps in the room.

The hospital sheet and bandages covered him, so I couldn't see the burns. According to the medical team, he'd sustained burns on over eighty-percent of his body. His crew in California got caught in a ravine with the wind whipping the fire quickly in the opposite direction.

Bill hadn't been able to get out in time and his emergency fire shelter hadn't been able to withstand the flames. No matter what had gone down between Bill and me, he'd been my best friend for years. My heart ached. A bit of his hair was visible on top of his head, his face relaxed in sleep. They'd told me he was in an induced coma and would stay that way until something changed.

I wished I could see him crack his sly smile once more. When it came to being out in the field, Bill was rock solid. Though we hadn't ended up on the same crew, we'd completed our training together.

Curling my hands over the bed railing, I spoke, "I'm here, man. You were on my list to call soon. Because I fucking miss you. Shit happens, and it just took me a while to figure that out. I know you were sorry, and I'm fucking sorry I stayed angry as long as I did. I'm hoping you're gonna pull through this, but it's not sounding good."

I had to stop and take a shuddering breath because my tears were choking me up. Funny, but I hadn't cried when everything went down with him and Katie. I'd just been pissed. That wasn't what I was crying about right now. I was crying because my friend was probably going to die. Hell, he wouldn't be alive right now if it weren't for modern medicine.

I rested my hand on his arm over the sheet. Regret was hitting me like a fucking truck, and I hated that it had taken this to get me to see him.

I wasn't what I would call a particularly religious man, but my mama had taken me to church every weekend growing up. Every so often, I sent up a prayer and did so now. I just wished Bill's pain would end. Whatever that meant. I'd faced death enough to know that death was a part of life. You could hold it at bay, but only for so long. If this was Bill's time to go, I just didn't want him to suffer.

I didn't know what the answer was. I understood why Bill's parents were considering taking him off life support, yet it seemed like a nearly impossible decision. Much as I wanted the news to change and for him to have a chance, I'd almost rather he just died on his own if that was the foregone conclusion.

I brushed my hand over the sheet covering his arm, barely a touch. "Well man, you said your piece when you called. Even if you can't hear me, I want you to know I did finally let it go. Katie was never right for me. She wasn't right for you either, and you figured it out too. I wish you could meet Jasmine. She's incredible. In hindsight, it's a damn good thing you let your dick get ahead of your brain.

Because if you hadn't, I might've married Katie and missed out on meeting Jasmine. I guess I should thank you for that. I'm gonna miss you, man."

Almost on cue, there was a knock at the door and then a nurse stepped through, followed quickly by a doctor. They looked surprised to find me there.

"His parents let me in the room, just to give me a few minutes alone with him," I explained.

The nurse smiled softly. Whether she knew a fucking thing I was feeling, I sensed her warmth. "Do you need a little more time?" the doctor asked.

"No, but thank you," I replied, stepping out of the room and walking down the hall to the waiting area where Bill's parents were sitting, along with mine.

My mom stood, immediately wrapping me in her arms, giving me what I used to call her "mama hug" when I was a little boy. At thirty-three, I'd been a man for years and stood a good foot taller than her. She didn't distinguish. Her hugs were simply all-encompassing. She saved them for moments like this—when words just wouldn't do.

As much as my heart ached with the sharp sting of grief, in a strange way, I felt more myself than I had in years. I could look back now and see that I had every right to be pissed off at Bill. But, he had apologized. I'd been just a little too bitter at the time to accept it. At least that had been released.

When my mama stepped back, her eyes were bright with tears. A mingled sense of grief and despair hung in the room.

Chapter Thirty

JASMINE

A napkin flew past my head, bouncing off my shoulder and landing in Maisie's lap beside me. Maisie simply laughed and tossed the napkin back at Lucy. Lucy was venting her various complaints about being pregnant, most particularly what she considered 'limitations.'

Maisie, who'd had two babies already, was simply rolling her eyes. Case in point, her reply.

"My God, you're just ridiculous. You don't have any limitations on your activity, and you'd think it was the end of the world. You're barely through your first trimester. The only reason you're showing is because you're so tiny. I'm a little chunkier," she said, slapping her hand on her thigh. "And two pregnancies didn't help matters, so don't even bitch to me."

Amelia added another eye roll to the chorus of them. Amelia had been a little bit ahead of me in school, but I knew her well. She'd been born and raised in Willow Brook, so she'd been here longer than me seeing as I'd only moved here at the beginning of high school. Unlike me, she had never left.

She added, "I know. Nothing has slowed her down at work, unless you count Levi worrying about her."

I flashed a grin in Lucy's direction. "Thank God, now he's got someone else to worry about other than me."

Lucy sighed, reaching up and adjusting the ponytail on her head. "I know. I'll get used to it, but good grief, you'd think I was the only woman who'd ever been pregnant before, with the way he acts."

Amelia nudged her in the side with her elbow. "Yeah, he worries in equal amounts to you complaining."

Lucy stuck her tongue out at Amelia and shuffled the cards. Conversation carried on, and I glanced around the table. We were at Cade and Amelia's place where, apparently, the girls had a casual cards night every few weeks, and it had been determined I should be included.

The group included Amelia and Lucy, along with Maisie, who I'd only recently gotten to know. Her grandmother had passed away and left Maisie her house in Willow Brook. Maisie was also married to a firefighter, Beck Steele, who was on Cade's crew.

Ella Masters, Cade's little sister, was also here. She was currently engaged to Caleb, who'd been her boyfriend in high school. I knew Ella the best, if only because we were the same age. Levi and Cade had been friends in high school together, so Ella and I had spent a ton of time together. Like me, Ella had left Willow Brook for a few years. She'd moved back and finally come to her senses with Caleb.

Rounding out our group this evening was Charlie Lane, or rather Dr. Lane. She was a newcomer to the group and was newly in love with Jesse Franklin, another firefighter. Charlie had initially intimidated me because she was a doctor, but she was nice and down to earth. She was a few years older than us with a sly sense of humor.

Someone said something about Levi's crew going out to another fire, and Lucy glanced in my direction. "Do you happen to know if Donovan will be back soon? You both live at Janet's B&B, right?"

Heat flooded my cheeks, and I hoped no one noticed. I grabbed my beer and took a sip. "As far as I know, he'll be back tomorrow," I replied, striving to keep my tone casual.

Lucy nodded and reached for her water, rolling her eyes as she did. "I can't drink. I don't think about alcohol very much, but apparently I like to have a beer on the weekends," she muttered.

Maisie laughed. "You only have six months left."

Amelia's gaze landed on me, her eyes considering. "So what's up with you and Donovan anyway?" she asked.

Um, what the hell? How did Amelia know anything about Donovan and me?

As I scrambled to reply to her question, Maisie smiled at me, her round cheeks plumping up as she did. She was about as cute as could be with her wild brown curls, freckles, and big brown eyes. "Yeah, what *is* up with you and Donovan?"

Something must've shown on my face. I completely gave up trying not to blush. It was a lost cause with my cheeks on fire.

Lucy smiled slowly. "Fess up. I'll be the go-between between him and Levi. Don't worry. I can hold him off."

It was on the tip of my tongue to say nothing, but it *wasn't* nothing. I was fairly certain I was falling in love with him, if I hadn't already. Clearly someone had either seen us together or heard something, most likely from Janet.

I took another pull on my beer and set it down, picking at the label with my fingernail. "I'm not sure. Why are you asking?"

Amelia's grin stretched. With her amber hair and eyes, she was tall and leggy. She used to intimidate me a little when I was younger, until I got to know her better. "Janet told me the other day that she thinks you two have a thing for each other," she explained.

"You know she likes to fancy herself as Cupid," Ella

offered from across the table with a sympathetic glint in her eyes. Despite that, I could tell I needed to resign myself to this grilling.

I glanced over to Lucy. "Don't you dare say anything to Levi."

"I won't offer him anything, but if he asks me, I can't lie. Donovan is totally awesome, so if ..." She let her words trail off with a sly smile.

I sighed. "Well, we might have been having a thing, but ..."

"What's a thing?" Maisie chirped, while Charlie chuckled from across the table.

I snagged a tortilla chip from the bowl in the middle of the table and ladled some salsa onto my plate. Between bites, I shrugged, unsure how to explain. "The thing is I don't know what the *thing* is. I guess nothing. Because he left, and I don't even know where he went or why he's gone. I'm taking that as a good reality check for me."

Curious eyes stared back at me from all sides of the table. Ella finally spoke. "Well, I can't imagine you would be upset if nothing was going on."

Maisie nodded, her curls bouncing. "Right. So back to my question, what's a thing?"

"Sex," I said bluntly. "Lots of sex."

Charlie burst out laughing and then immediately apologized. "I am so sorry. It wasn't that funny, it was just the way you said it."

My blush was fading, if only because I wasn't bothering to hide anything. I took another nibble on a chip. "Well, that's about all I can chalk it up to. Things are still pretty new or whatever, but I'd like to think, if he wanted *more* than just something physical, he would've told me why he was leaving. But seeing as he doesn't consider me important enough to let me know what's going on, I'm taking it as a wake-up call. My luck with men isn't so great."

Lucy narrowed her eyes at me. Before she spoke, Amelia

did. "Well, Janet thinks he likes you. A lot. Donovan's a nice guy. He keeps to himself. I don't think he really gets around much. I don't even know if he dates."

Maisie pursed her lips and cocked her head to the side, twirling a curl around her finger. "No, I don't think he does. And he *is* a really nice guy. Rock solid. Always nice around the station. He's awesome with Emily," she said, nodding in Charlie's direction, referring to Charlie's niece.

"I know. He came over to help Jesse deal with one of our trucks, and he was so patient with her. She loves all of the firefighters. She totally looks up to them. They're all like stand-in uncles for her," Charlie added.

"This isn't helping, you know. I don't need to know how great he is. I need to get my head on straight," I mumbled.

"Why are you pissed off at him?" Lucy asked pointedly, her perceptive blue gaze pinned on me.

I fiddled with a chip in my hand, spinning it around. "I don't know. He hasn't given me any reason to think there's more going on. I sure as hell don't know what's going on for me, but he just left and didn't say a word. That doesn't exactly inspire trust. I'm feeling a little like an idiot these days. Plus, am I crazy? It's probably just a rebound for me anyway. It was only like a month ago or so that I walked in on Glen fucking Lisa."

Maisie spoke up immediately. "Donovan would never do that. Not that I know much about his personal life, but he is rock solid, and he's a total mama's boy. His family comes to visit every year, and they stop by the station. Last year, his mother brought in this crazy chocolate cake that she makes. It was fucking heaven. You should've seen him with her. Pretty sure he would do anything for her. He even calls her *Mama,* which is like the cutest thing ever."

"He's totally got that sexy southern drawl going on," Ella piped up.

"All right, girls, cut it out. If I mattered, I think he would've told me why he was leaving. The last thing I needed to be doing is jumping in and ..." I paused when a rush of emotion hit me.

I'd been about to say *falling in love*. Correcting myself, I finished, "Falling in lust."

"So I'm guessing the sex is good," Amelia said from my side with a sly grin.

I picked up my napkin and tossed it at her.

Meanwhile, Lucy had stayed quiet. She finally spoke. "Look, I'm no expert, but some people might say I have problems with being too defensive."

That got everybody laughing, myself included. I adored Lucy, and she was like a sister to me now that I'd gotten to know her. But no one would ever accuse her of being a softy, or for letting something slide. To this day, I was fairly certain Levi still thought he was the luckiest guy in the world, and perhaps wondered if he'd tricked her into falling in love with him.

At her glare, we managed to stop laughing. She continued, "Anyway, it seems like you like Donovan. I'm not so convinced it's a rebound. I don't think you were ever really in love with Glen. I think you tried to tell yourself you were. But you'd be a lot more broken up over him if you were. I'm just saying. If Levi fucked around on me ..."

Her words trailed off, and Maisie nudged me with her elbow. "Pretty sure there'd be a throw down fight."

Lucy rolled her eyes. "I'd probably kick somebody's ass, his included, but I'd also be torn up. Seems to me like Glen hurt your feelings and you feel stupid, but you dodged a bullet. I think we can all vote that Donovan would not fuck around on you. He's just not that kind a guy."

I was still smarting inside, both with myself and with Donovan. There were a few more comments, but it appeared the girls picked up on my cues. I wasn't ready to go further into this topic, not right now.

Later that night, I let myself in to Janet's B&B after Lucy dropped me off. Since she wasn't drinking, she was my designated driver. Walking up the stairs, Donovan's absence hurt, like a little knife cut on my raw feelings. After having called that first day or two, and texted a few times, he hadn't done so again. Now I was trying to interpret what that meant when I knew I wasn't being reasonable. I was the one who hadn't called him back, so maybe he was giving me space. I hadn't asked for space, but my passive refusal to respond to him appeared to have sent that message.

Letting myself into my suite, I kicked off my boots and dropped my purse by the door. I walked to the window to look out over Main Street. August was right around the corner and the days were starting to get shorter. It was past nine, and the sun was disappearing behind the mountains, leaving nothing but a lingering burst of orange and gold in its wake as the darkness came to claim the daylight.

A half-moon rose over Swan Lake, its light glimmering on the water. I took a deep breath and let it out. It felt good to be home, really good. There was even a sense of relief, which I certainly hadn't expected in my abrupt return here to lick my wounded pride. I just wished I could think straight about Donovan.

I fell asleep, missing his warm strength holding me, and wondering if he was okay. The next day, when I still hadn't heard from him, I shifted back into anger. I had a bit of a temper, and I was hurting. I kept trying to convince myself I was overreacting, but I lost the internal argument.

When my phone buzzed, and I saw a text from him telling me he was landing in Anchorage late this afternoon, I ignored it. Four whole days, and I still didn't know why he'd left so abruptly.

Chapter Thirty-One

DONOVAN

The plane landed with a slight jostle as the wheels hit the runway. Looking out the window, I watched as everything raced by, the airport slowly coming into focus. As soon as the pilot announced we could turn on our handheld devices, I pulled out my phone, powering it up and hoping to see something, anything, from Jasmine.

Fucking nothing.

I didn't know how I knew, but I knew she was pissed. I just needed a chance to talk to her and wanted to do it face-to-face. I felt like we'd skipped about fifty steps in our relationship. I was in love with her, and I knew it with deep certainty. It was just that this thing with Bill had thrown me sideways. I'd needed to process it on my own, or at least this part of it.

In the four days I'd been in Denver, there'd been another flicker of hope that had disappeared as quickly as it came. His parents had decided to take him off life support and pull him out of the induced coma. He'd been conscious for all of fifteen minutes. It had been brutal, but he didn't appear to be in pain.

I'd gotten a chance to say goodbye and even seen a glimmer of his old smile before leaving him with his parents until he passed away. The saving grace was he seemed at peace.

While I had found as much peace as I could over Bill's death, the wrinkle in those long days was Katie showing up. God only knew how she heard about it. The interconnected world of social media had likely sent the information her way. I hadn't even known she lived in Colorado. Apparently, before her and Bill broke up, she moved there with him. She showed up, crying, and then fucking trying to apologize to me and tell me she'd made a mistake by screwing around on me with Bill. I couldn't quite believe she'd had the nerve to come to the hospital, where Bill was dying, and tried to get back together with me. But then, if nothing before had illuminated who Katie was, that sure as hell did.

The only good thing that came out of seeing her was realizing the concept I'd had about love when I'd been with her wasn't love. I'd been too damn young. I had wanted what my parents had and let my cock lead me there. As if my cock had a brain, or heart. Uh, no. Katie had still been beautiful with her long dark hair, her blue eyes, and her willowy build, but I was older and wiser now.

I politely listened to her cry and then wished her well.

Seeing Katie had only brought my feelings for Jasmine into sharp focus. With every single beat of my heart, I couldn't wait to get back home, back to Jasmine.

She'd boxed me out. I thought I knew why, yet we hadn't talked and put any words to the intimacy winding around us and ensnaring us in its web.

I needed to see her.

Landing in Anchorage, I texted her as soon as we were on the ground. *I'll be home in about an hour. We need to talk.*

I rented a car and headed back to Willow Brook. In my life, there were only two places that felt like home. Georgia, with its winding roads in the mountains, humid summers, and Mama's food was one of those places. I'd left Georgia when I was young enough to not want to cling to any place.

Until I landed in Willow Brook, no other place quite felt like home. As I drove out of Anchorage, leaving the city behind me, that sense of peace settled over me. Despite my grief, my raw emotions, and my uncertainty about Jasmine, I knew I was where I belonged.

It was late, late enough that the sun was making its bow behind the mountains. Glancing ahead where the highway went west, the mountain ridge in the distance was a silhouette against the sky with a watercolor of pinks and purples above. The smudgy light of dusk felt weighted tonight. So much like my mood—a little gray and a lot of regret.

I slowed when I passed a mama moose and her twin calves nibbling on alders by the highway. The babies were all legs as they carefully picked their way through the tall grass to reach the branches that their mama pulled down for them. Fields of fireweed were ethereal in the falling darkness, the fuchsia flowers bright in the silvery light.

I took a deep breath and let it out with a sigh, relieved I'd had a chance to say goodbye to Bill. I'd keep on missing him, but I'd let go of the bitterness, once and for all.

Now, I just needed to make it right with Jasmine, to say what I should've already said when I knew it to be true. Maybe the timing wasn't right, maybe she was skittish, and maybe I'd let my own baggage get in the way of telling her how I felt, but I wasn't going to let any of it get in the way now.

Pulling up at the B&B, I didn't realize I'd practically been holding my breath. Her little blue hatchback was there. I jogged inside, taking the stairs two at a time. The hallway light was out. I let my bag slide to the floor outside my door and turned to knock on hers.

Silence greeted me. I knocked again. "Jasmine, it's me, Donovan. I know you're here."

Nothing. Without thinking, I reflexively reached for the

doorknob and turned it. It was locked. The need to see her was fierce, beating like a drum in my chest. I wanted to kick down the fucking door. I needed her, and not just because I needed to explain why I'd been gone.

I tried several more times, knocking and calling her name, with nothing more than an echoing silence in return.

"Fuck," I muttered to myself.

My grief over Bill and my frustration with her spun together inside as I turned away. I wasn't going to beg. I didn't have it in me, not tonight.

I let myself into my suite and took a shower. After snacking on whatever I could find in the kitchen, I fell into a restless sleep, missing Jasmine and angry with her at the same time.

Chapter Thirty-Two

JASMINE

After Donovan stopped knocking and calling my name, I kept staring at the door. Part of me desperately wanted him to come back. But I was still pissed off.

I looked at my phone screen again, his last text glowing back at me. *We need to talk.*

"About what?" I muttered aloud.

Since my card game with the girls, I'd felt even more out of sorts. I was such an idiot. When Donovan texted me, all I could think was how he hadn't even mentioned that Janet asked him to help with my studio. I had no idea why that bothered me, but it did. Whether it was rational or not, somehow, I'd convinced myself that if he took us seriously, he'd have said something.

He wanted to talk. I did not. I felt so stupid. I was at peace with letting go of Glen. Oddly, coming to terms with how I felt about Glen brought how I felt about Donovan into painfully clear focus. He mattered. A lot.

I was an idiot because I'd fallen for an emotionally unavailable man. Hooray. Score one for my stupid heart.

I barely slept that night, restless, anxious, and on edge,

again and again wishing Donovan would come back to my door.

Weary, I finally fell asleep in the wee hours of the morning, only to wake late with a start, like ten a.m. late. I never overslept. I was all out of whack. At best, I'd probably gotten three delirious hours of sleep.

Rolling out of bed, I couldn't help the hum of anticipation that started up in my body. Knowing Donovan was back, right across the hallway, was going to make for a rough few weeks. I promised myself I was going to try to be sane about this and take a step back. Because I was in *way* too deep. Even if he had a perfectly good reason for why he couldn't be bothered to tell me why he'd be out of town, my reaction was what showed me how in over my head I was.

I took a quick shower and slipped on a pair of jeans and a T-shirt. Before anything else, I needed to take some measurements and go to my parents' garage to drag my old kiln out of storage.

I felt silly when I left because I was almost tiptoeing. Donovan had to be gone, or so I told myself. I knew from Lucy that Levi's crew was working today because they had a controlled burn project. Nothing but silence greeted me as I crept past his door and hurried down the stairs.

I stopped by Firehouse Café first, getting much-needed coffee, then headed to my parents' house. When I arrived, my mother was standing on the porch, talking with Lucy.

Lucy was just now beginning to show a little bit more, her slightly rounded belly visible even under the baggy T-shirts she tended to favor. They both turned as I walked up the steps onto the porch.

"Hey, what's up?" Lucy asked.

My mother answered for me. "She's here to take her kiln out of the garage. You are *not* allowed to help," my mother said with a pointed look at Lucy.

Lucy rolled her eyes. "You know I work in construction, right?"

I laughed, enjoying having my mother's attention on Lucy instead of me for once. Cresting the top step to the porch, I leaned against the railing. "It's a miracle Levi's even letting you work," I offered with a wink.

"Letting?" Lucy asked, her eyes narrowing.

My mother chuckled softly. "Oh honey, we're just all so happy for you."

Lucy took a deep breath and rolled her eyes. "Me too, but I didn't count on all this extra worrying." With a shrug, she moved on. "Anyway, did you figure out what you need to do for your studio?"

"Janet lined up Donovan to do the work because she needs some other stuff done there," I explained, wishing my cheeks weren't getting hot.

Lucy knew far more than I wanted my mother to know about Donovan and me. I wasn't worried about her saying anything, but my mother was astute.

Lucy simply nodded, a hint of a smile in her eyes. "Well, if you need anything after all, just let me know."

My mother was conveniently distracted by her cell phone ringing. As she took the call, Lucy followed me into the garage off the side of the porch. The moment we were in the garage, she pounced. "So, what's going on with Donovan?"

I shrugged. "Nothing."

"Is he back yet?"

I was nodding before I realized it. "Yes, he got back last night," I said tersely.

"Have you talked to him?"

"Not yet."

"You can only avoid him so long, you know."

I glared at her, resting a hand on my hip. "I know. It was late. I'm sure I'll see him soon."

"I don't usually stick my nose in things, but I'm going out on a limb here. It's obvious you like him. Don't be stupid," she offered with a pointed look.

At that moment, my mother stepped into the garage from the entry from the kitchen. "Do you need help, dear?"

I hurried over to the corner where the kiln was stored. "I'm sure I can get it, Mom. I'm not gonna take it today. I just wanted to make sure I could get to it."

Lucy followed me over, and before she had a chance to touch anything, my mother was all but shoving her out of the way. I chuckled, enjoying Lucy's discomfort.

I realized my mistake the moment she glanced toward my mother. "Have you met Donovan?"

"Of course I have," my mother replied. "He's helping Janet with her B&B." At that moment, I saw the light bulb go off in her head. "I wasn't even thinking about how he's your neighbor there. Donovan is the nicest guy. He has been a godsend for Janet. It's a blessing his house isn't done yet. He's getting her B&B all taken care of without charging her a penny. The materials alone are expensive, so his help makes a big difference. I know the café keeps her busy and she makes a good profit, but I don't like her worrying about things."

"His house will be done soon," Lucy offered, piquing my curiosity.

She caught my eyes, smiling slowly. "You didn't know that? We're finishing his house for him. He started it last summer, but then he said he realized it was going to take forever trying to do it by himself in between fires. So, he hired us. Another month or so, and it should be done. You'd better take advantage of his help while you've got it."

Lucy wasn't saying anything that gave anything away, but I knew she wasn't going to let the topic of Donovan drop until I talked to him. Turning away, I moved a few boxes out of the corner until I came to the one at the bottom. "Here it is," I said, smiling over my shoulder.

Shifting the other boxes out of the way, I pulled my measuring tape out and quickly measured it, entering the measurements in my phone.

"What are you measuring it for?" Lucy asked.

"I need a stand for it. It's been years since I used this kiln, so I wanted to check the measurements."

Somehow, I got the topic off of Donovan as we walked into the house, my mother offering us coffee once we reached the kitchen.

Lucy demurred with a sigh. "No coffee for me." She patted her stomach. "I can do without the alcohol, but I hate missing my morning coffee."

"Oh, you'll make up for it," my mother added. "Wait until the little one's born, and you're hardly sleeping through the night."

I glanced at my watch. "I need to get going. I want to take some measurements in Janet's garage too."

"I'll walk out with you," Lucy said.

We both got kisses on the cheek from my mother as we headed out. Lucy elbowed me in the side on the way down the stairs.

"Don't be stupid. I'm gonna tell Levi if I have to."

"Tell Levi what?" I asked, spinning to face her.

She burst out laughing. "I'm not telling Levi anything. But maybe that'll be a wake-up call."

"What is it with you? Usually you're all about 'live and let live.' Why is this a thing for you?" I asked, honestly curious.

Her teasing gaze faded. "I don't know. I like Donovan. He's totally a good guy, and it seems like you really like him. After Glen fucked you over, I figure you deserve an awesome man."

"Yeah, but you don't even know ..." My words trailed off when she rolled her eyes.

"I can't see the future. You're right. I don't even know how he feels about you." I bit my tongue because she hit it spot-on with what I'd been about to say. "I just think it's worth at least trying to talk to him," she finished.

At that, her phone rang, and she pulled me into a quick hug before stepping away.

I returned to town, parking at the B&B before walking over to Firehouse Café and letting myself into the back garage. I jotted down some more measurements for what I wanted where, and then looked at my watch. God, I so wanted the studio ready. I would've given just about anything today to bury myself in throwing pottery. It would've given me something to do to take my mind off Donovan.

Instead, I hurried over to the B&B to grab some of the cleaning supplies Janet kept downstairs. She told me I could help myself, as long as I replaced anything I used up. There was probably twenty years of dust in the garage, so I settled in to clean for a few hours.

Later that evening, I realized I'd left my purse with my inhaler in the B&B. With the doors and windows to the garage open, my asthma hadn't really been a problem, but I realized I should finish up. I returned, dusty and dirty and ready for a shower. When I walked into the B&B, a gust of sawdust hit me in the face. Donovan was working downstairs. I hadn't even noticed his truck was here because I'd come in from the back.

In a flash, I was coughing heavily. For the second time in a few weeks, I was in the midst of the run up to another bad asthma tack. My purse with my inhaler was upstairs. I didn't know if Donovan heard me because the saw was running.

As I heaved, frantically trying to catch my breath, I suddenly felt his presence. His arms came around me as he lifted me against him.

"Jasmine? What the hell is going on?" he asked, his words sharp.

I couldn't answer. I could hardly breathe and felt my lungs constricting. I managed to look at him and saw awareness dawn in his eyes. As a hotshot firefighter, I knew he was a trained medic. He carefully set me down and ran upstairs, his feet thudding against the treads.

As I gasped and desperately tried to get air in my lungs, he was back at my side in seconds, where I'd fallen against the wall in the stairwell. He held an inhaler to my mouth, and I breathed in the heavenly air. I knew it was technically a dose of medicine, but to me, it meant oxygen to my lungs.

After a few moments, I was breathing somewhat normally. I was about to tell him that I needed to get out of there. Because even though he'd stopped whatever he'd been doing, fine sawdust was still floating in the air.

I didn't need to explain though. As soon as he saw that I was breathing okay, he lifted me up, efficiently bundling me into his arms and carrying me upstairs.

He didn't ask where I wanted to go. All I knew was I wanted to stay right there in his arms. He kicked open the door into his suite and carried me inside. Setting me down on his couch, he held the inhaler up to my mouth again, giving me another dose.

My skin felt clammy, and I had that funny lightheaded feeling I got when I made it through to the other side of an asthma attack. The combination of not getting enough oxygen and then the bliss of getting enough of it all of a sudden was dizzying.

I was so relieved Donovan was here. He was quiet, just sitting beside me. When I finally rolled my head to the side, I found his concerned gaze on me.

"You okay now?" he asked, his voice gruff.

I nodded. "Uh-huh," I managed, my voice raspy.

I glanced down at the inhaler held in his hand. "That's not mine."

"No, it's not. I have a medical kit. It's a little more tricked out than most. Now I know to keep an extra stock of these around," he murmured.

We stared at each other. Even though I felt dizzy, it was *so, so* good to see him. I tucked my head against his shoulder. He dipped his head, pressing a kiss to my forehead.

Emotion rushed through me. I couldn't tell if everything I was feeling was more intense because I'd just had an asthma attack. That never failed to leave me feeling punch-drunk for a few minutes. I was beyond relieved Donovan was here. I forgot my frustration with him and simply relaxed into his side.

After a few shuddery breaths, with his arm resting over my shoulder and his fingers sifting through the ends of my hair, I managed to speak again.

"Thank you."

"You don't need to thank me," he murmured, the low sound of his voice sending a familiar hot jolt through me. Mingling with my dizziness, I was tingling all over at his mere presence. "You could've mentioned you had asthma."

I shrugged, burrowing a little closer into his chest. "I don't think about it very much. I don't have attacks often anymore. I was cleaning next door and it was a little dusty."

His fingers were still sliding through my hair. My tension eased, the relief of him being home so immense I felt tears wicking up from the knot in my throat. Only Donovan had this effect on me. In a matter of seconds, I was a bundle of emotions. He glanced down just as I looked up. My tears must've shown in my eyes.

"Why are you crying?" he asked, his concerned gaze sweeping over my face.

The truth slipped out. "I missed you."

As soon as I spoke, I was scrambling inside to clarify, to take it back. "I get all emotional when I have an asthma attack. I don't mean to sound weird," I said quickly, stumbling over the words.

Donovan was quiet for a beat, his eyes studying me. We were sitting in the corner of the couch. He angled to face me more fully, his back resting against the armrest of the couch. Lifting his other hand, he brushed a lock of hair off my forehead, tucking it behind my ear and sending a trail of goose bumps over my skin, heat following in their wake.

"I missed you too." His words fell into the quiet, something flickering in his eyes. "I should've explained why I needed to leave so quickly. An old friend was injured in a fire. He died."

"Oh, I'm so sorry, Donovan. I didn't know."

I suddenly felt bitchy for being angry with him.

"Of course you didn't know. I didn't tell you. For a bit there, it looked like he might pull through. But then he got an infection. That was it."

Uncertain what to say, I reached over, catching his hand in mine and giving it a squeeze.

"There was some baggage with Bill. He was my best friend growing up. We went to college together and did our hotshot training together. I came home one day after being out for a couple weeks at a fire and found him with my fiancée. Like I said, we had some baggage."

Donovan's gaze met mine, regret swirling in the green and gold depths. My heart squeezed, realizing how painful that must've been. I had a similar experience in the sense of finding someone screwing around on me. Yet, Lisa was more of a casual work friend. Most definitely not a best friend from growing up.

I said the only thing that came to mind. "I'm so sorry."

Tears glistened in his eyes, his throat moving as he swallowed. "Yeah. It sucked. He tried to apologize about a year or so after, when she screwed around on him." There was no bitterness in his tone, just acceptance. "I was still too pissed off to deal with him. If you're wondering why I didn't want to talk about it, it's because I was feeling like shit and I never took the time to mend fences with him. And now he's dead. I'm as okay as I can be, but it sucks."

He was quiet then, leaning back and running his free hand through his hair. His shoulders rose and fell with a deep breath. I could hear the steady beat of his heart with my head resting against his shoulder.

Drawing back, I took a breath. "I'm sorry I didn't answer the door last night. I was ..." My words ran out because I didn't know what I meant to say. I wasn't sure now was the time to announce that I was falling in love with him and I'd been an emotional mess as a result.

He spoke, filling the silence. "It's okay. I'm a little rusty when it comes to relationships. I should've told you as soon as I got the call about Bill. Honestly, I just shoved all that shit away for a bit." He paused, his eyes widening at whatever he was thinking. I adjusted a little, still nestled in the crook of his shoulder, but shifting so I could see him better. "Don't go worrying I've still got a thing for my ex, Katie, either. I was long over her. When all was said and done, I should've thanked Bill. It wasn't like things were awful with Katie, but we were young. It took that for me to see her true colors. So don't think that," he said solemnly, his eyes locked with mine.

I hadn't been thinking that, but I supposed it was reassuring to know he was concerned I might've been. His gaze coasted over my face, and it felt as if he could see right into the center of my heart.

"Katie came to the hospital."

My breath drew in sharply. "Why?"

I didn't say it aloud, but it seemed like a shitty move. At best, a horribly tactless move. To know that Katie had screwed around on Donovan with his best friend, and then screwed around on his best friend with somebody else, well, I couldn't fathom why she'd show up at the hospital under those circumstances.

Donovan chuckled at the look in my eyes. "Lord knows what she was thinking. I guess she felt bad and wanted to say something to somebody about it. They had Bill in a drug-induced coma, so she didn't get to say it to him. One good thing came out of it."

"What's that?" I asked.

"Everything came into focus," he replied.

His fingers were trailing across my shoulder, his touch light. A shiver ran through me at the look in his eyes.

"What's everything?"

"You. What you mean to me."

"Oh," was all I managed to say to that.

My pulse was pounding wildly, and I still felt a little fuzzy from my asthma attack.

"I'll just get right to the point, sugar. I wasn't looking for this. I sure as hell wasn't looking for you. But I love you. I don't expect you to feel the same way I do. Maybe not now. But I know what we have isn't something you find every day."

He paused, as if giving me a chance to say something, yet I couldn't form a single word. With my pulse pounding and a giddy sense of joy spinning in my chest, I simply stared at him.

"You see, sugar, seeing Katie brought it all into focus. I thought I loved her once. And I suppose I did, in the way I could love someone when I was only twenty-six years old. But I never felt the way about her that I do about you. I'm not a stupid man, so I'm not about to let you get away. We can go as slow as you need; like molasses, if that's what works for you. But I'm telling you right here, right now"—he paused, lifting a hand between us and tapping me right over the heart with his fingertips before tapping his own heart —"this doesn't come along every day. My mama would never let me forget it if I let you get away."

By this point, I was fairly certain my heart was going to fly straight out of my body. I felt like a bird in a cage, wings flapping loudly to the beat of my heart.

"Oh," I said again, wonderingly.

He dipped his head, pressing his lips to mine before drawing back swiftly and swiping his thumb across my bottom lip. My lips tingled where he touched me, my breath hitching as I tried to slow the wild spin of joy in my heart and body.

I finally gave up, the smile blooming from my heart and tugging at the corners of my lips. "We don't have to go slow," I finally said.

"We don't?" he asked, his mouth kicking up at the corner.

Oh geez. His grins were dangerous for my sanity. They made me hot all over, stole my breath, and kicked any functioning brain cells to the curb.

I shook my head slowly. "I mean, it's not like we've gone slow so far."

His green and gold gaze seared into me. "I suppose not, but I know you just came out of your own break up. I know I'm not your rebound. But I just want to make sure it's what you want."

In a flash, I realized my own clarity about my feelings for Donovan had crystallized because of Glen.

Shaking my head again, I reached out to trail my fingertips along his jawline, savoring the subtle prickle of his stubble. "You're not a rebound. I know that. Maybe because of the timing, it might seem like that. But you're not."

When my words trailed off, I shrugged. "Glen wasn't what I thought, he wasn't who I really wanted. He did me a favor too. If it weren't for him, I might not have found you." I paused, taking a deep breath and letting it out with a shuddering sigh. My heart was kicking and screaming inside my chest, clamoring for me to say what I knew to be true. "I wasn't quite ready to say it, but I am now. I love you too. If I didn't, I wouldn't have gotten so pissy about you going away without telling me where you were. Sometimes I can be a little dramatic," I offered with a roll of my eyes.

My temper didn't flare often, but it was definitely there, especially when my feelings were concerned.

"That'll never happen again," he said flatly. Then he brought his lips to mine again, tugging me into his lap.

This was no chaste kiss. In a hot second, his tongue was delving deep in my mouth, tangling with mine. Shimmying closer, I tunneled my hands into his hair and held onto him with everything I had.

Chapter Thirty-Three

DONOVAN

With a lapful of Jasmine and her soft luscious body, I lost myself in her mouth. She kissed like a dream. There was no hesitancy with her. But then, it had been like that since the first time I kissed her—like being dipped into a fire and loving the burn.

She was straddling me, and I could feel the heat of her hot, tight pussy through the layers of fabric between us. Suddenly remembering she'd just had an asthma attack, I shackled my need. With every ounce of discipline I owned, I drew back from the unholy temptation of her mouth, smoothing my hand through her hair and down her spine.

"As much as I would love for this to go a little further, you just had an asthma attack. I'm guessing you need to take it easy for a little bit," I murmured.

Jasmine narrowed her eyes and actually pouted. I burst out laughing.

Pouting wasn't the kind of thing she usually did. As fucking hot and sexy as she was, there was no artifice to her, none whatsoever. Which only made her hotter and sexier to me.

When I laughed, she rested a hand on her hip and rolled her hips over my aching cock. I sucked in my breath, the air hissing through my teeth. "I'm serious."

She took a deep breath, and I could still hear a slight hitch in her lungs. My mind spun back to what couldn't have been more than fifteen minutes ago when she started coughing, and I'd looked into her eyes and realized she simply could *not* catch her breath.

As I'd raced up the stairs to grab my medical kit right away, knowing I had an inhaler, I recalled an elderly man I'd carried out of a fire once. He'd had asthma and had been deep into an attack. They'd told me later that his age had been a major factor, yet he died.

Jasmine took another breath, letting it out with a sigh. "I'm fine. See."

My heart thudded so hard inside my chest, I thought it might burst. I lifted a hand, brushing her hair back from her face and sifting my fingers through the silky locks. "I know. We don't have to rush. Plus, I'm filthy and I need a shower."

Uncertainty flashed in her eyes as she caught her bottom lip in her teeth, worrying it. I sternly ordered my cock down. She wasn't doing it to be sexy, but my cock sure thought she was.

"It doesn't have to be a thing," she said softly.

"A thing?"

Her mouth twisted with another sigh. "My asthma."

"It's not a thing. I'm just pointing out the obvious. You were on your way to a pretty serious attack there. Now I know I need to stay stocked up on this," I replied, gesturing to the inhaler sitting innocuously on the coffee table now.

She rolled her eyes and giggled. I was relieved to see the worry fade from her face. "I need a shower too," she said, shifting gears quickly.

Adjusting her in my arms, I stood and lifted her with me. I wasn't ready to let her go. Even though my week had been shit

—Bill had died, and I was still reverberating from that shock —right now, with Jasmine in my arms and her legs curling around my hips, I knew I was exactly where I needed to be.

The air between us had cleared. The blunt truth about how much she meant to me and how deeply I cared was out there. I was the luckiest fucking guy in the world because she loved me too.

I carried her into the bathroom, reluctantly easing her down. Once the hot water was flowing, and we climbed in the shower with steam cocooning us, I realized my judgment had been rather shortsighted.

Between leaving for the fire and then going down to Denver, I hadn't been skin-to-skin with Jasmine for two weeks. I glanced over to see soap bubbles rolling over her curves, her dusky pink nipples pebbled under the water. Before I even realized what I was doing, I reached out to cup one of her breasts, rolling my thumb back and forth over a taut nipple. With the soap rolling down out of her hair, she lifted her eyes, her lashes spiky with the water. In the mist, her sapphire eyes stood out.

"I thought you were treating me like I might break," she murmured with a slow smile.

The evidence of my arousal was obvious, with my aching cock thick and swollen.

As if to be helpful, she added, "Steam is really good for my lungs."

Then my lips were on hers, and her legs were winding around my waist. I held her high against me, turning us together and bringing her back against the tiled wall. I drew back, catching her bottom lip with my teeth and giving it a tug. I bit back a moan as her slick pussy rocked against my cock.

"I love you," I murmured on a ragged breath through the steam and water raining down around us.

Her head fell back against the tile as she opened her

eyes. "Love you too," she said on the heels of a gasp when my cock slid over her swollen clit.

I didn't want to wait. Reaching between us, I adjusted my angle and sank home inside of her snug, wet, clenching heat.

My forehead fell to hers once I was seated deeply inside of her.

"Fuck, Jasmine. You feel so good."

With her eyes right there and our lips brushing against each other as we spoke, she replied, "You do too."

Her heel spurred my ass and made me forget how much I missed her. Holding her tight, with the hot water and steam cocooning us, spinning us into a world where only we existed, I drove back and sank inside of her again and again. Her pussy clenched and throbbed around me. I felt her body tightening and shudders rippling through her. Only then did I reach between us, pressing my thumb over her clit and watching as she cried out.

My own release thundered through me, heat twisting at the base of my spine and whipping like a lash, the force so intense, my knees almost gave out. Her forehead fell into the crook of my neck. We stayed like that for several moments, catching our breaths in the steamy heat of the shower.

Chapter Thirty-Four

JASMINE

My feet were resting on Donovan's lap while he leaned back into the couch. He was conveniently wearing his jeans and no shirt. I was thinking I'd be content to just look at him all the time.

It was ridiculous actually. He was so fucking sexy—all rugged, hard, muscled planes. Before I even thought about it, I leaned forward and dropped kisses over his chest.

He chuckled, his eyes canting down to mine, glinting with mirth. "I don't think I can handle another round, sugar. I'm fucking exhausted."

"You don't need to handle anything," I replied. "I just wanted to taste your skin."

We'd ordered pizza and lounged around his suite. Our shower had left me giddy, fizzing with joy inside. He told me a little bit more about Bill, what had happened while he was in Denver, and more about his family. Apparently, his parents were coming up to visit in a couple of weeks.

He wanted me to meet them. That wasn't the least bit terrifying.

For a flicker, I experienced a beat of fear. It all seemed so real, so big. But then Donovan dipped his head and dropped a kiss on the inside of my wrist. I remembered that when I was with him, it was always okay, it was always right.

We had the television on, but we weren't really watching it. I drifted off to sleep at points. Seeing as I had hardly slept at all last night and I'd busied myself to the point of distraction today, that wasn't a surprise.

"Have you met my parents?" I asked, realizing he may have and I just didn't know it.

As soon as my question came out, I remembered my mother had mentioned meeting him. "Oh wait, my mom told me she knew who you were." Suddenly, I remembered that I had an older brother who was friends with Donovan. Not that I'd forgotten, I'd just conveniently put it out of my mind. "I think we need to tell Levi about us."

"Glad you mentioned it. I was thinking that myself before I went to Denver. But I figured it was your call, not mine," Donovan replied.

"Just so you know, he's kind of a typical older brother. You may not think that because he's so laidback and always teasing. But he's not with me. Well, sometimes he's not."

Donovan lifted a shoulder in an easy shrug. "I'd be over-protective if I had a little sister. I get it. If he needs to haul off and hit me, I'll deal with it."

"He won't hit you! That's not okay with me. I'll tell him we're serious, and he'll deal with it."

Donovan chuckled. "I'd punch me."

"Even if I told you not to?"

He nodded, the sly look in his eyes making my belly do a quick little flip.

"Sugar, most men don't like to think about who wants to fuck their little sister. I love you, but I'd be flat out lying if I didn't say that's what started this. That first night I saw you, I wanted you."

A little thrill raced through me. "You did?"

"Oh yeah. You're gorgeous when you're angry. Hot as

fucking hell. We haven't even had a proper fight yet, but I can already tell you I'm gonna love it. We're gonna have amazing make-up sex."

My heart was doing that wild and crazy beat again, about to fly right out of my chest. My cheeks heated as I looked over at him. I couldn't quite believe he'd wanted me the first time he saw me. My thoughts must've shown in my eyes.

He brushed his thumb across my cheek. "Yeah, I have it that bad, sugar."

EPILOGUE

Jasmine

More than a year later

Standing on the deck behind Midnight Sun Arts gallery, I leaned on the railing, looking out over the water. Kachemak Bay glittered under the sun. The mountains rose tall on the far side of the bay, their peaks snow-tipped and bright against the blue sky.

An icy wind gusted off the water, and I tugged my jacket tighter around my shoulders. I took another deep breath of the bracing salty air before turning and walking back inside. I bumped into Donovan as he was walking down the hallway.

"Cold?" He smiled. "It's busy in the gallery," he murmured as he stepped closer, caging me in his arms against the wall. I looked up into his hazel gaze, taking in his dark hair and the chiseled lines of this face. He still took my breath away. My pulse skittered wildly while my belly spun in a flip.

I kept thinking the effect he had on me would start to fade. No such luck, but I wasn't complaining. He pressed closer against me where we stood in the back hallway, currently in a private place. My breath hitched when he traced my lips with his fingertip. Teasing, I caught it in my teeth, swirling my tongue around it, savoring as his eyes narrowed and darkened with desire.

The saving grace in how much power he held over me was the fact I had as much over him. I knew how to bring Donovan Ryan to his knees, and he knew how to do the same to me.

"Don't make me crazy," he murmured, dipping his head and fitting his mouth over mine. His tongue swept in swiftly, sensually curling around mine before he drew back. He dropped his hand, sliding it down across the side of my breast and into the dip of my waist before palming my ass as he rocked his arousal into me.

Just like that, and my panties were a lost cause. Someone called my name, and Donovan's mouth curled into a delectable grin.

"Duty calls," he murmured. "We'll finish this later."

One more roll of his hips against me, and my sex clenched, my nipples tightening.

"No fair," I muttered.

He chuckled as he stepped back. "You started it, sugar."

My cheeks were hot as I leaned against the wall, shaking my head. "You're the one who started it."

His gruff laugh echoed through my body, sending little pinwheels of pleasure through me. Dear God. I was probably headed for an early death based on the effect he had on me.

I pushed away from the wall as he held his hand out, curling his strong grip around mine. He led me back down the hallway and into the gallery. It had been a busy year. Time had folded into itself. It was winter, and every Winter Solstice, Risa had a big show at the Diamond Creek location of Midnight Sun Arts. They had an event at every location, but this location was her baby. Or so she said. She'd invited me to come down and mingle with the guests for the show.

Over a year and a half ago, in the summer, or thereabouts, Donovan had taken a weekend to get my studio in working order. Then I got busy. I was selling plenty of my work. My home had always been Willow Brook in my heart. But now home was also Donovan.

We got married last spring. He'd declared he didn't want to wait. I hadn't wanted to wait either. Levi never did punch Donovan. I took that as a win, although there had definitely been a few tense moments.

I was now the proud aunt of Glory, Lucy and Levi's baby daughter. They named her after my mother, Gloria, but Glory stuck as her nickname. She was as feisty as I expected with Lucy as her mother.

Janet's B&B was no longer our private love nest. Although we'd pretty much christened every room of that place through last winter before I finally gave in and moved into Donovan's new house. Which was now *our* house.

With Donovan's hand warm in mine, I threaded through the crowd. I wasn't the only artist here tonight. Risa was the one who called my name, and she came over to check with me, her eyes bright as she slipped her arm over my shoulders.

"We're going to run out of your stuff after next week by the time I ship all these orders. Just so you know. Seeing as we haven't even gotten through Christmas yet, you might want to get busy next week."

A little flash of anxiety zipped through me, but I ignored it. Lately, my motto was that some problems were better to have. This was definitely a good problem to have.

With a grin, I replied, "Absolutely. I'll do my best, but you know I'd rather have this problem than the other."

She chuckled just as someone called her name. She

started to spin away, but turned back quickly. "I can't help it. I have to say it. Told you so," she said with a wink, referencing her comment last year that she was confident she'd be able to sell my work. With a wave, she hurried off to talk to whoever had been calling her.

Donovan was a good sport, always coming to events like this with me, although it definitely wasn't his element. One of the things I loved about Alaska was the hodgepodge of people. In the gallery tonight, there was a mix of artists, fisherman, business people, and more. The sentiment that tied everyone together was the warmth and sense of community.

Later that night, Donovan was leaning against the headboard on the bed in the small suite we'd rented in the B&B beside the gallery. His muscled chest gleamed in the shadowy light. He held his hand out as I stepped out of the bathroom. It was a miracle I was even standing at this point.

He'd just fucked me thoroughly and sent me flying more times than I could count. But he did that often. Tugging one of his T-shirts over my head, I climbed onto the bed beside him, propping up the pillows behind me as I curled into his shoulder.

"So, we drive back in the morning?" I asked.

"Yeah, assuming the weather cooperates."

He chuckled, his eyes flicking to the window. I followed his gaze. We'd left the curtains open because there was no one to look inside. A set of French doors led out onto a small balcony. The moon was high above, shimmering on the water, its silvery light illuminating the snowflakes falling.

Glancing back to me, he continued, "It'll have to get a lot worse than this. But if it does, we'll just hole up here."

Then his lips were on mine, his warm embrace holding me strong and sure.

———

DONOVAN

Another few months later

I walked outside, ignoring the biting cold and taking a deep breath of the winter air. It was a clear, chilly day, and spring was right around the corner. I had a surprise for Jasmine, but I had one last thing to do.

Letting myself into the small building at the back of our property, I scanned the space as I closed the door behind me. When I'd bought this property, this building was the only thing here and had once served as a two-room cabin. I thought I had everything just so. The last thing was to get her kiln installed today.

I'd invited my parents up for a few weeks, if only to keep Jasmine distracted while I finished this project. Mama had insisted Jasmine take her to Anchorage today. Things were much better than I ever could've imagined. Jasmine and I had been married for over a year now. If anything, my love for her had only deepened in that time.

I wouldn't lie, the sex was amazing. But that wasn't why I loved her, although it did pretty much make me a slave to her.

I was just about to pull my phone out to call Levi when there was a sharp knock at the door. Opening it, I found him standing there with Cade. "We're here. We've got the kiln in the back of Cade's truck," Levi said, by way of greeting.

"Awesome. Let's do this," I replied.

In short order, we had her brand new, shiny kiln set up in what was going to be Jasmine's new studio. She was still using the studio behind Firehouse Café, but sometimes she was gone for hours upon hours. I'd learned that once she got going, she lost all sense of time. I didn't mind it one bit because she loved it. Yet, I wanted her to be able to work more easily, especially in the winter. I didn't like worrying about her driving home at odd hours after bursts of inspiration.

In the meantime, the owners of Midnight Sun Arts had decided to add another gallery to their small local chain here in Willow Brook. It would only be open during the summer, but Risa was already hounding Jasmine to help her with it. Jasmine had declared she did not want to be in charge of sales, but she'd help with the rest. Unbeknownst to Jasmine, they were going to use her almost-former studio as storage for the gallery.

As we were walking out after Cade had already driven away, Levi paused by his truck. He'd been right pissed at me when he first found out about Jasmine and me. Like I told Jasmine at the time, I'd have been pissed too. He never did punch me though.

"You're a good man," Levi said, reaching out and clapping my shoulder. "I might've been pissed as all hell at first, but I wouldn't trade you for another brother-in-law, not for a second."

I chuckled. "I love Jasmine. But I'm pretty sure you know that by now. I'd do anything for her, anything at all."

Levi held my gaze, nodding once. "I know." At that, he turned away.

A few hours later, my mama and Jasmine returned to the house. Mama came up to me, dropping a kiss on my cheek and enveloping me in one of her warm hugs. Even though she hadn't even been baking today, somehow, she still smelled like cinnamon and sugar. But then, she always smelled like that to me.

Leaning up to whisper in my ear, she said, "I'm going to go upstairs for a nap. You take Jazzy out and show off that studio."

And then she pinched my cheek. Because she still did that, and I let her.

Jasmine was putting away some groceries, her amber hair up in a loose knot atop her head.

"Hey, sugar, you got a minute?" I asked, as I walked up behind her, slipping my arms around her waist and dipping my head to breathe her in.

She closed the kitchen cabinet, turning in the cage of my arms. My cock, of course, stood at attention. No matter that this was an entirely inappropriate time for me to be getting randy. My father would probably be in any minute from whatever the hell he was doing out in the yard, and my mother was upstairs, for God's sake.

I sent up a little prayer of apology and caught Jasmine's lips in a quick kiss. Just that—one swipe of her tongue against mine—and I was hot for her. With a force of will, I drew back. Her cheeks were pink, and her gorgeous blue eyes were dark.

She bit her lip, a grin curling one corner of her mouth. "Now is not exactly the time," she said softly.

"I know," I replied, stepping back and catching her hand in mine. "I've got something to show you though. Come on."

She was definitely curious, her eyes widening as she looked at me. She didn't hesitate and came along as I tugged her out of the kitchen. In the year and a half since the house had been finished, we'd had one summer to do some work in the yard. Just now, the snow was melting, and I could hear the rushing sound of a stream in the trees behind the house. Spring was called mud season in Alaska for a reason. Everything melted and turned the ground muddy for weeks at a time. The streams were overflowing with the snow coming down off the mountains. Jasmine, ever practical, was wearing a pair of leather boots, and she trudged easily through the yard with me.

I'd been working on the studio every chance I had while she was away during the day for the last month. Normally, I'd have been able to knock out a project like this in a few days.

The outside of the old cabin still needed work, but the inside was transformed.

When I reached the building, I glanced to her.

"Why are we going to this old cabin? Please don't tell me you got some kind of animal and neglected to mention it to me."

I chuckled. Jasmine had heard plenty about the potbellied pig that my family had when I was growing up. I still missed that pig. Ben was his name. He lived a long life, but he'd passed away a few years ago. I was still figuring I could sweet-talk her into getting one.

"Oh, no," I said, "I'm saving that argument for later. Come on."

Opening the door, I flicked on the light.

Jasmine followed me inside. Her breath hitched sharply, her eyes widening as she looked around. "Oh my God! When did you do this?" she squealed.

Before I even had a chance to answer, she was flinging her arms around my neck and kicking her feet up. I caught hold and held her fast against me.

Leaning back, her eyes were bright with tears. "This is the best present *ever*! I mean, I love my studio in town, but ..." Her words trailed off.

"I thought it'd be nice for you to have a place here to work."

She dipped her head, burrowing into my shoulder. "Thank you so much," she mumbled, her voice muffled as she spoke. Drawing back, she shimmied out of my arms and looked around.

"You bought me a new kiln?" she asked, her tone wondering. "How did you get that?"

"I might've had a little help from Levi and Cade. My parents also might've come to visit now because I wanted to have this ready before your busy season."

She stood still for a beat before walking slowly around, her gaze sobering. Her footsteps echoed in the mostly empty room. Spinning to face me, she took a few steps, closing the distance between us. Stopping in front of me, she reached out and caught one of my hands in hers. She leaned up, tracing her fingertip over my lips.

Her touch was like a blaze of fire. Just like that very first night I met her.

"I'm so damn lucky. In case I don't say it enough, I love you," she said, as she leaned up and pressed her lips to mine.

"Sugar, I'm the one who's lucky."

Somehow, we ended up having a quickie in her brand-new studio, christening her worktable.

Later that night, after we walked back to the house hand in hand, and Jasmine let my mother take over in the kitchen, I lay in bed beside her. The moonlight lined her silhouette in silver.

I'd go anywhere in the world to be with Jasmine. Because she was home. I trailed my fingertips over her shoulder, and she sighed, shifting her bottom back against me.

I woke the following morning with her warm and soft in my arms, and the bright sun rising against snowcapped mountains. This was life with the woman I loved, the one who owned my heart and soul, held tight against me. She was my everything.

Thank you for reading Play With Fire - I hope you loved Jasmine & Donovan's story!

Up next in the Into the Fire Series is Melt With You - Harlow & Max's holiday story. A tech billionaire collides with a sassy firefighter heroine - opposites attract doesn't quite capture it.

Keep reading for a sneak peek!

Be sure to sign up for my newsletter for the latest news, teasers & more! Click here to sign up: http://jhcroixauthor.com/subscribe/

Somehow, while attending a wedding almost in the middle of nowhere in Alaska, I'd ended up handling taxi duties. Go figure. According to the latest update sent to me via frantic text from the bride, there was only one straggler left. Within minutes, I was rolling to a stop in front of the hotel. My phone buzzed in my pocket. Sliding it out, I glanced down.

Harlow May is her name. Find her!

This from Ivy Nash, the bride and the woman Owen Manning had fallen so hard and fast for, I was still questioning his sanity. Ivy was lovely though and perfect for Owen. I considered teasing her and telling her Harlow was gone. But no. It was Ivy's day, so I'd behave.

On it. She'll be delivered to the wedding shortly.

I'd expected this last guest, who seemed quite important to Ivy, to be waiting outside. Not so. Harlow May was late.

I thought I recognized Harlow's name. I surmised she was the daughter of an investor for Owen's company. I happened to be familiar with her father through business connections. Owen and I had met at MIT some years back. He remained one of my closest friends. Off the Grid was his baby, his world-class multimillion-dollar engineering firm situated in the middle of fucking nowhere Alaska.

After another few beats of waiting, I strolled into the lobby. The wedding was taking place on top of a mountain at Last Frontier Lodge. There wasn't enough room there for all the wedding guests since the resort booked out so far in advance, so the other guests were staying here. Just as I was about to go to the desk and ask for Harlow to be called, a woman came hurrying out of the elevators.

Inside of a millisecond, I was completely distracted, enchanted, and then some. She had straight, glossy brown hair that hung almost to her waist and dark brown eyes. Aside from the fact she was flat out beautiful, she wore a cream silk dress, the outfit as out of place as a giraffe in the midst of a room full of dogs, what with most of the guests around her dressed for the outdoors.

I watched as she hurried through the front entrance, following after her. My stride closed the distance between us, my eyes locked on the swing of her hips. She had curves for days, filling out the silk dress. The silk swung just above her knees in a ruffle, hugged her hips like a lover and dipped in at her waist, only to flare out again to cup her breasts.

Stepping through the doors, I walked directly to her, my body tightening the moment I reached her. "Harlow May?"

Her espresso gaze swung to mine. "Yes. Are you the driver?"

I bit back a laugh. "I presume you're attending Owen and Ivy's wedding?"

Harlow twirled a long lock around her finger. The motion made me want to tangle a hand in her hair and muss it. I didn't, though it took an act of will. At her nod, I gestured to the car. It wasn't my vehicle. It was Owen's decked out black SUV with every tech feature you could imagine and entirely electric. It felt as if I were temporarily living a borrowed life.

"Am I late?" Harlow asked as she stepped towards the SUV.

Her scent drifted up to me, a hint of honey and vanilla. "I don't know if you're late, but you're the last one," I said. She'd missed the first three scheduled trips, but I no longer cared.

I opened the door for her, glancing down to see a flush crest on her cheeks. She slipped into the front seat and buckled her seatbelt. Once we were en route to the lodge, my eyes flicked sideways, landing on the curve of her thigh. My hand itched to slide over the silk, to feel the heat of her skin penetrating through it. I didn't know what it was about her, but I hadn't been this curious about a woman in, well, longer than I could remember.

"So Harlow, how do you know the bride and groom?"

I thought I knew the answer to my question, but I figured I'd ask anyway.

"I met Ivy and Owen through my father because he's an investor in their company. I'm here for the wedding because Ivy's become a friend. Alaska was on my bucket list too."

"Alaska is quite beautiful. It's my first time here myself."

I rolled to a stop at an intersection, glancing over to find Harlow's gaze on me. "I don't think I caught your name," she said.

She crossed and uncrossed her legs, tempting me to touch her again. Forcing my gaze forward, I turned onto the road that wound up into the mountains.

"Max. Max Channing," I replied.

"Are you just a driver, or here for the wedding?"

"I'm a friend and driving as a favor," I offered.

I couldn't have said why, but I preferred Harlow didn't know how our worlds might intersect. Within minutes, we were rolling to a stop in front of Last Frontier Lodge, the spectacular setting for Owen and Ivy's wedding. Diamond Creek, Alaska was one of Alaska's coastal jewels with the mountains dipping their toes in the sea here.

As I opened the door for Harlow to step out, I caught a glimpse of blue silk between her thighs. I was a gentleman. I wasn't prone to trying to catch sneak shots of women's panties. But sweet hell, Harlow was a magnet for me, and my eyes had a will of their own.

Of all the factors I had considered in coming to this wedding, encountering a woman so delectable I could hardly keep my body in check wasn't on the list. Not to mention, I wasn't on the best terms with her father. In fact, the last time we'd crossed paths, I'd told him he was a fucking asshole. Because he was.

As I walked behind her up the entrance stairs, I idly wondered what she did. Yet, now wasn't the time for chitchat. We had a half an hour before the wedding started. As we walked through the door, I rested my hand on her back, guiding her inside and savoring the heat of the silk against her skin.

If Harlow noticed my touch, she didn't react. We walked through the crowded lobby and restaurant, and onto the back deck. Guests were milling about, yet Owen and Ivy were nowhere in sight. I glanced down to Harlow. "Seating's over there. Check with Delia," I said, gesturing to a woman who ran the restaurant at the lodge and was also a wedding guest.

When Harlow glanced at me, I noticed how her dark lashes curled against her cheeks. I couldn't have looked away if I tried when a slow smile stretched across her face. I wanted to kiss her.

"Actually, I'm a bridesmaid. Thank you for the ride," she said softly before turning away. She paused beside Delia, her dark hair a contrast to Delia's honey blond. They briefly conferred, and then Harlow slipped through a side door back into the lodge.

Meanwhile, I had duties to attend to. I walked back into the lodge to hunt down Owen. I found him in one of the rooms set aside for dressing with Derek Bridges. Along with

Owen, Derek was one of my closest friends back from our days at MIT.

Owen was leaning against the dresser, ready in his suit and tie while he laughed at something Derek said. He glanced my way. "Did you round up everybody?"

"Of course I did. Just ferried the last guest. Harlow May. She's Howard May's daughter, right?"

Owen nodded, his blue eyes crinkling at the corners with his grin. "Yes. Harlow and Ivy are close."

Derek stood from where he was seated by the windows. "Aren't we all relieved Howard couldn't make it to the wedding?" he asked with a wry grin.

"I gather his daughter is nicer than he is if she's one of Ivy's bridesmaids," I replied.

Owen chuckled. "Ivy adores her, and she's nothing like her father. In fact, he's cranky because she's refusing to work for him."

Just as I was about to counter with a question—because I was *that* curious about Harlow—there was a knock at the door. With a grin, Garrett Hamilton poked his head around the door. "I've been ordered to come fetch you boys."

In the short time I'd been here, I'd met the Hamilton family in a whirlwind. They owned this ski resort, which was primarily run by the eldest brother, Gage. Garrett was a former corporate lawyer. He still practiced law, but he'd said goodbye to his high-flying career in Seattle and moved up here to marry Delia.

Glancing toward Owen, I asked, "You ready for this?"

Owen, with his jet-black hair, ice blue eyes, and calm demeanor, actually looked a tad apprehensive. His shoulders rose and fell with a breath as he pushed away from the dresser. Adjusting his tie, he met me at the door with Derek behind him. "Ready as I'll ever be."

Garrett had already started to walk down the hallway. "Let's do this," Derek added, clapping Owen on the shoulder. "Now would be the time to speak up if you have any doubts."

We had started to file out when Owen came to a complete stop, turning back to face us. "I have no doubts. If you're wondering, I'm half terrified Ivy might suddenly come to her senses. If she does, I don't know what I'll do," he said flatly.

His eyes met mine, the depth of emotion contained there almost startling. "I don't think you need to worry about that," I heard myself saying.

Barely a hint of relief entered his gaze as he turned around.

We filed down the hall and onto the back deck of the lodge, which had been transformed into an outdoor wedding chapel. As I took my place beside Derek at the front, I contemplated that Owen had once been just as unlikely as me to settle down. Yet, here he was, head over heels in love with Ivy.

He had his reasons for keeping to himself, as did I. I still couldn't quite imagine caring that deeply for someone. I'd all but written the idea of love out of my life. As the pastor began the ceremony, I scanned the crowd. My eyes made their way to Harlow who stood with two other women beside Ivy. The moment I saw her, lust lashed at me. I could most certainly imagine a night between the sheets with Harlow.

I couldn't quite get a bead on her. She was quiet and gave off an air of steely strength. I wanted to know more.

Forcing my gaze off of her, I took a moment to scan the horizon. Mountain peaks rose all around us. The air was crisp and cool. Kachemak Bay was visible in the distance, the sun striking sparks on its surface. On the heels of a breath, savoring the crisp mountain air, I turned back and watched one of my closest friends get married.

I wasn't much for weddings usually. Yet, this wasn't a typical wedding—outdoors on the back deck of a beautiful lodge with the mountains and the ocean serving as the cathedral for the ceremony. My eyes were drawn to Harlow —as if she were my own personal magnet.

With a forceful mental shake, I tore my gaze free. Relationships were another part of business for me, a way to meet my needs and nothing more. Love, the flash in the pan, crazy love that Owen had stumbled into with Ivy, well, that wasn't for me.

HARLOW

After the wedding ceremony, the sky started to cloud, and the guests were herded inside. The lodge was busy even though it was only autumn. They catered to tourists for every season. I leaned against the bar, sipping my pomegranate martini. I didn't drink often, but I did enjoy a good martini. I was working on my third at this point, but I figured what the hell? I was at a wedding for one of my dearest friends, happy to escape the pressures of my life.

When Ivy had asked me to be one of her bridesmaids, my only hesitation had been whether or not my father was coming. Ivy, being the friend she was, had been sympathetic but still begged me to come. She'd also gleefully called me when my father bowed out. Owen had invited him out of courtesy since he invested quite generously in their company.

"Hey, hey," Ivy's voice called.

Spinning around, I leaned my hips against the barstool and smiled.

"Are you glad you came?" she asked when she reached me.

She was glowing in her cream silk dress with her amber hair and eyes. I was so happy for her. She and Owen were perfect for each other, the kind of perfect that didn't come along very often.

"Of course I'm happy I came. I think I might stay a little

longer than I planned. When do you leave for your honey-moon?" I asked.

Ivy leaned against the bar beside me, glancing over her shoulder to catch the eye of Gage Hamilton. He was the owner of the lodge and had been taking turns bartending with his brother Garrett. He was quite handsome with his gray eyes and dark hair. He was also quite taken. Not that I felt any kind of spark with him, not at all.

"Give me what she's having," Ivy said to Gage.

He flashed a smile and mixed her drink while he carried on a conversation with another customer.

"We're leaving tomorrow," Ivy replied. "I wish you would stay longer."

"Why? You won't be here."

"Because it makes me happy to think you can have some downtime. You can stay at the house if you'd like. I know how you feel about hotels."

I hated them. Well, hate wasn't the word. They just felt so impersonal. Much of my childhood had been spent in hotels. My mother died when I was young, and work was all that mattered to my father. He traveled a lot and carted me around with him, rotating through babysitters as needed.

I glanced to her as she took her drink from Gage. "Really? That makes the idea more tempting."

"Of course. We'll be gone for two weeks. The house is all yours. You can stay there when we get back too."

I cast a smile her way and shook my head. "I might take you up on saying while y'all are gone, but I'm not crowding your house right after your honeymoon."

Ivy shrugged. "We've been living together for years. My God, it's almost embarrassing it took us this long to get around to the wedding. We've been engaged for three years. Why don't you just move up here anyway? You're always saying you want a change of pace."

Home, as it was at the moment, was coastal North Carolina, where my mother was originally from and where my father's company had its base. Lately, I had found it smothering because all my father wanted was for me to join his company, and I refused. In fact, I'd gone behind his back and done the craziest thing ever. Or not, depending on how you looked at it.

It was quite tempting to pull up stakes and move to Alaska. I would have a built-in best friend and settle into a life far from my father. Even though Ivy and I had only met over the past year, we'd bonded quickly. That was saying something for me because, with all the travel when I was little, I hadn't had many opportunities to make friends. Ivy and I met at a function for the company she shared with Owen and connected instantly.

Catching her eyes, I shrugged. "We'll see. Meanwhile, tell me about Max."

Max, the driver who'd picked me up at the hotel, sent heat sliding through my veins and my belly spinning in flips. Max was *way* too handsome for his own good, and I was *way* too curious for mine.

Even if it didn't make a lick of sense because nothing would, or could, happen with Max, I was still curious. I'd sworn off men. For a perfectly good reason. I had an unerring accuracy for being attracted to men who were assholes. One after another stomped on my heart. The most recent had been the most devastating. I'd gotten pregnant and had a miscarriage, and it had torn me to shreds.

Ivy looked at me, her eyes taking on a gleam with her slight grin. "Max is a hot one, isn't he? He's known Owen forever, since MIT. And..."

She was cut off when Owen approached, sliding his arm around her waist and dipping his head to drop a kiss on her neck.

My heart pinged. I was so happy for her. Owen loved Ivy to pieces.

"We're supposed to cut the cake," he said with a sigh.

Ivy pushed off the bar. "Now? Why are there so many

rules about weddings?" she asked, looking to me as if I could answer.

I shrugged. "Don't ask me."

Owen chuckled. "I'm told if we don't do it soon, they'll need to move it back into the kitchen."

I followed them, meandering over to the back of the guests surrounding the table where the cake was displayed. I caught myself searching for Max. I wanted to know more about him, and that was bad. Because when I got curious about a man, that was when I did stupid things. Just as I was telling myself it was a good thing he wasn't around, I sensed his presence.

He strolled to my side. I couldn't keep from peeking looks at him. He was obscenely handsome with his midnight black hair and ice blue eyes. I wanted to dive in and take a swim. He held a glass of scotch in his hand. Even his hands were sexy, strong and slightly rugged as if he'd worked with them. My mind flashed to a vision of his hands on my body, heat blooming through me in response.

Restless, I took a gulp of my martini. Mistake. It burned my throat, and I started coughing.

"You okay?" Max asked.

His voice was low and sent a shiver over my skin. I tried to say I was fine, but I just kept coughing. His hand slid down my spine. With my dress open at the top, his touch sent fire shimmering under the surface of my skin.

He turned, guiding me away from the small crowd gathered around Ivy and Owen. My coughing outburst was drawing attention. Max walked me back to the bar where Garrett was now serving drinks. Max paused by the corner of the bar near the windows. His hand rested on my back, the heat of his touch filtering through the silk of my dress. I slowly managed to stop coughing.

Glancing up, I found his blue gaze watching me. "Went down the wrong pipe?" he asked.

With a sigh and another breath, I nodded. My eyes

watering, I reached over to snag a bar napkin. Dabbing at them, I set my martini down. "I'm not fit for company at things like this," I said with a little laugh.

Max was quiet for a beat and then his mouth hitched at the corner. Oh sweet hell. He should *not* smile. My belly felt funny and slivers of heat spun through my veins. He looked away, glancing over his shoulder towards the cake cutting. "I think we missed the fun."

I chuckled. "The most important part already happened."

"How long are you staying?" he asked, his gaze swinging back to me.

His question took me off guard. "I'm at the hotel until tomorrow. You?"

He shrugged. "Don't know. It's beautiful here."

As I looked up at him, my body—my traitorous body—sent naughty thoughts through my mind. The view of Max was quite beautiful. He was ridiculously handsome. Yet, I knew that wasn't what he was talking about. I managed to keep those thoughts in my head and nodded politely. "It is."

Garrett came to the corner of the bar. I'd been here two days now and met most everyone in Ivy and Owen's circle. I'd quickly come to learn that the Hamilton family was comprised of beautiful people. Garrett was no exception with his glossy dark hair and blue eyes. His gaze was sharp and assessing as he looked between us.

"Another drink?" he asked, his eyes flicking to my almost empty martini glass.

"Yes, please," I said quickly. I needed something to take the edge off. Having Max nearby made me restless and prickly all over.

"You?" Garrett asked, his eyes shifting to Max.

Max shook his head. "All set, but thanks. I'm the shuttle, so no drinks for me."

Garrett chuckled as he prepped another pomegranate martini for me.

———

The rest of the evening was a blur. I drank too many martinis, danced, and felt the burn of Max's gaze on me every time our eyes collided. I wanted him. Badly.

Even in my tipsy state, I kept reminding myself that whenever I wanted someone, it was usually a bad decision on my part. I didn't do casual well. I never had.

I tended to fall hard and fast, confusing attraction for something else. My therapist, the one I saw after my last relationship blew up in my face, had gently pointed out that perhaps I was looking for the love I'd never gotten from my father.

I'd been looking high and low for love most of my life. With my mother gone and a father who approached parenting as something to pencil in on his calendar and hand off to others, I'd craved love for too long. As such, I misinterpreted cues and read far too much into small gestures.

Max was particularly tempting with his dark hair, the strong lines of his face, and his eyes. One look from those cool blue eyes, and it felt as if he was undressing me, his gaze lighting little fires on my skin everywhere they landed.

Somewhere along the way, I ended up in his arms out on the deck. Seeing as he was one of the groomsmen, and I was a bridesmaid, it only made sense we would dance at some point. Not many men enjoyed dancing, and I loved it. Max surprised me. While he gave off a somber, controlled air, he danced like a dream, twirling me easily around the deck. When the music shifted into a slower song, he pulled me close, just when I was thinking I needed to make my escape.

With the heat of desire sliding through my veins and the feel of his strong embrace, my body reassured my mind that it wouldn't hurt to enjoy it for a few minutes. He smelled good, crisp and musky at once. My head barely reached his shoulder. With one of his hands gripping mine and the other splayed on my lower back with his fingers teasing over my bottom, I could feel the moisture building between my thighs, the silk of my panties wet.

"So, Harlow, tell me what you do?" he murmured.

A rather common question and perfectly expected. Yet, these questions were loaded for me because they reminded me of how I let my father down over and over again.

I shoved those thoughts aside and answered "I just finished my training to be a hotshot firefighter."

Max's steps stuttered slightly, and I couldn't help but laugh, glancing up at him. "Did I surprise you?"

His eyes canted down to mine, and my breath caught in my throat as butterflies spun in my belly. This man was too much.

He was quiet for a beat, his gaze searching mine as a slow grin stretched across face. "Yes, you surprised me."

Between his grin and the slightly rough edge of his voice, a shiver ran through me. I ordered my mind to ignore the crazy signals of my body. Manners, I had manners.

"And what you do?" I managed to ask.

I felt the shrug of his shoulders, the motion making me aware of his muscled chest pressing against my breasts. My nipples tightened, giving me away. He appeared to be considering his words.

"Business," was all he finally said.

I was just tipsy enough to be less than polite. "Vague much?"

He smiled again, sending my belly into a series of flips. "I'd rather not think about work tonight."

The song ended and a more upbeat song began. When Max stepped back, I felt bereft, my body nearly following him like steel to a magnet. I managed to stop myself. Conveniently, Ginger Nash, Ivy's sister-in-law, was approaching with two glasses in her hands.

"Champagne?" she asked, pausing at my side.

Ginger was funny and smart. Her brown hair was up in a twist, and her blue eyes were twinkling. She squeezed my arm as I accepted the proffered drink and took a gulp. "I'm so glad you're here," she said with a wide smile. Ginger seemed to have decided we were best buddies even though we'd only met days ago. She was easy to be around with her sly sense of humor and warmth.

She glanced to Max, arching a brow. "Aren't you handsome?"

Max barely reacted, his lips quirking.

"Oh, don't worry. I wasn't flirting. Just making an observation. I'm happily married," Ginger said dismissively.

Max merely arched a brow this time, his eyes glinting with mirth.

"It's a wedding though," she continued. "Maybe you should find someone to sweep off her feet."

Max threw his head back with a laugh just as Cam Nash, Ivy's brother and Ginger's husband, approached. Cam was a totally nice guy and dreamy. He'd retired from being a world-class skier and was a ski instructor here at the lodge.

Cam slipped his arm around Ginger's shoulders, nodding in my direction and grinning at Max. "Ignore Ginger. She always wants to set everyone up."

Ginger nudged him with her elbow and took a sip of her champagne. "What's wrong with being romantic?"

Cam, who shared Ivy's coloring with amber hair and eyes, cast a smile her way. "Nothing at all, but not everyone wants to be set up."

Unabashed, Ginger shrugged, her eyes bouncing from Max to me. "You two match. Just saying," she offered with a wink.

———

Available now!

Melt With You

If you love steamy, small town romance, take a visit to Diamond Creek, Alaska in my Last Frontier Lodge Series. A sexy, alpha SEAL meets his match with a brainy heroine in Take Me Home. It's FREE on all retailers! Don't miss Gage & Marley's story!

Go here to sign up for information on new releases: http://jhcroixauthor.com/subscribe/

FIND MY BOOKS

Thank you for reading Play With Fire! I hope you enjoyed the story. If so, you can help other readers find my books in a variety of ways.

1) Write a review!
2) Sign up for my newsletter, so you can receive information about upcoming new releases & receive a FREE copy of one of my books: http://jhcroixauthor.com/subscribe/
3) Like and follow my Amazon Author page at https://amazon.com/author/jhcroix
4) Follow me on Bookbub at https://www.bookbub.com/authors/j-h-croix
5) Follow me on Twitter at https://twitter.com/JHCroix
6) Like my Facebook page at https://www.facebook.com/jhcroix

———

Into The Fire Series

Burn For Me
Slow Burn
Burn So Bad
Hot Mess
Burn So Good
Sweet Fire
Play With Fire
Melt With You
Burn For You
Crash & Burn

Swoon Series

This Crazy Love
Wait For Me
Break My Fall

Brit Boys Sports Romance

The Play
Big Win
Out Of Bounds
Play Me
Naughty Wish

Diamond Creek Alaska Novels

When Love Comes
Follow Love
Love Unbroken
Love Untamed
Tumble Into Love
Christmas Nights

Last Frontier Lodge Novels

Take Me Home
Love at Last
Just This Once
Falling Fast
Stay With Me
When We Fall
Hold Me Close
Crazy For You

ACKNOWLEDGMENTS

Huge shout out to my readers for cheering on my books, sending me funny notes & making every book I write a labor of love. This firefighter series has been an absolute joy to write, and y'all keep asking for more, which means so much!

Many thanks to Jenn Wood for editing with a sharp eye and making sure I gave Jasmine & Donovan the story they deserved. Gracious thanks to Terri D. for her eagle eyes in proofing this story & not letting me miss anything.

My proofreader angels are the last line of defense - Janine, Beth P., Terri E., Heather H., & Carolyne B. - thank you ladies! Yoly Cortez never fails to dazzle with her covers, and this one was no exception.

My dogs are always there to get me out on morning runs *every* day, which is my best time for story forming. They're also incredibly generous with wags and snuggles. Last and never least, DBC.

xoxo

J.H. Croix

ABOUT THE AUTHOR

USA Today Bestselling Author J. H. Croix lives in a small town in the historical farmlands of Maine with her husband and two spoiled dogs. Croix writes contemporary romance with sassy women and alpha men who aren't afraid to show some emotion. Her love for quirky small-towns and the characters that inhabit them shines through in her writing. Take a walk on the wild side of romance with her bestselling novels!

Places you can find me:
jhcroixauthor.com
jhcroix@jhcroix.com

 facebook.com/jhcroix

 twitter.com/jhcroix

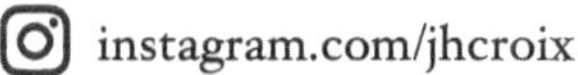 instagram.com/jhcroix